Hit & Split

Moving from my established world of non-fiction into fiction comes with nothing but uncertainties. Therefore, I'd like to seize the opportunity to dedicate this first fictional yarn to my beloved wife. I'd also like to thank the real Lucy and Kirk for their invaluable insights into the British Police system, and Joe Halt for the same courtesy regarding the US equivalent.

Table of Contents

Part 1. The Incident.

1.

How to kill him?

No, how to kill him wasn't the question. It was how could the guy die unremarkably?

Toby was sitting on the bed, fully clothed, his legs stretched out, feet crossed, shod in a dirty pair of trainers. He was glaring at the TV, which was turned off. The blinds were closed, the lights off too. The digital alarm clock illuminated the side of his face, which reflected back at him on the TV screen. He glared in the direction of his own reflection, but his stare was directed at the question, not the reflection.

Toby exhaled slowly, there were many things to consider; the bugger was huge for a start, and it was better to assume the man really knew how to use his size, so a fair 'one on one' fight would be too dangerous.

He shook his head at the idea of a fair fight, what a ridiculous concept.

The man needed to die and Toby needed to survive, so the fight would be as unfair as possible. His size had to be turned into a disadvantage and Toby's smaller stature needed to be in his favor, so a really enclosed space might work? He grimaced; it could also backfire spectacularly.

A vehicular accident? Too many variables; neither man was on their home turf and therefore there was no established routine to utilize. Essentially, Toby had no idea where the guy might go next, so helping him have an accident was just

2

not going to happen. Shame really, as car accidents were suitably unremarkable.

An overdose? No, the guy's size was an obstacle again. How could he restrain somebody that big while administering the dose? Same problem with a staged mugging; the guy was too likely to come out on top.

Toby shook his head, wishing he could just shoot the guy. But traveling with weapons was a professional no-go. In the movies, people arrive in a foreign land with all the cool toys and gadgets they could wish for. In the real world, you picked up whatever you needed on location, and in some places, that was harder than others.

Toby glared harder, starting to see the beginnings of an idea; maybe expecting the guy to die unremarkably was unrealistic in this case. Toby realized he'd been looking at it wrong, he'd only considered methods whereby the mark would die in a manner that didn't create ripples, when what really mattered was the anonymity of who'd created the splash. He swung his legs off the bed, picked up the room key and shoved it into the pocket of his jeans.

2.

Madyson was going stir crazy on the Air Force base. It hadn't taken her long to realize there was only so much foreign TV you could watch and so much bumming around the house you could do before you needed to get out. The downside was that going out, out there, was really outside her comfort zone.

Back home in the States she understood her friends, she lived in a world of musical workouts, of jogging with strollers, comparing shopping purchases, and of course, bragging with those friends over an expensive coffee. They bragged about cars, houses, and kids, but mostly they bragged about their husband's successes. And that was where Madyson always won. Most of the other husbands earned more money than hers, but it didn't matter; her husband was special while theirs were dull, his life was secret, theirs tediously open. And she knew exactly how to play it to her advantage.

Until recently, they'd been living in Virginia, the home of the US Intelligence community. Her hubby couldn't talk about his work, not even to her. He had no social media accounts, and in that region the implications were deafening. The other women were better in every tangible way, but she was married to something otherworldly. Her life was mysterious and glamorous, her husband dark and threatening. At least that was her version.

The reality was different; stateside, he'd gone to work

every day, and she was pretty sure that work meant sitting in an office with a computer. Presumably, the information he worked with was sensitive and vitally important to national security, but he was still a nine-to-fiver. And then he'd been posted to Great Britain, England, the United Kingdom. Jeez, she couldn't even understand what she should call the place.

So she'd gone with him and been smacked in the face with the biggest culture shock of her life. Back home, her friends were predictable; they were groomed and polished, warm, polite, and ever so slightly insincere in their jostling for social supremacy. Here, the women she'd met hadn't been at all what she'd expected. She'd been hoping to befriend the Kate Middletons of England, and while her spy hubby was totally internet anonymous, she'd imagined stocking her friends-only social media gallery with envy-inducing images of her and her new English besties. Instead, most of the women she'd encountered had a hard, threatening edge to them. Some of the shop workers had been reassuringly polite and insincere, but the average person made precious little effort to fake the niceties.

But those local people were just one cause of her discomfort; the roads were the stuff of nightmares. She'd never seen anything like it before, some roads were barely the width of a US sidewalk, and the edges were strewn with completely irresponsible dangers: huge ancient trees, big metal light poles, hedges built from rocks, tall curbstones. And as if that wasn't unfriendly enough, they weren't even straight; it was as if somebody had taken a sharpie and

scribbled a wiggly line, then said, 'That's the road, build it.'
What was wrong with these people?

No, going out here was an uncomfortable exercise, with
just one exception; she got to drive her own SUV. A
wonderful perk of her hubby's job was having it shipped at
no charge, and now every time she clicked the unlock button
and climbed into it, the familiar smell took her back home.
She closed her eyes, started the engine, and was suddenly
stateside, driving to the mall with the sun shining, wearing
big Jackie O shades, with the local radio cranking out
familiar tunes and a DJ talking in a soothing accent.

Then she opened her eyes, flared her nostrils and tensed
up at the sight of drizzle on her huge windshield. She peered
forward to see grey skies and matching concrete buildings,
pulled the lever into the drive position, and pointed the huge
black vehicle toward the base's security gate, winding down
her window as was required.

"Good morning ma'am, how are you today?" asked the
English soldier on gate security.

"Fine, I'm just heading out for the morning," she replied
before pulling on the electric window button with her
fingernail.

"Enjoy yourself and drive safely, ma'am." the soldier
replied to her closing window. A second soldier wearing a
similar red beret opened the barrier allowing her to
accelerate toward the junction of the public road.

"I'm very well, ma'am, thank you for asking." the

Military Policeman sighed as the back of her SUV accelerated past him.

"We're just mall cops to her, mate." said the second MP as he closed the base security barrier.

3.

The lack of distractions in Toby's hotel room had allowed him to flesh out a plan for this job but it had also left him feeling lethargic, a hazardous state for him. So he jogged from his grotty little hotel to the local vice district; it had got his heart pumping and his mind suitably alert, allowing him to slow to a brisk walk. Now he was searching for the right kind of degenerate human being.

Two girls to the left, tiny metallic skirts, equally shiny thigh-high boots, plastic-looking tits, and, oh, the closest one had an Adam's apple, so not girls after all. Toby, his face showing no emotion, just continued by.

There has to be one close, Toby thought to himself. He tilted his head ever so slightly left, checking out the side street behind the hustlers, empty. His pace didn't change, a slight tilt to the right for a view into the next side street, bingo, a long-haired guy leaning on the wall. The man was just out of sight from the main street but with enough of a vantage point to watch his sex workers. It was a warm night, and Toby easily spotted a recognizable bulge under the waistline of the man's t-shirt. Mark acquired. Toby kept his head low and crossed to the other side of the street. Once he'd cleared their view, he hung a quick right into the next side street.

He needed another right turn as soon as possible; anything would do, ahead he could see a narrow opening between the apartment blocks, potentially a choke point, but whether it was viable or not, needed closer inspection. He slowed as he approached, placing his feet more cautiously on the ground. As he reached the corner, he stopped and slowly leaned his head into the alleyway.

The alley was narrow, barely wide enough for a single vehicle, there were two dingy recessed areas to the right, but it was too dark to see what they led to. Toby stepped into the alley, placing his feet gently to stay silent. He could now see the alley was about a hundred feet long and led into the street on which he'd seen the longhaired pimp; he continually edged forward.

Toby could hear sounds ahead but couldn't place them over the gentle noise of cars and distant music. They seemed to be coming from one of the cutouts ahead of him. He edged closer, finally reaching a close enough point to recognize the sounds. There was no doubt what was going on; the sound of male grunting and a higher-pitched attempt at faking pleasure told him everything. As he reached the corner of the first cutout in the alley, he once again stopped to confirm his suspicions, seeing a man's back thrusting up and down into the prone form of somebody else wearing thigh-high boots. Toby ghosted past them, unseen.

Clear of the alley's only risk, he silently jogged to the alley's end, peering around the corner one more time.

The long hair was still positioned in the same spot; much like a family dog instinctively choosing to position itself between separated pack members. Toby took a deep breath because now it was all about minimizing the risk, as it

9

always was. You didn't need to be a superhero in these situations, just pragmatic and efficient. In this particular case, there were two primary considerations; stealth and Toby's own safety. In preparation, he'd taken a plain white face cloth from the laundry cart at his hotel room. He had no weapon but didn't really need one for this.

Toby slipped on some gloves, stepped out into the quiet street and started to silently approach the long hair. Occasionally the man turned his head to the side, but Toby was hugging the wall and therefore helped by the shadow which it created. As he neared the man's back, Toby removed the face cloth from his pocket and then, resisting the urge to clumsily accelerate the last few feet, he prepared his hands for the task.

Toby stood immediately behind the man, having successfully closed the gap to an arm's length, he took a deep breath and then put both hands into action. Toby's right hand pulled on the man's hair, yanking his neck backward, as Toby's left hand shoved the washcloth into the man's mouth. The stealth part was done, but the man's next instinct would be to defend himself, which of course, Toby knew, so Toby had already whipped his right hand down to the man's waistband and placed it on the pistol's grip.

Toby's left hand instantaneously thrust upwards into the man's nose, causing a disproportionate amount of pain. Ignoring his muffled grunts, Toby's right hand pressed the man's own gun into the soft tissue of his waist. The man's hands instinctively moved forwards in a gesture of surrender and the noises stopped.

This was all well and good, but Toby wasn't new to this, and experience was everything. Maybe the gun was all the guy had, but in plenty of other cases, it hadn't been, so Toby wasn't taking any chances. He switched the pistol to his left hand, and still standing directly behind the man, he reached forward with his own right hand, pulling the man's right hand back toward him. Toby then felt for the man's thumb, took a strong hold and rapidly whipped it to the side, snapping the thumb joint and disabling the man's ability to hold anything in his dominant hand.

The muffled noises recommenced, but much louder, Toby quickly raised the gun and struck the back of the man's head in the appropriate spot, the long hair slumped straight to the floor.

Toby checked all directions for newcomers, and finding no threat, he removed the washcloth from the man's mouth, sharply tugged some hairs from his head and took off in the opposite direction from which he'd come.

Toby now had a weapon more useful than a facecloth.

4.

Madyson steered her huge SUV to the right of the base's exit road, accelerating past one of those weird road signs that must have only had significance to military personnel. This one was a white circle with a black diagonal struck through it, to her it seemed like the badges the men wore on their funny uniforms. Her husband didn't have to wear one of those uniforms because he was higher up the chain of command -that's what he called it.

She put her foot to the floor and the big SUV effortlessly accelerated up the hill. She'd been meaning to share some photos with a couple of the girls back home and already knew there was a cool old castle just up the road. She unlocked her phone with her right hand as she steered with her left, her foot still pressing hard on the go-pedal.

As Madyson crowned the hill, she felt a brief moment of confusion before she squealed in panic and while trying to relocate her right foot, she whacked into something, losing consciousness instantly.

Madyson's head hurt and she didn't know where she was. She opened her eyes and slowly raised her head, a cream-colored air-filled bag was pressed against her boobs and she gradually realized she was sitting in her car. Her poor car, what the hell had happened?

She pushed the airbag downward, opening up her view

through the windscreen. The glass was covered in cracks and blood, and a mangled face was pressed against the other side. Madyson's muscles contracted in horror, slamming her back into her car seat. Then she felt her stomach convulse and her airway filling with fluid; she strained her neck forward as her mouth involuntarily splayed open wide and then she puked all over herself. She could hear sirens approaching, but different sounding from the ones she was used to. Of course, she wasn't stateside anymore. Only now did she start to experience some sense of the situation, "Oh God, oh no, oh shit no." She pulled on her door handle and swung her hips to get out of her truck but was held stationary by her seat belt. She recoiled at a sharp pain in her chest, pressed the button to release her belt and stumbled out of her truck. As her feet hit the floor, she felt another wave of vomit forcing itself upwards and thrust her sore upper body forwards, allowing it to gush forth again.

"Are you alright, madam?" asked a female voice. Madyson didn't know how to respond. Turning to the side, she saw a woman wearing a fluorescent nylon coat with 'Police' written on it in blue and white. Taking in the scene a little more, Madyson noticed a white police car with the side marked in blocks of blue and the same viciously bright green as the woman's coat. "That's right, let it out." said the Policewoman placing her hands on Madyson's shoulders, helping to support her, "the ambulance is nearly here."

Madyson inhaled deeply and hunched forwards again allowing another wave of vomit to escape. The Policewoman was talking again, but Madyson just wasn't listening. It was starting to become apparent what had happened. This was bad, really bad. More sirens arrived and different voices were talking to her, but it was all just white noise. She was put onto a stretcher and a breathing mask was placed on her face, some doors closed and then the foreign sounding sirens restarted.

5.

Every job was dangerous, every single one, but some were off the charts in their danger levels. It could be due to different things, such as where the job was happening -and this job was in one of those countries you really didn't want to hang around in. So Toby wanted it done, in quick time. He had a gun and now he wanted to use it, so he could get the hell out of town. Jail here really wasn't something he cared to contemplate.

It was a balancing act though, rushing something could bring him closer to that which he was trying to avoid. He was pondering this back in his hotel room, but unlike before, he was pacing the room as he planned. Apparently, the sense of urgency was hard to suppress.

Earlier that night, he'd watched his mark check into a hotel. Toby had found a good observation point; watched the man check-in, and waited for evidence of the room he'd taken. Five minutes in, there had been no moving curtains, no windows opening and no indication of a new occupant for any of the street-facing rooms. So, Toby had relocated to the rear of the hotel, where he'd been pleased to find the mark lounging on a third-floor balcony.

Toby had checked into a neighboring hotel in readiness. Since then, he'd planned the whole operation, carried out the mini op with the pimp, and would still have time to finish up and exit the country. But he had to slow himself down enough not to screw it up. *All the Ps*, he reminded himself;

15

proper preparation prevents piss poor performance. Those Army sayings had a way of staying with you. He continued to pace, "Still a soldier," he reassured himself, "Proper soldier."

The pacing stopped, "Right, let's do it." He wrapped the pistol in a hotel hand towel and slid it into a small black rucksack. Then, he took another couple of pairs of latex gloves from his duffle bag and left the room.

Standing outside the man's hotel in the small hours of the morning, Toby quietly rolled a wheelie bin into a position where he could get enough height to pull himself up onto the lowest of the hotel's balconies. From there he'd found it child's play to continue upward until he'd reached the appropriate third floor balcony. Toby had already observed the man for the last twenty-four hours and had every faith he would be a creature of habit; meaning he'd probably wake early and be in the shower before daylight, which would work out nicely for Toby. So, for now, it was a waiting game.

6.

Madyson was sitting in a hospital bed, having finally encountered the first group of people in this country who'd been really nice to her. She'd been told by the doctor she had bruised ribs and was suffering from shock. She was shocked alright, what the hell had happened? None of it made sense yet. A nurse smiled as she opened the curtain, which had partially obscured Madyson's bed.

The Policewoman who'd helped Madyson back at the scene had already come and gone. She'd been with a male colleague and they'd taken a statement from her, although they'd been frustratingly evasive in response to her questions about the other person, the one who'd been splayed across her SUV's hood.

As Madyson sat on the bed, still shell-shocked, she heard her husband's voice, which caused a huge wave of relief to wash over her, unexpectedly resulting in her starting to cry, and before he'd even reached her bedside, the crying had turned into uncontrollable sobbing.

As her husband approached, he could see his arrival had triggered these emotions. He took her hand, "Maddy, are you okay?"

Madyson couldn't hold back the sobbing, making her breathing erratic and creating a barrier to getting her words out.

"Listen, you don't have to worry. We're here now." he

continued.

We? She thought, then noticed that two men in suits had entered with her husband.

"I don't know what happened." she finally managed to respond. Her husband smiled with just the corners of his mouth, his eyes telling a different story. Maddy noticed as one of the suits turned and looked at her with an expression she couldn't recognize, but he'd turned away again before she could give it much more thought.

"It doesn't matter Maddy, we're diplomats." her husband replied.

Madyson couldn't grasp the significance of the comment, it seemed so totally irrelevant. As she turned to the side, she noticed the nurse was still there and that she was looking at Maddy's husband with what appeared to be shock on her face, but then the expression changed. The nurse strode briskly away, with a look of clear disgust having replaced her original expression.

It was all overwhelming, there was simply too much going on, and Maddy was painfully aware that she wasn't keeping up with it all, "But what about the... person?" she asked. Just the thought of it made her feel like she was going to heave again.

"We're diplomats, Maddy," her husband repeated with more force, "You don't need to worry." He turned toward the nurse who'd just left, calling out loudly, "Nurse, can my wife leave?"

The nurse was stunned, "What?" she hesitated, trying to grasp the implications, and then quickly realizing she needed to buy some time she suggested, "I'll need to check with the doctor, sir, let me track her down."

Maddy's husband didn't hesitate with his response, "I only want to know if it's safe for my wife to check herself out."

The nurse wasn't dim, so she persisted, "As I said, I need to check with the doctor first." and without giving him time to reply, she picked up the phone in the nurse's station.

Maddy's husband shook his head and said to the accompanying suits, "We're not waiting. Let's go."

Madyson was still struggling to keep up, "But..."

But her husband and his two aides were already pulling her to her feet. "Sir!" called over the nurse, "Really, I must insist you wait for the doctor. You might be endangering your wife's safety."

"Bullshit," growled Maddy's husband as his posse strode past the nurse's station.

7.

Toby was catnapping when he was startled by the muted sound of music. Opening his eyes, he found himself on a balcony, breathing warm moist night-time air, and then his grogginess turned to purpose as he remembered why he was there.

He leaned his head closer to the sliding balcony window and listened for clues as to what was happening inside. He could hear the radio, a clock radio no doubt, and the sound of running water. Toby put on his latex gloves, reached into the little black rucksack next to him and pulled out the long sturdy flat-bladed screwdriver he'd appropriated from his own hotel's maintenance room. He pushed the blade under the window runner at a forty-five-degree angle and then lifted. With the window raised in its runners, he jiggled until he'd got the clearance he needed, then lifted it off the runners, moved it aside, and quietly entered the mark's hotel room. Now inside, he could hear the shower running and see the excess steam escaping from the bathroom door ahead of him. He took stock of the room, reminded himself of the man's size and decided to position himself in the farthest corner, out of range of the man's long arms.

Suitably positioned, he checked the stolen gun's magazine, its safety position, and that he'd got one in the barrel. He then took a pillow from the bed and turned the room light off.

As he stood in the darkness, his nerves started to kick in.

It was a natural response, one that training and repetition taught you to cope with, but they never fully left you, so he just sucked it up and waited. Eventually, the shower stopped, and the only noises were faint ones as the man dried himself in the bathroom. Finally, the light leakage from the bathroom door increased and the man's figure walked into the bedroom's small entrance. Stark naked and with a slightly confused look on his face, the man peered into the darkness.

Toby's nerves evaporated away; the guy was huge, except for where it counted. Brushing aside that distracting thought, Toby refocused, he raised the pistol, covered the muzzle with the pillow, and started to speak, "Good mornin' mister bomb-maker, this is a gift from all the British Army lads you've murdered." And the room was momentarily filled with ear-splitting noise.

The man dropped hard, but Toby's ears were already ringing, masking the sound of the thud. Toby walked over to the lifeless body, found his shot's accuracy pleasing, and then gently rested the few hairs he'd previously pulled from the pimp's head, next to the bomb-maker's right hand. Knowing the clock was ticking, although not as urgently as in some other parts of the world, he hurriedly returned the window to its runners, checked everything was how he needed it, and then left the way he came.

At street level, Toby rolled the wheelie bin back to its original location, before tossing the pistol inside it. He knew it'd be found, thereby directing any investigation further in the wrong direction. He hesitated as he replayed it all in his head, checking for potential errors, then pulled his ghost routine once more and disappeared into the dark.

8.

"I don't understand," said Madyson, "stop the car, Jeff. Tell me what the hell is going on."

The driver turned to Maddy's husband, who gently shook his head. The driver obediently continued in the direction of the airbase. Jeff massaged his own forehead before replying, "Look, Maddy, really, what have I got to say to you?" he shook his head as if dealing with a slow-witted child, "You hit a cyclist, at speed, while driving on the wrong side of the road."

A horrible shiver traveled through her body, "I was on the wrong side of the road?"

Jeff didn't want to attack his wife any more than was necessary but couldn't suppress the answer, "Yes, Maddy, they drive on the wrong side of the road over here."

She hadn't done too much driving since her SUV had arrived, but her unintentional visits over the centre line had only been fleeting so far. She'd really thought she had the hang of it. "Holy crap, did I really?"

Jeff couldn't bring himself to reply, she'd potentially stirred up a huge shit storm and somehow this conversation was only making it seem worse.

But Madyson was hung up on the trivialities, how once she'd got moving, it was usually quite easy to stay on the left, but every so often at a junction, she'd been out of her depth momentarily. She started crying again, but silently

23

now, all she could feel was guilt and horror at what she'd done.

She was trembling, "And the other person?"

The car stayed silent for a while. Eventually, Jeff replied, "So far, he's hanging on, but you hit him hard, so it doesn't look good."

Her breathing started to feel panicked, "Where are we going?"

"We're getting out of here."

The confusion filled her head once more, "What do you mean?"

"Madyson. You hit a cyclist head-on because you were driving on the wrong side of the road. And you did this in a foreign country. We're not fully versed in their laws for an incident like this, but at first glance it doesn't look good. For now, we're using our diplomatic immunity and getting onto a US Air Force transport plane, so we can get stateside ASAP."

This can't be happening. Maddy felt like she was losing her mind.

The absence of a response from his wife prompted Jeff to add, "Or do you wanna roll the dice and risk prison here?"

She had so many more questions, what would happen if the person didn't....if they didn't get better? What would happen once she was back in the US? What would the local British Police think of her just leaving like this? But Jeff had just presented her with an even worse scenario. She scrunched her legs into her chest, trying to ignore the pain sensations it triggered and continued to weep.

9.

"Um, hello, I don't really know who I need to speak to." said a young female voice.

"Well, what do you want to talk about?" asked a male voice.

"I think it would be news?" the voice didn't sound convinced.

The man could already tell from her concerned tone of voice this was real, so he tried to be as reassuring as possible, "Don't worry, my name's Bill, Bill Addison. I work on the news desk. Just tell me what's going on; in any old order you want, then we'll figure out if it's news from that. Sound good?" Bill knew when not to ruin things by prematurely asking for a name.

"Yeah, okay." she replied, "So what happened is….no wait. I work in accident and emergency….oh wait." the line went quiet, "Do I have to tell you my name?"

"Nah, luv, I couldn't care less. Unless you want to be mentioned. Or if you wanna get paid for the story?"

No response. So she had morals, not greed. Bill couldn't care either way, "If neither of those applies, then just tell me what you've got. Anonymous is never a problem for us, coz we do our own investigating anyway."

Somehow that comment reassured the caller exactly as Bill had intended, so the young woman started afresh, "A patient was brought into the hospital where I work. She'd been in an RTC, sorry, a Road Traffic Collision." The nurse hesitated.

"I know what an RTC is, luv. Go on."

"She was an American," the nurse took a deep breath which Bill could hear clearly, "anyway, we'd just finished checking her over, when some other Americans arrived and took her. I tried stopping them, but they didn't care and took her anyway."

"Yeah?" various possibilities had been unleashed inside Bill's imagination.

"These other Americans, did they kidnap her?"

"Oh no," the girl sounded horrified, but then thought about it and wondered whether that would've really been any worse, "No, you see, she'd hit another road user, and the Police had interviewed her before these other Americans had arrived..."

Oh shit, Bill thought to himself. He could now clearly see which direction this one was taking.

"And I heard them say it didn't matter as they were diplomats."

Bill exhaled away from the phone. *This one's gonna be big.* "Diplomats? So she was the diplomat? Or were they all?"

"Well, I'm not sure, but like I said, I think it might be news." she hesitated again, "I just thought that if she hit a cyclist and hurt him, and now she's been taken away by

27

people talking about diplomats... Is that important enough to be news?" she asked.

"It might be, luv," Bill replied. But he needed specifics so that he could find out more, "Can you tell me the name of your hospital or the names of the local plod who interviewed her? Or anything that will help me follow up and see if this woman has done what you think?"

"I suppose so," replied the nurse.

Bill Addison was good at his job and he knew it. He'd finished up with the nurse, but only after managing to persuade her to give him a contact number. He'd promised her whatever it seemed she wanted, but knew he couldn't risk hitting a total dead end, so he'd covered that base. "Listen up everyone," he yelled. The room was still filled with chatter, but the overall noise level dropped in response to his call. Bill put his fingers in his mouth and let out a deafening whistle, then repeated himself.

With everyone's attention properly gained, he started, "Look, we've got a big one here, forget chasing royals and celebs, we've got an American diplomat who had a head-on collision with a cyclist. We don't know where it happened, but we know what hospital she got taken to. So we can work out where she was based, by starting with what's closest to that hospital and then working our way outwards. I wanna know where the accident happened, whose fault it was, who the first responders were, what the Police have to say. I want her name, her husband's name, her husband's job, where she was born and where he was born," people had already started responding, both via keyboard and by chatter, but he wasn't done, so he bust out another infuriatingly loud whistle.

"Jesus Christ, Bill, enough of the bleedin' whistling." moaned a young male colleague.

Bill ignored him to continue, "I wanna know if they're nice people or arseholes, I wanna know if they're good drivers or they've already got speeding tickets and all that. I wanna know who the other person is and how they're doing."

The room noise continued to escalate, "Remember, this has got to be about the people. Yeah, we need to know what happened, but it's about the personality of who did what, and who got hit. And..." he let out another monstrous whistle.

"Seriously?" asked the same man.

"And, most importantly, my source said that the yank driver was bundled away from the hospital, and all the talk was about not worrying as they're diplomats. So, if we are looking at somebody pulling a diplomatic hit and run, that's what's gonna make this big; the simple morals of it."

10.

Toby had already successfully crossed the border into a neighboring country, one more closely allied with Great Britain, the knowledge of which had enabled him to unwind slightly. For him, the job was done and it was simply time to go home, have a beer with the lads and then see what the bosses had planned for him next.

Not all of the tasks he was given were so grave, but it didn't concern him. He'd long since come to terms with the fact that what he was doing didn't conflict with his personal sense of right and wrong, no matter what others may have thought. Of course, nobody outside the department would ever know what he did, but that wasn't the point.

Last night's case was a stellar example, one piece of rubbish removed from this earth, and nobody with a shred of decency would ever mourn him—end of story. Toby was more concerned with returning his rental car and making his flight, than looking backward.

He pulled into the car return bay, fidgeted impatiently while the jobsworth painstakingly inspected the car for any microscopic damage and then had to sprint toward the terminal to ensure he made his flight. As he fed his boarding pass into the machine, his phone received a text, but with more pressing issues, he shut the device off so he could take his turn in the security line.

Having cleared security, he had to hurtle through the crowds to make it before the departure gate closed and then standing at the empty gate breathless, the attendant had to ask permission before allowing the latecomer through.

As Toby finally walked down the aisle looking for his seat, he heard the flight crew shut the doors. With barely enough time to stash his bag and buckle up, he powered on his phone to check the content of the text. As his phone rebooted, the device's theme tune played rather too loudly, embarrassing him enough that he tried muffling the noise by covering it with his t-shirt. He smiled awkwardly at the elderly woman sitting to his side, then checked the text, 'Tobe, call me m8. Urgent'. Toby winced, he'd never have enough time to call his brother-in-law, and sure enough, the flight attendant had already started hovering, "Sir, all phones should already be turned off."

Toby heard the elderly lady let out an overly dramatic sigh, clearly done for audience enjoyment. He grinned cheekily at the attendant, apologized, and held the power button once again.

As his phone screen went black, he turned to his neighbour, and smiling, he offered, "Hi, sorry about that, I'm flying home, are you off on your holidays?"

11.

Madyson couldn't comprehend the pace at which things were happening. She'd been bundled into the back of a huge military cargo plane and was looking at something which the uniformed guy had described to her as her seat. Whatever it was, a seat it was not; it was comprised of a yellow plastic board for your butt and a color-coordinated plastic net for your back. She winced; the flight back was how many hours?

The co-pilot waited for her to take her seat, buckled her in and then returned to the cockpit, taking his place next to the pilot, "Who's the passenger?" he asked as he sorted out his own buckles.

The pilot shook his head, "Wife of a spook."

The co-pilot grimaced, "Why the urgent ride from us?"

The pilot wrapped his hand around the microphone of his helmet com and nodded for his right-hand man to do the same, then continued in a lowered voice, "She had a wreck in her personal car and they're using his diplomatic status to…" he lowered his voice, "…bail."

The co-pilot frowned incredulously, then, lost for words, just shook his head.

Back in the cavernous cargo bay, Jeff finally broke the silence he'd maintained since pulling Maddy from the British hospital, "Madyson."

32

She rolled her eyes. He hadn't contracted her name, which meant he was going to lecture her. She didn't bother responding.

"Talk me through it. What happened exactly?" Jeff stared at her. His eyes were cold, angry even.

Madyson looked down at her knees, then at the painted metal floor of the jet, trying to recall how such a promising morning had deteriorated into this, "I wanted to run into town, get a coffee, do some shopping, just get out really. You don't know how boring this is for me." She looked up at him, pleading with her eyes, hoping for some sympathy from the man she'd followed halfway across the world.

Jeff looked at her even harder. The word 'boring' didn't seem like her smartest choice of adjective. Now he couldn't bring himself to reply.

She looked back down at the floor, sighed, and felt tears welling in her eyes once more, "I went out to the car, started it, the security guards opened the gate for me."

"They're Military Policemen, Maddy, not security guards. They're soldiers with power. Power over you when you're inside that base."

"So you don't wanna hear what happened then?" Maddy asked feistily.

Jeff ground his teeth together and continued to glare.

Maddy refocused on the metal flooring in front of her feet, "They..." she petulantly avoided using the correct term, "let me out of the gate and I turned right toward town." She squinted, trying desperately to remember what happened next, then her eyes quickly widened.

Jeff watched her reaction; it's what he'd been looking for, "What, Maddy?"

She just shook her head. Her crying became audible again.

At that exact moment, Jeff felt furious with his wife for the very first time in all their years, "What, Maddy" he boomed at her.

"I unlocked my phone, okay?" She spat out, her face pleading with him again.

He closed his eyes, rocking his head backward in disbelief. "You were screwing around on your cell phone?"

She put her hands to her face, rubbing the tears from her cheekbones, "Yes, just for a second." she looked back at the floor in total shame, "Yes."

Jeff looked away in disbelief, threw his hands in the air, then suddenly unbuckled and strode away from Maddy in the direction of the cockpit. Walking straight in, his furious voice betrayed his mood, "Are we gonna go or what?"

The pilots both turned in disbelief, "We'll leave as scheduled, sir." replied the pilot with a slightly sarcastic tone to his voice.

"We'll leave now!" Jeff snapped back in an unflatteringly high-pitched voice.

Both pilots turned to look Jeff in the eye fully. The co-pilot suppressed his desire to retaliate, respecting his superior's right to take control. "We don't our take orders from you, Sir," the pilot managed surprisingly calmly.

"You don't think your superiors take their orders from mine?" Jeff was intent on winning now.

The pilot considered Jeff's question, then shook his head gently, "No. No, sir, I don't believe they do. Although if you can have your superiors request that my superiors order me to take off, earlier than scheduled, I'll get right on it. Sir."

The pilot turned his head away, empowering the co-pilot, who added, "But you'll need to sit back down and buckle up to do that." The absence of the word Sir seemed inordinately noticeable. Jeff left the cockpit, even angrier than before.

"Well, that makes sense." said the co-pilot to his colleague.

"How's that?" the pilot didn't get his meaning.

"The wife uses diplomatic immunity to duck out of trouble, the husband is a grade-A Langley asshole, and lucky us, we get to fly 'em both home."

The pilot grinned, "Well, that jackass interrupted our preflight checklist, so I guess we're gonna have to start over."

"Do you know how bad this is?" Jeff snapped at Maddy, knowing he'd get no response, "You drove on the wrong side of the road, you were distracted by your phone, and you slammed a kid into the next century. But not stateside, you did it in the UK. They're our number one ally. How do you think they're gonna feel about this?"

Maddy quickly looked up, "But we have diplomatic immunity, don't we?"

There we go, Jeff thought. *It's taken all this time for her to realize what's really going on.*

"Yeah, we do." he replied, "but you'd better hope that kid pulls through. Right now, this would be a charge called 'Driving without due care and attention'. But if the kid dies, you're looking at something they call 'Causing death by dangerous driving' and I don't know if our diplomatic status would hold for that. This is all unchartered waters, Maddy."

She swallowed hard, having nothing to offer.

Jeff was trying to run it all through his head, which triggered a question, "So where's the phone?"

Maddy squinted in thought. *Where was her phone?* She had no idea. She'd blacked out, did she faint like in an old movie? It didn't matter. Moving on, she remembered that she'd unbuckled after getting hung up in the car and after that, everyone else took over.

Jeff could see her thought process, "Where is your phone, Maddy?"

She winced and looked up at Jeff, terrified now, "It's still in the car, I think. It's probably on the floor."

36

Jeff's head rolled back again. So her phone was almost certainly in the car, which would have already been towed away as evidence. *When will they actually look at the car?* he wondered, before asking her the pressing question, "What were you doing on your phone?"

Her face filled with shame again, "I was going to take a photo, to post online."

He shook his head again. He couldn't bring himself to ask what she needed to take a photo of so badly, "So, had you taken the photo? Or just unlocked your phone?"

Remembering this stuff was so hard. Maddy knew how important it was but just couldn't remember. The whole thing had happened so quickly and it had been so overwhelming, that she wasn't sure of anything. "I know I'd unlocked it, and I think I'd opened the camera app." her expression wasn't at all confidence-inspiring.

Jeff was still shaking his head, if she'd taken a photo, then it would be date stamped and that would be indisputable evidence of her negligence. He didn't know whether their diplomatic status would be upheld in this unique situation, but he knew they had to get that phone back. He also knew it'd be way better for them if the damn kid could survive.

12.

"Sir?" called WPC Lucy Bell.

"Yes, Bell," the Inspector replied.

"That was the hospital on the phone. The lad hit by the American driver just died."

"Poor lad." he paused to sigh. "Alright, Bell, that means the charge has changed. Remind me, when you attended the scene, did the Area Traffic Car attend?"

"No, Sir," Lucy replied.

"Then you need to head over to the Accident Reconstruction Team as this will move up from a driving without due care charge, to a death by dangerous one, and they'll have to investigate the new charge. They're gonna need you and your existing file on the case, so before heading over there, I want you to make sure all your I's are dotted, and your T's are crossed. I don't want any of my constables turning up unprepared."

"On it, Sir." Lucy located the appropriate file, opened it, and checked her work. Satisfied, she headed out of the door in the direction of the recon team.

Lucy entered the ART room, where a sole uniformed Sergeant was typing into a computer, "Can I help you, Constable?"

"Yes, Sarge, name's WPC Bell; I attended an RTC this

morning. A lad on a bicycle had been hit by a car, and the evidence pointed to a driving without due care and attention charge."

"I heard about it. Has something changed?"

"The boy just passed and as it's probably a death by dangerous driving charge now..."

"Why the death by dangerous?" he interrupted.

"Coz she was driving on the wrong side of the road."

The Recon cop scrunched up his face and stopped typing, "Why was she doing that? Was she on her mobile phone?"

"No, Sarge. Well, she might have been, but she was an American, so it's also possible she forgot what side to drive on." Lucy answered.

The recon officer considered her answer, "Is she on holiday?"

"No, Sarge, she's a wife from the Air Force base."

Now he turned away from his computer altogether, swivelling his chair to face her better, "Have you got your file?"

"Here," Lucy Bell handed him her complete file.

"Did you sketch the scene?"

"I did," she leaned in and flipped the file pages to the appropriate one. "I also shot some photos on my mobile phone and then later I printed off an aerial view which shows the base and its proximity to the accident scene. She'd have exited the gate here, taken the road I've highlighted in green, and then this is where she hit the boy." Lucy pointed.

The recon officer nodded approvingly, "Nice work WPC, Bell was it?"

"Yes Sir, and thanks," Lucy replied.

"I know the road," he continued, "it rises here, right?"

"Exactly." they were both studying the aerial view.

"And where does it crown?" He asked.

"Right here." Lucy's finger stabbed the spot where the impact occurred.

"So she left the base, turned right out of the gate, went up the hill and then hit him right where the road crowns." Lucy nodded in acknowledgement. "And she was driving on the wrong side of the road." he summarised

Still nodding, Lucy turned back to her sketch of the scene to prove her case, "There were skid marks here and here. The driver's SUV came to a stop here, as you can see they're both on the right-hand side of the road, with her vehicle facing in this direction."

He took a deep breath, "The victim?"

"A sixteen-year-old lad, local boy."

"The poor parents." He sighed, "Okay, so this is good work Bell, but it's just the beginning. We'll have to redo all the paperwork to reflect the new charge before handing it over to the CPS. Have you done a death by dangerous before?"

"No, Sarge."

The recon officer looked up at Lucy and sighed, "You can call me Kirk instead of Sarge all the time, okay?" Lucy nodded her acknowledgement. "So then WPC Bell, when we up the charge to a death by dangerous one, there's more work to be done. There's more forensics, more witness statements, more lovely paperwork." Kirk fell silent, thinking through what needed to be done. "Considering the driver is a foreign national and one that's here by invitation by our Government, we need to make sure everything is perfect before we make an arrest. So we'd better get going straight away."

Lucy looked at Kirk, then at her file, "Oh, you mean, I can?"

"Why not? This is your work, so I'm sure you want to see it through. Let's start by heading out to the scene before it gets dark."

13.

Toby had caught up with some sleep on the flight home and was now standing half in the aisle and half in his seat, waiting for the first rows to exit the plane. As the people ahead of him finally started to clear a route, Toby cheekily asked his elderly neighbour if he could lift down her bag, knowing it would throw her judgement of him. Astonished, she accepted and then happily chatted to him as he patiently helped her down the narrow aisle and off the plane.

As they stepped onto the jetway, Toby saw two uniformed Police ahead. They were checking the faces of each passenger as they walked past. He approached, his head full of potential scenarios, still arm in arm with the grumpy old lady. As he neared them, the younger plod gave his elder a nudge, blatantly nodding in Toby's direction.

The two officers started toward Toby, making the old lady look ahead, then backward, then suspiciously at Toby.

"Mister Toby Miller?" asked the elder plod, and suddenly the old lady pulled her arm out of Toby's and walked off; her expression of disgust at having been tricked into trusting him plain to see. As she accelerated away, looking like she needed a shower to clean herself of him, Toby stopped without saying a word and started sizing up the two Policemen, wondering out of habit who'd put up the better fight.

Like many soldiers, he believed the civilian Police to be inferior in every way and decided there was no way he was going to let these two detain him, not without some humiliation and bruises. But then Toby started to wonder if he'd misread the whole scenario.

What really struck him was how the two plod weren't trying to look threatening, which they'd have surely done if they'd been sent to place him under arrest. Their manner was different and he couldn't quite place it. In reaction, his expression turned to one of total confusion and finally, he managed to respond with a cautious "Yes."

The younger of the two cops was getting a troubling kind of vibe from Toby, but they'd been ordered to locate him out of professional courtesy, so he brushed aside his instincts and took point, "Mister Miller, we've been asked to escort you straight through immigration, would you mind coming with us?"

Toby started walking with the two old bill, trying to figure it all out, without having to ask them for help. It couldn't be anything to do with the job he'd just completed - that was way above their pay grade, as was all of his work. So it had to be personal. Suddenly he remembered the text that he'd glimpsed before his flight home and how it had completely slipped his mind with all the rushing around.

Think man, he told himself. What had he got? His brother in law had asked him to call about something urgent, but he hadn't done it. Now because he was being escorted by these two plod, he couldn't return the call anyway, so it would have to wait. But was this unrelated? Unlikely.

What the hell could connect the two and be so urgent that he was getting rushed through border control? It had to be something personal and serious. He inhaled deeply; this wasn't looking good.

Toby reluctantly accepted how desperately he needed to know and stopped walking, "Is it my sister?" he directed his question to the plod who'd done the majority of the talking.

Toby's doubts and concerns had removed all trace of his previously threatening demeanour, altering the younger cop's attitude toward him, "I'm sorry, we don't know." he turned to look Toby in the eye and Toby could see the sincerity.

So now a copper was genuinely sorry. *What the hell was going on?*

The younger officer continued, "We were just asked to rush you through. All we know is there's somebody waiting for you on the other side, somebody who could pull enough strings to make this happen."

Any of his superiors had enough clout to swing that, so it didn't narrow things down at all. Toby's eyes searched the crowds in some futile attempt to find answers.

They reached the UK Border Agency booths and the elder of the two plod signalled for Toby to stop. As they waited for the first available immigration officer, Toby studied the scene, finding that every face in the endless line of people waiting to clear UK immigration was looking at them. A young couple left a booth in the middle of the hall and instead of accepting the next person in line, the immigration officer waved to signify that Toby and his Police escort should be next. She scanned Toby's passport, looked at his face, and handed it back without asking a single question. Toby had never seen anything like it.

On past trips to the US, he'd enviously watched as the separate line for their own citizens moved about ten times faster than the line for visitors. In the UK, there was no preferential treatment for their own people, it simply wasn't British. And so, within seconds of taking his passport back, Toby and his Police escort were walking out into the bustling arrivals area.

Toby was starting to feel like he had no control of his situation and it felt bizarre. He looked around the arrivals area, hoping to find something which would offer him more clarity and suddenly caught a glimpse of his old Commanding Officer wearing civilian clothes.

Toby froze to the spot.

Captain Bowyer had seen them already, thanks to the bright uniforms of the two Police and before greeting Toby, he offered his hand to each of the cops, "Thank you, gents." He nodded to them and they went on their way, the younger one taking one last considered look at Toby before disappearing back into the secure area.

"Who is it, Sir? Is it my sister?" asked Toby, fighting the emotion he could feel welling inside.

"No Miller, I'm sorry, but it's your nephew, Luke."

Neither man felt unnecessarily abrupt in getting straight to the point; it was the Army way and it was expected.

But the Captain's words had made Toby's breathing go to shit. Instantly. He had to regain control of himself, but his eyes were filling too, "May I ask what happened, Sir?" Toby was standing rigidly, almost to attention, although it wasn't a conscious decision.

Fuck. Captain Bowyer despised this part of the job and he'd done it so many damned times. To see such brave, strong soldiers weakened by news like this was agonizing, "He was riding his bicycle and he was hit by a car, he put up a really good fight but," the Captain was fighting his own emotions now, "his injuries were too severe."

Toby had fought back a little self-control, but his nostrils were flared. It all was turning to anger now.

The Captain winced. Sergeant Toby Miller was one of the best soldiers that Captain Bowyer had ever served with. He'd fully expected Miller to be drafted into an elite regiment like the SAS, but the fact that he'd been swiped from his Company by the suits at GCHQ for occasional use by some undeclared British Government agency, showed just how rare a soldier Miller was. Seeing him like this was all the more challenging for the Captain, so how could he possibly tell him the next part?

"He was a strong lad Miller. You should be very proud." Toby was nodding mechanically. Bowyer readied himself to deliver the sting, "I am sorry Miller, but the driver of the car was the wife of a US diplomat, and since the accident, they've left the UK, which they're able to do under diplomatic immunity agreements."

An immense wave of confusion hit Toby, "But they're our friends," he knew how naive it sounded the moment it came out.

Captain Bowyer looked at Miller, nodded, glanced down at the floor uncomfortably, then back up at Miller, "Yes Sergeant Miller, of course they are, which is why we're not going to read anything into that, it's early days. I've got a car waiting, let's go."

Toby had known Captain Bowyer for years now and unlike most gormless Army officers, which the men in the ranks universally referred to as Ruperts, Bowyer was a good man. Toby followed the Captain's orders, as he'd always done.

14.

"The boy just died." somebody called across the newsroom. Then frustrated, the same voice yelled, "Oi, listen!" even louder. Having successfully lowered the overall volume, they took another shot at sharing the update, "The boy hit by the American diplomat, he just died in hospital."

Now Bill Addison stood up to address the already attentive room, "Alright people, this will change the charge brought against her by the Police, which changes everything. You all know what we're writing about now, but has anybody figured out what's happened with the driver?"

The room fell as silent as a newsroom possibly could.

Bill was pissed off, "Are you bloody kidding me? Will somebody find out if this bloody woman is still here or not? For God's sake, people, it's the most important part of this whole story." The noise level quickly increased again.

"Danny!" Bill yelled above the racket, "get out there and shoot the bloody scene, shoot where the accident happened and shoot the gates of the Air Force base, we need images to go with everything. And everyone else, find out everything you can about this damn driver, will you?" Bill waved his arms in mock despair. "The clock is ticking," he roared.

15.

Lucy and Kirk parked their police car immediately behind the scene of the morning's incident. They placed Police Caution signs to ensure they wouldn't become victims of another careless driver, then walked over to the fatal spot.

"Her SUV was here when I arrived." Lucy stood in the spot using her arms to indicate the direction of travel for the vehicle.

"Hold that," said Kirk, and he walked further on to place himself in the oncoming direction, he then turned and faced Lucy from the position that young Luke would have been in. Standing there, he could imagine it all too easily from the young man's perspective and while Kirk was the consummate professional at work, this was more than just a job. It was simply impossible not to be emotionally invested in situations like this. *At least it would have been quick*, he thought to himself.

"So the victim" avoiding constant use of the actual names of the victims helped officers to do their jobs "would have been cycling in this direction." Kirk looked down at the area where the road met the narrow footpath. "The road's edge is in good condition with no pothole damage, and so there's no reason for the victim to have been positioned out too wide within his lane."

Lucy watched as Kirk inched slowly toward her, studying the ground the whole time.

As he stopped and knelt, she joined him, "Yeah, I noted that on my sketch."

Kirk nodded. It was a small scuff, the width of a bicycle's tyre, he then backtracked, "So this is from the lad's bike, but the SUV's tyre marks don't start until back there."

Lucy was nodding, "So she made impact here, but only lost braking traction over there." she pointed to two very separate spots.

Kirk had seen this before, the gap was incriminating, "It's too far between impacting the cyclist and the point where the road shows signs of her deceleration."

Lucy was a local WPC who dealt with a huge variety of call-outs, but this was her first time working with a specialist, and she found it fascinating.

"Alright, so where's the vehicle now?" asked Kirk.

Before answering, Lucy considered the current time, "It should have been dropped off at the police pound by now." She was intrigued to know what was going on inside Kirk's head but was content to wait for him to share in his own time.

Kirk nodded to her, then walked the same steps a second time and still nodding, he decided he was ready to share. "This is a preliminary inspection, but it appears that the driver struck the cyclist first and then applied the brakes second." He was still intently studying the most subtle of marks on the road's surface. "And as you've already shown, she was travelling down the wrong side of this single

50

carriageway road, but what I'm now wondering is whether she was even looking where she was going at the time of the impact."

A shudder ran down Lucy's spine, she hadn't considered that possibility.

"We're going to need to go all out on this one. Forensics need to go over her car, so we'll need that done immediately, which means sending them straight to the pound. We need to interview the ambulance staff. We'll need your official statement, statements from the hospital staff and...." Kirk walked the route a third time, shaking his head.

"And once forensics are done with the SUV, we'll need to close the road and do a recreation, using her car."

"Oh, so how does that work?" Lucy had never heard of this before.

"Well, we drive the scene in the actual vehicle, if it's still in drivable order. If it's not, we'll do it in an identical vehicle. We'll do several runs to ascertain the speed at which it was travelling. We need to use the same vehicle, on the same road, and in the same weather conditions so her solicitor can't try and discredit the investigation's findings as inaccurate. And Bell, what was the driver's name?"

"Lutz, Madyson Lutz, with a Y."

"Then finally, we'll need to place Mrs. Madyson, with a Y, Lutz, under arrest for the charge of causing death by dangerous driving. After that, the courts can decide her fate."

51

16.

"Are you going to be alright, Miller?" asked the Captain.

"Of course, I'll be fine Sir," Toby replied.

When Army Drill Sergeants put new recruits through basic training, the recruits were always told that when an Officer asked how you were doing, the only acceptable answer was 'Fine thank you Sir' and it frustrated Captain Mark Bowyer that every single one of those men persisted with the same attitude and the same answer, no matter how many years passed, and no matter what obstacles life threw at them.

"I'm not asking you as your CO Miller. I'm asking you as a friend, because I hope that after all the years we've served together, you think of me as a friend too."

Toby turned and looked at his CO, "I do, Sir, but really I'll be fine Sir. Thanks for the lift." and with that, Toby swung open the passenger door and stepped out of the unmarked British Ministry of Defence car.

In Miller's case, it's probably not just bravado, thought Captain Bowyer as he checked his mirror and accelerated away.

"Tobe." Whispered the haggard looking woman, stepping out of the house.

Toby dropped his bag and ran up the front path, wrapping his arms around his sister's slim frame, "I'm sorry, Trace. I'm so bloody sorry."

He could feel her slump in his arms as she gently started to sob. The pair just stood on the front steps in each other's arms as the world cycled and drove by obliviously, and as he supported his sister's weight, Toby finally released his own tears, something he wasn't sure he'd ever done before.

In this area, the locals thought of Toby as a hard case, not a man to be crossed, but Toby knew the tag of hard case really belonged to his big sister, yet here they both were, crying in the bloody street. But the tears just gushed forth and Toby couldn't stop them. He tightly held his sister while they finally shared their grief, as they'd both unknowingly been waiting to do.

Toby's sister Tracey finally opened her eyes and, looking over Toby's shoulder, noticed an elderly neighbour walking his dog past the end of her front path. The man removed his woollen flat cap in a simple gesture of respect, and Tracey instantly collapsed in Toby's arms, wailing.

It triggered a release she'd never imagined possible, "Why?" she heard herself squealing. "Why did they take my bloody boy?" She was screaming at nobody in particular, "My beautiful baby boy." her body was lurching and twitching in spasms. "Why?" Her voice was pleading now, but Toby could barely make out her words. Suddenly Toby wanted to kill someone, but not to avenge fallen comrades and not out of duty. He wanted to kill then and there, because he felt anger like he'd never known before. He felt hatred, pure hatred, and with that he'd found the way to stop his tears.

17.

WPC Lucy Bell and her surrogate recon squad training officer had travelled from the accident scene to the Air Force base, to interview the Ministry of Defence officials working on the main gate, which at this particular base was a pair of Royal Military Police soldiers.

The civilian Police weren't in a position to enter the base and make an arrest; this interview was merely part of the complex process required to fulfil (and ideally exceed) the Crown Prosecution Service's requirements for prosecution.

"So do you know Mrs. Lutz?" asked Kirk, who'd introduced himself formally as Police Sergeant Treavett.

"Know her no, but we've seen her coming and going since she's been on base," answered Lance Corporal Smith.

"And how long has that been?" asked Lucy.

"Well, she's been passing through this gate for," the MP tried to find something accurate to link the memory to, "I'd say five weeks now."

"You seem quite certain. Why is that?" Lucy continued with the same MP.

"Well, you see Ma'am, she was an attractive woman and I'd just had a falling out of sorts with my own girlfriend, and so, I might have thought some foolish thoughts when I first met her." Lucy smiled sympathetically, triggering an embarrassed chuckle from the young MP. "Although since we've seen her coming and going more, I'd say that initial attraction has since gone."

"And why is that?" asked Kirk.

The second MP answered that question, "Because she's snooty and cold."

"What about her driving?" asked Lucy.

"Well, that's hard to say," it was Lance Corporal Smith again, "we can see their confusion within this short exit road, but because of the hedge and then the treeline, we have very little visibility once they're out on the public road."

The two civilian Police nodded as Lucy took notes.

"How is the boy?" asked the second MP, "is there any update? We'd heard he was injured quite badly."

"He was Lance Corporal, and unfortunately, this afternoon he passed away in the hospital."

"Bollocks." the first MP said under his breath. "So she'll be facing charges then?"

"Our investigation is ongoing," Kirk replied.

"Of course," replied the second MP, "we know the drill. I always knew something like this would happen eventually, though."

"Why's that?" asked Lucy, intrigued.

"Well, when we have duty on the gate here, we see them coming and going, and they're just really bad at adapting to driving on the left-hand side of the road. I know it's not easy, I've done a posting in Belize, and so I know it's a hard adjustment to swap sides, but..." he shrugged instead of finishing his point. "And they're not the most skilled drivers, to begin with."

"What do you mean by that?" asked Lucy again.

Kirk answered this question for his own colleague, "I think the Lance Corporal is referring to the differing standards required to gain your driving licence. What's our test now? A fifty-question theory test, followed by nearly an hour of observed driving, following about forty to fifty hours of lessons with a fully qualified Driving Standards Agency Instructor?"

"Sounds about right. And in America?" asked Lucy.

"About fifteen minutes." the second MP chipped in.

"Is that true?" Lucy asked Kirk, the second MP looking slightly wounded that she doubted his knowledge.

"It can be, it varies from State to State, but the standard is certainly less demanding than the majority of other western countries," Kirk responded. "But we start with no assumptions about Mrs. Lutz's abilities as a fine driver. Our duty is to simply find and present any applicable evidence."

Lucy felt slightly reprimanded but nodded in agreement as his point couldn't be disputed.

18.

Toby followed his sister through the front door of her house, straight into their living room.

"Alright, Tobe." said her husband, looking up from the sofa.

"Alright, Damien," replied Toby, his eyes red from his recent uncharacteristic outburst.

Seeing Toby's eyes, Damien involuntarily looked away, scared by the idea of having to discuss anything involving Toby crying openly. Keeping his eyes averted, he asked, "Fancy a cuppa mate?"

"Yeah, that'd be nice." Toby nodded before walking over to him. Once Damien had got to his feet, Toby startled Damien by wrapping his arms around him, then releasing him before saying, "I'm so sorry mate."

Damien's head pivoted back slightly, his eyes welled up, and he said, "Thanks, Toby," before rushing off toward the kitchen.

"How's he doing, Trace?" Toby asked his sister.

Tracey wasn't holding herself normally; she slumped as if she'd just done a few rounds in the boxing ring. She shrugged, "He'll be okay. What choice 'ave we got?"

Toby didn't know how to answer. He was so far out of his comfort zone, this emotional stuff was never his strong point, and neither was knowing how to say the right thing to people. He knew it was a problem - he'd just never figured out how to fix it. He needed to steer things back onto something where he could be of use, randomly picking the accident investigation as a starting point, "Have the Police been? I mean since they first came."

Tracey knew what he meant -since they'd initially had to inform her of the severity of her baby boy's accident, "Not since the first time, no." she answered.

"Who's dealing with it? What's their name?" Toby asked.

"Bell, a lady copper. I think Lucy was her first name."

"I'll follow up with her." Toby could barely recognize his sister. Even to his insensitive man eyes, it was obvious that she was spiritually crushed.

She shook her head apathetically, "You don't have to do that, Tobe."

"Yes, I do," replied Toby, the steel back in his voice. *I really do.*

19.

The C130 touched down at Langley Air Force base in Virginia. Madyson was still awake, an unusual occurrence for her after such a long flight. Jeff was too, and although they'd both remained awake and seated opposite each other, they'd undertaken the entire flight in absolute silence. The day's events weighed heavily on them both.

The plane felt like it was taxiing itself to the appropriate point, something they couldn't confirm due to the absence of windows in the fuselage, still the heavy silence continued.

Finally, the plane came to a halt and noises outside signaled movement. Maddy and Jeff unbuckled themselves and walked toward the rear of the huge jet as daylight started illuminating its gray interior, instantly transforming the drab gray into something so bright it strained their eyes. Maddy waited for her eyes to adjust, half expecting Jeff to take her arm and guide her down the jet's huge pivoting exit ramp, but he'd already walked halfway down it on his own.

Having reached the bottom, he turned to look where she was, saw her delay and looked impatiently down at the floor. She suddenly felt a vertigo-like moment. Her balance felt off, but it wasn't the balance she needed to walk down the ramp; it was the balance of life itself. It was new. Everything was new; a shiver ran down her spine. Her whole life had changed.

Maddy looked down at her husband of three years, her love of five, and saw a man for whom she was suddenly a source of irritation and stress. How could one thing so dramatically change everything? She hesitated as if the act of walking down the ramp was an acceptance of this horrific new reality.

Jeff merely continued to stare at the floor.

Maddy felt the emotion rising inside once more, but finally she fought it. She lifted her head high and walked down the ramp, straight past Jeff. She was going to survive this, with or without him.

20.

"The vultures have arrived." Lance Corporal Smith nodded in the direction of a grey-coloured estate car that was parking in the entrance to the base, directly opposite Lucy and Kirk's police car. They watched as a photographer sprinted to the other side of the road, framing what had to be a wide angle shot of the Air Base's entrance for their breaking story.

Neither the MPs nor the civilian Police were surprised at their presence. It was their speed that always caught everybody off balance.

"Here we go." said the second MP, who resumed his correct position to the far side of the base barrier, the first MP moving back to stand by the hut that held the computer system, which scanned and logged all entries and exits, plus the base phone, their wet weather gear, etc.

Kirk nodded in the direction of their own car and reminded Lucy of the expectation of silence from her in such a fresh investigation.

"Following the death of Luke Rigg, will the Police be pursuing a charge of death by dangerous driving?" asked Danny throwing his camera over his shoulder in order to start his digital voice recorder.

Kirk simply smiled blankly and continued walking toward the police car. .

"Is it true that Mrs. Lutz has already used her diplomatic

status to leave the UK?"

Both Lucy and Kirk hadn't seen that coming, Kirk's eyes widened involuntarily, and Lucy paused before opening the car door.

"Holy cow!" said Danny, "You didn't bloody know." With that, he ran back to his own car, opened a laptop computer and initiated a phone call.

"What the hell's going on, Sarge?"

21.

As Madyson finally walked down the exit ramp of the C130 plane, she saw a pair of suited men walking toward them.

"Jeff." the younger of the two clearly knew Maddy's husband already.

"John." replied her husband, shaking his hand.

"And this is National Security Advisor Bob Taggart." John gestured toward the older man he'd arrived with. Jeff moved to shake the newcomer's hand too, "Mister Taggart, it's an honor to meet you, sir."

"Uh-huh, under far from ideal circumstances, though. Still, we look after our own. I assume this is Mrs. Lutz?" asked the President's Security Advisor.

Maddy shook his hand silently.

"So you've been updated on the news?" asked the President's Security Advisor. Clearly, they hadn't, so he filled them in, "The Brits will be looking to pursue us with a charge they call death by dangerous driving."

Maddy's knees wobbled momentarily, but she forced herself to focus on her own problems, "What does that mean?" she asked.

Bob Taggart shrugged, "I'm not sure it matters really, you have diplomatic immunity due to Jeff here, and we simply won't allow them to take you back there. Not under any circumstances."

Jeff suddenly looked uneasy, "I'm not sure if this is appropriate right now, but it's highly time-sensitive."

"Go on, Mister Lutz," replied Bob Taggart.

Jeff took a deep breath, he was accustomed to impressing his superiors with the information he had to offer. He'd dreamed of one day being put with one of the President's closest men and of making an impression. But this wasn't the impression he'd planned on making, "We might have another problem."

Advisor Taggart opened his palm, a gesture intended to encourage open discourse.

"It's possible that my wife was using her phone at the time of the accident, and we already know that she'd drifted onto the right side of the road, so would it be better to recover the phone before it's discovered inside her truck?"

Advisor Taggart rolled his eyes.

22.

"Where's Frodo?" asked Toby, taking the last gulp of tea from his mug.

His sister's shoulders slumped, Damien stepped in to spare her more pain, "Follow me, mate." Damien led the way up the narrow staircase, turning at the top toward what Toby already knew was Luke's room.

Toby felt another wave of grief welling inside him. Luke's room was unchanged from his last visit, still the same posters of Premier League soccer players, Italian cars and tanned blonde girls in bright swimsuits. There was still the 'Please Drive Carefully' road sign he'd stolen on their trip down to Devon a couple of years back. What had changed was the room's sense of purpose.

Sitting in the middle of the bed was a doe eyed spaniel, its cream coat spotted with golden patches. It looked at Toby, the recognition was clear, even visible in the wriggling end of his tail, but it remained firmly planted to the centre of Luke's bed.

Toby frowned and felt the tears welling again, "Are you kidding me?"

"We think he's waiting for Luke," Damien mumbled.

"Oh, for fucks sake." Toby cursed, "Can you give me a moment?" his breathing was getting patchy again. Damien simply nodded and left Toby standing in the doorway to his son's room, former room.

Toby's eyes were leaking bloody fluid again. "What are you doing, you daft dog?" Toby sat next to it and slid the dog toward him, "He's not coming home, fella." Toby was now full on crying again.

"I'm taking Frodo out for a walk," Toby said as he strode toward the front door.

"Thanks, Tobe." his sister was sitting on the sofa, shoulders hunched. She didn't move a muscle as she said it.

"Oh, wait, Tobe," Damien called louder just as Toby touched the doorknob, "the King's Head just opened. You remember the way, right?"

"I do, thanks, Damien. Later."

Toby ambled along, feeling guilty at enjoying the refreshing cool evening air, "I'd like to speak to WPC Bell, please." he said into his mobile phone.

"Who's calling?" asked the other end.

"Nice phone, mate," said a voice behind him, "yeah, that'd look really good on my ear."

"You have got to be joking," Toby said without turning, then stopped. "I'm actually on the phone to the old bill." he turned, "Don't you see how stupid that is?"

Of the two teenagers in front of him, one looked serious, but the other looked down at Frodo, then up at Toby and his eyes opened like an owl. "Jay, that's bloody Luke's uncle.

Leg it mate," then turned and took off like an athlete.

"You don't scare me, you old fag." said the remaining one.

Toby ended the call and slid his phone into his pocket. In reaction, the kid pulled out what looked like a kitchen knife. Toby lunged in and before the kid could even raise the knife, he'd already punched him full force in the adam's apple. The teenager dropped to the floor, a gentle tinkling sound accompanied that of his thud.

"What the hell is wrong with you?" Toby had the kid by the collar of his t-shirt now. "I should beat the bag out of you, you dumb little shite." It's all he'd been wanting to do since he'd arrived in this bloody town, but he looked down at the idiot youth and knew that taking it out on him just wouldn't scratch his itch.

"Listen, Jay, that was your name, wasn't it?" The kid nodded, wheezing. "You've gotta find something better to do than this, seriously." Toby was about to loosen his grip and leave but thought better of it, tugging him up off the pavement by his shirt again. "You like to think you're tough?"

The kid didn't dare nod at the man who'd just disabled him with one cheeky punch, but the fact that he didn't shake his head for a no response was answer enough for Toby. "But I just put you down that quickly." The kid looked emotionally wounded now. "Kid, you need something better to do than this. You need to join the bloody Army, and they'll teach you to fight. Better than that." Toby tilted his head to make a joke of it.

He loosened his grip on the boy's upper body slightly. "Where do you live, Jay?"

"Down the street, number thirty-three," the boy answered as quickly as he could.

"And you thought you could lift my phone? What are we, like twenty houses down from yours?" Kids like this were the staple diet of the Armed Forces; loads of testosterone, but no clue. "I'm almost lost for words, Jay." Toby finally let his shirt go.

Still positioned over the boy to stop him from getting up, Toby stared at him as he thought it through, "You're gonna go home and tell your Mum, you've got a Mum, right?" Toby had to check as broken homes were the new norm.

"Course I got a bloody Mum."

"Well, you're gonna tell her that you tried stealing Toby Miller's phone and that he forgave you. Alright? But you are gonna tell her, Jay." Toby surprised him with a hard slap on the cheek. The kid flinched and looked like he was on the verge of tears.

Toby whipped back from over the top of the boy and pulled him up by the arm, surprising him yet again before reiterating his point. "Now you go and tell your Mum. I'll be in the King's Head if anyone needs me. You understand?" Toby lowered himself to reassure Frodo as the kid took off just as quickly as his friend before him.

23.

Lucy and Kirk had just pulled into the police car pound, now they were walking around, waiting for the forensics team to arrive.

Kirk was pacing around Madyson's SUV. Lucy was intent on learning as much as she could from the specialist, "So what would normally happen in this situation, Sarge?"

Kirk raised his eyebrows. "You're not going to call me Kirk, are you?"

Lucy looked a little uncomfortable, "Not yet, Sarge."

"Fine." he shook it off, "There's nothing normal about this situation Bell. Normally once we've got a car in the pound, we let forensics get to it when they can, but if that reporter was right and there's diplomatic immunity involved, then everything's different."

He went on, unable to stop talking or walking, "Diplomatic laws aren't clear enough. They're open to interpretation and decisions are often made at the Whitehall level. Right now, we haven't had any official statement of a claim to diplomatic immunity, so we can still have forensics look at the vehicle. But who knows what would happen if the Chief Constable received a call making the diplomatic claim official? Would we still get to inspect the vehicle? Or would it be hands off? It could go either way, so if we can get our forensics done before that call, then it's our evidence and it can't be taken back. You see?"

"I do, Sarge." but the overall situation was still too murky for Lucy, "So if we get all our evidence together, can we still hand it over to the CPS? I mean, what's the point if there's diplomatic immunity?"

"That's two totally different questions. Firstly yes, we can absolutely hand it off to the CPS. They'll decide whether to press charges and the CPS are fiercely resistant to outside interference." He raised his eyebrows as he already knew he had to contradict himself. "Although we'll need to request a meeting with the Chief Constable and lay out what we've got, as he'll want in on the decision as to whether we press charges too. The way we handle this will be judged publicly, this case will shine a spotlight on the whole Eastern Constabulary, his Constabulary. However, those considerations should make no impact on how we build the case. In fact, the only way I see it is that we have a duty to build the most cast-iron case of our lives."

"Even if we can't prosecute due to the diplomatic immunity?" Asked Lucy.

The truth was that Kirk wasn't sure; he stopped pacing. "What if Whitehall decided to press the Americans for the return of Madyson Lutz, but we hadn't built a sufficiently strong case?" Kirk asked her back.

Lucy nodded her understanding and found herself checking her own watch, impatiently wondering where the forensics team was.

"Sir." the man spoke into his phone in a barely audible whisper.

"Yes." replied the voice on the phone.

"I'm inside the secure area, but local law enforcement is already at the vehicle. How do you want me to proceed?" He studied the male and female Police Officers as they continued their conversation.

There was a long delay before the voice finally answered, "Abort."

Lucy's mobile phone was buzzing inside her jacket pocket. She checked the screen to see it was the police station's number, "Bell." she answered.

"We've got a caller who's asking for you, his name is Toby Miller, says he's the brother of the RTA victim's Mum. Can I put him through?"

"Absolutely", Lucy replied.

Lucy waited for the line to click before identifying herself, "This is WPC Lucy Bell."

"Hello, my name's Toby Miller. Luke Rigg is my sister's boy." A pause. "Was my sister's boy."

"Hello, Mister Miller. I'm sorry for your loss."

"Yeah, me too. I wanted to talk to you about it."

"I'm sorry, but I can't discuss an ongoing investigation."

"What? Even with the family of the victim, how does that make any sense? I just wanna bloody know if this Yank woman is going to come back and take responsibility." Toby was getting annoyed again.

"Wait, how are you aware that she left the UK?" asked Lucy, surprised, confused even.

Toby scrunched his face in thought. Bowyer had told him, shouldn't he have? Toby couldn't be sure and wasn't about to drop his CO in it, "Came down through the chain of command."

"What chain of command is that?" asked Lucy.

"Army." Toby kept it nice and simple, starting to believe this plod was worrying about all the wrong things, "Excuse me, but it's my nephew I want to talk about, not my job."

"I'm sorry, Mister Miller, let me take down your number and call you back when I can give you more information."

WPC Bell noted Toby's details and headed back to the Lutz woman's SUV, pleased to see a forensics team finally suiting up. "Sarge?" she called over to her new colleague.

"Bell?"

"That was the uncle of the deceased. He's serving Army and he already knew that Mrs. Lutz had been flown out of the UK." It wasn't a question, but her tone made it sound that way.

Kirk scrunched up his face, folded his arms and sat his bum on the bonnet of their police car, "So the Army knew

72

before us? They're Ministry of Defence, maybe they felt obliged to inform the boy's uncle, as he's one of theirs. But that means the MoD knew she'd gone." His face was scrunched in confusion. "She must have flown out on military transport, but did the Americans tell our MoD it was her on the flight before she'd left, or after?"

Lucy really tried to understand the significance, "What difference would it make?" she knew there had to be one.

Kirk still had to rearrange the mounting facts inside his own head, "Well, they still haven't informed us. Us, meaning the Police. So what does that mean? If the MoD didn't know she was on that flight, then they're playing catch up, the same as we are. And that means they'll be looking at us to put together a strong case, in order to request extradition for Mrs. Lutz."

"But if the they knew ahead of time that the Americans were flying her out and didn't share that, it seems to imply there's already an acceptance of her claim for diplomatic immunity." It was a lot to process, which reminded Kirk that the forensics team had finally started to process the vehicle.

24.

"I'll have a pint of Spitfire, please," Toby said to the man behind the bar.

"Coming right up," he answered, placing a spotless glass at just the right angle under the tap, "Aren't you Tracey's brother?"

"I am."

"I just heard about Luke on the news before I unlocked. I'm sorry, would you tell your sister how sorry I am?"

So it was public. Toby sighed. He was going to have to get used to everybody saying they were sorry. "Of course."

Why did everybody say they were sorry, he wondered. The obvious answer was that they were sorry, but why were they all sorry? He took his pint of beer, "Thanks." They were sorry because your life had just gone wrong and theirs hadn't, and they felt sorry for you and probably felt guilty that theirs was unchanged; better than yours, you'd hope. He poured about a third of the pint down his neck in one go.

So what was the deal with the lady copper? She was more concerned with asking questions than answering them. Plod, so no surprise there. But she'd been surprised that Toby knew about the American doing a runner, that's why she wanted to know how he'd found out. He knocked back about another third of his pint.

The Captain had told him. Toby squinted in confusion, then took out his phone, smiled at the idea of the dopey kid who'd tried to steal it and then dialled Captain Bowyer.

He answered the phone with, "Sargeant Miller, how are you doing?"

"Fine, Sir," Toby replied.

The Captain rolled his eyes, "You should go out and have a beer Miller, unwind a little."

The Captain was right. Toby caught the barman's attention, then pointed to his glass.

"So what can I do for you, Miller?"

"I was just wondering how you knew the American driver had already left the UK Sir, about the diplomatic immunity part."

The Captain exhaled audibly, "You should come by the barracks, Miller. Why don't you swing by tomorrow, let's say oh eight hundred hours. Then we can discuss all of this."

"Yes Sir, oh eight hundred. See you then."

Toby knocked back the remainder of his first pint, then settled in to enjoy his second one more slowly. *Oh hell*, he suddenly had a horrible thought. It sounded like the lady copper hadn't expected Toby to know about the American's flight home, but what if his sister didn't know either? Toby leant forward, dropping his head into his hands. *If she doesn't know yet, how the hell is this going to affect her?*

25.

"Sarge?" Lucy called. She'd been so intent on watching the forensics team at work that she'd been getting in their way, and on their nerves, before they'd even started on the car. But now, she'd been ideally positioned to watch as they discovered Madyson's phone. "They just recovered a phone from underneath the driver's seat, it's locked, but its presence and location indicate it must have been in use around the time of the accident."

Kirk started nodding, "Good. That's very good. After forensics are done with it, we'll see if we can get it unlocked." he walked over to Lucy, his own phone illuminated in the palm of his hand, "Look, the whole world knows about this thing now, the same story is on every news site. They're all going with the story that Lutz left the country, shortly after checking herself out of the hospital. But we've still had no official confirmation of that fact."

He started toward their car, "We need to let the forensics crew get on with their job and get back to the station. Now this evidence is ours, no matter what happens, so we can take what we've got upstairs."

Toby had left his second pint of beer on the bar and sprinted back to his sister's house, where he could already hear the chaos from the end of her front path. She'd obviously seen the news, and he hadn't been there with her. Everything was going wrong.

He paused briefly, readying himself for what must come next, then noticed Frodo cowering down by his ankles. As he bent down to reassure the dog, a police car flew down the street, abruptly stopping just a few feet away. Toby started down his sister's front path and watched as the sole Policeman exited the car and sprinted straight to his sister's front door. Irritated, Toby stopped halfway up the footpath and took out his mobile phone.

"WPC Bell? You need to get here now. You caused this mess." he gave Bell the address, hung up while she was still talking, and entered his sister's house.

"You need to calm down, madam." the baby-faced Policeman had his arm out, as if to protect himself.

"Calm down? How dare you tell me to fucking calm down? My boy is dead, the bitch who killed him has run away, coz you let her go, and I have to find out like this." she was gesturing franticly at the television set, her teeth bared like a wild animal.

"Madam, if you don't calm down, I'm going to have to place you under arrest." the officer had chosen his route, poorly perhaps.

Now Toby stepped in, "You arrest my sister and you'll be facing a long fucking stay in hospital, you gormless little twat." he hadn't even raised his voice to deliver the threat.

"What the hell is going on in here?" boomed a huge authoritative voice.

Toby was surprised to see it had emanated from a slim WPC who'd just entered the room.

Her baby-faced colleague attempted to answer her question, but Toby snapped "NO." in a way that silenced the whole room. "Bell?" he asked her.

"I am. Mister Miller, I'm assuming." the room had already quietened down.

"Yeah, Toby. Now look, Officer Bell, my sister's boy got ploughed by a big SUV earlier today." He was angry but calm, the group unanimously respected his right to speak. "he was taken to hospital; he'd been smashed but was alive. Hard to deal with."

"I know, and I'm so sorry," replied Lucy, sizing Toby up as she spoke.

"Not done talking." Toby glared at Bell, "My sister goes to the hospital, and her boy dies." His sister started to shake with tears once again, dropping into Damien's ready arms, but Toby went on, "Really bloody hard to deal with." He raised his hand to silence everybody, "Now she finds out from the TV news that the driver has split, claiming diplomatic immunity after killing her boy. Now we're right on the verge of impossible to deal with."

Lucy could only look down at the floor.

"So how didn't you know this? How come you hadn't told her?" Toby quickly raised both hands, forcing the silence once more. "And then this pillock arrives threatening to arrest her, for being upset." the baby-faced officer tried speaking, but Kirk, who'd entered behind Lucy, interrupted him with, "Constable. Outside please."

"Yes, Sarge." replied the young officer reluctantly.

"I am sorry." Lucy offered to Toby, then his sister. Toby looked into Lucy's eyes and finally saw a hurt human being instead of an arrogant copper.

"Can we come in and sit down, please," Kirk asked.

Toby's sister nodded, and Toby, who'd found himself in charge of the room, felt obliged to officially confirm, "Of course, you can." He cleared them some space on the second sofa.

"Can you please tell us what is going on?" Toby asked respectfully now.

Kirk took a deep breath then shared as much as his position would allow, perhaps a little more, feeling that it was the least he could do.

26.

The sun was setting on America's East Coast when Jeff Lutz was called into John McAdam's office, "Good evening Jeff, how are you coping'" asked McAdam.

"It's a little overwhelming, Sir."

"I'm sure it is, and your wife?"

Jeff hadn't asked her. In all honesty, he was furious about the whole situation. Her screw-up whilst under diplomatic immunity might yet turn out to be free of consequences, at least in terms of traditional justice. But there was no doubt that she'd just derailed his career. Your wife didn't get to cause an international incident without paying the price. It simply didn't work that way. "I'm not sure yet, Sir." was all he could offer in response.

"Of course, it's still early days." John McAdam took a deep breath and straightened some of the papers on his desk. "So Jeff, you mentioned that your wife had maybe been using her phone at the time of the incident. Correct?"

"Yes, Sir, to the best of her knowledge, which is sketchy as she blacked out."

"Oh, I'm sorry to hear that. I hope she'll be okay." Jeff was truly surprised at how insincere the comment had sounded. McAdam went on, "We sent in somebody to retrieve the phone from her car. Of course, we can demand to have the car returned, but that kind of thing takes time. So we attempted to reduce the amount of incriminating evidence they're undoubtedly compiling against your wife by trying to recover the phone at least. Anyway," he messed with the same pile of papers, "we were too late. Essentially, that's what it comes down to. Too late. Local law enforcement was already there with the vehicle when our operative arrived."

"How many local cops, Sir?" Jeff asked.

McAdam looked at Jeff as if it were the most ridiculous question he'd ever had the misfortune to hear, "Two? Two hundred? What does it matter? Your wife's negligent driving has caused a diplomatic incident. This mess will strain the relationship we have with our strongest ally. Now you don't seriously think we'd even for a second consider making this bad situation even worse, do you?" McAdam's volume was unchanged, his patience not so.

"No, Sir, that's not what I meant." Jeff was flustered.

"And for what? She hit a juvenile with her car whilst driving on the wrong damn side of the street. If she wasn't on her cellphone, is everything suddenly better?" McAdam glared at Jeff, holding his stare for an uncomfortably long amount of time. "The Brits have choices. They can either accept the claim of diplomatic immunity, in which case the dust will eventually settle, and it will go away. Or they can decide to make a fuss, which would mean they'll request that we return your wife. We're not about to return one of our own, as that would mean we waived her diplomatic immunity to allow extradition. How could we do that? No American would ever want to operate overseas again if they thought it came with the risk we'd throw them to the wolves.

So your wife is good, whether we like it or not."

McAdam looked at the same pile of papers and reverted to a more light manner, "So, now we need to confirm various matters. As far as the Brits are concerned, what was your status there?"

Jeff could sense the ruin which lay ahead for him, "Communications Officer."

"For who?"

"Unstated, I was simply attached to the USAF."

"Have you or your wife ever contradicted this fact whilst overseas?"

"No, Sir."

McAdam took a moment to reflect, then continued, "The story has broken back in the UK, and it's a goddam mess. It won't be long before it breaks over here, and we can't control how it's presented. Now Jeff," McAdam leaned forward and looked him in the eye, "you remain invisible to the press. Period."

Jeff nodded.

"And if that becomes a problem, you need to prepare yourself for a potential move."

Jeff slumped in his chair.

"The President is embarrassed enough. We will not add to this by making him suffer the humiliation of the international press identifying one of his CIA analysts to the world. Clear?"

Jeff neither replied nor nodded. He merely inhaled with his eyes firmly closed, as he finally appreciated just how buried his career really was.

27.

"This is a unique situation, from so many different perspectives." said the man in the slim-fitting business suit.

"I appreciate that." answered a uniformed Captain Bowyer.

"It's a bloody mess, that is what it is. The American's wife has stirred up a storm of epic proportions, and how this pans out depends on the approach the Americans take. It will also be affected by how hard the press push. It will even be shaped by how the great British public reacts. It's liquid. Nobody can tell where it will take us yet."

Bowyer was aware of all this. The suit wasn't the only smart man in the room, "But Miller?" he prompted the suit from GCHQ.

"Yes, Miller. Shame she couldn't have hit somebody else's nephew, really."

What a crass thing to say, "Like yours, for example?"

The man threw Bowyer an angry glance, "I don't have one, but there's no need for that."

Captain Bowyer wasn't in the mood to back down. What was it about people when they stepped up to that level? They were so concerned with playing their game of chess that all of the pieces became irrelevant; their own manoeuvres were all that mattered. "No matter whose nephew it might have been, they'd have been crushed by it. But this nephew's name was Luke, and by all accounts, he was a bright kid who could've done anything in life. If she hadn't..." Bowyer just stopped.

"But she did, and Miller's going to be angry, and Miller's a bloody potent weapon, Her Majesty's Armed Forces saw to that, and now we've given him more training, more responsibility, more deadly skills. He's capable of a lot, and he's pissed off with her, so what if he lost it and went vigilante? He could cause catastrophic damage to the bond we have with our American allies."

Bowyer was aware of that too. "But he won't."

"Tsh, you don't know that."

"I know him better than you. Besides, for now, I'm taking responsibility for him, and I'm not worried about doing so."

"I do hope you're right, Captain. I think it's time we brought him in though, don't you?"

Toby Miller was standing in the corridor outside the Captain's office, wearing jeans, a t-shirt, and a light padded jacket, but only now did it dawn on him that he'd maybe been expected to arrive in his old uniform. A wave of panic swept over him.

"Sergeant Miller" called a loud voice. Miller instinctively marched quick time into the Captain's office, which felt and sounded so wrong in jeans and squeaky trainers.

"There's no need for that, Miller. Stand easy."

"Sir." Miller snapped back, as he relaxed his posture appropriately.

"Sergeant Miller, you've impressed lately and so you've earned yourself an easy duty back here in the barracks. How does that sound?" asked the Captain.

"Spectacular, Sir." Toby boomed.

"See, Miller couldn't be happier." Captain Bowyer said to the suit.

"Spectacular." said the man in the suit lazily before standing up, "Captain Bowyer." He nodded, shook his hand, and then as he walked past, he also acknowledged Toby, "Miller."

Toby stamped his feet to attention and held a rigid salute.

"Alright then, thank you." was all the suit could offer as he left the room.

"Oh, for Heaven's sake Miller, at ease man. In fact, sit down. Must you really?"

"I was just showing the gentleman the due respect, Sir." Toby was grinning as he relaxed his salute.

"Well, let's not get into that and what in God's name are you wearing, man?" asked the Captain

"It's popular amongst the youth these days, Sir." Toby was really turning up the cheek now. The Captain laughed and Toby took a seat, "Am I being RTU'd, Sir?"

"Look, Miller, you've worked hard. Everyone's happy

with your performance everywhere you go and we've decided we owe you some time in barracks, so that you're able to be with your family while they get through this. So, in answer to your question, no, you are not being Returned To Unit. Barracks just means the nights and weekends are yours. It's the best we can do."

"I appreciate it, Sir." he really did. This felt like a blessing.

"And the whole Company is here right now, so you'll be able to catch up with your old mates." The news made Toby's heart lift because he knew that his old friends would lift his mood, which would help him do the same for his poor sister.

28.

Madyson thanked the driver who'd taken her back to her house, stepped out and thanked them again for helping her with the bags. As the driver took off, she stood outside her house, taking in the sight of such a huge residence. She felt like a stranger, having quickly become accustomed to the smaller housing, which was the norm back in the UK.

The fact that she was standing out front added to the odd sensation, because she never used the front of their house; nobody here did. You walked through your house into the garage, a three-car garage in their case. Then you opened your garage door with the remote control before backing out and using the service road to reach the normal roads. You came home the same way, always using the garage door.

So here she was, looking at the front of her own house, which seemed more of a facade than it ever had previously. Even the road seemed fake now; it served no real purpose for the local residents. *Except for the mail trucks,* she reminded herself. Which also reminded her she'd have to get the mail deliveries back to normal. She slumped and shook her head in disappointment.

Normal. Normal seemed so distant.

Normally, she'd have driven home, but her car was... She threw her hand up in front of her mouth. *Oh no, is it still on that road in England?* Maddy moved her hand to her forehead and started trembling with emotion again; her eyes welled with tears. How could she fix that? Here she'd probably call for a tow truck, but there?

One bad thought seemed to lead to another. The Police have probably been doing whatever they do over there. Her car was probably evidence; *Oh My God*, her eyes bulged.

But what about when they were done with it? Would she have to call them? And have it... What? Repaired? Shipped back? How would that phone call go? *Hi, I'm Madyson Lutz. I don't know if you remember me...*

She started trembling, then dropped her bags and carefully sat herself down on the cold hard curbstone.

Normal, she thought again. She hadn't been able to book a ride-share service home because her phone was gone too. There was no normal left.

Maddy had been strong since the plane had landed, but the weakness was creeping back, and ever so gently, she started crying again, sitting on the side of the deserted street in front of her huge house.

29.

"Sir." the lady seated at the polished oak desk spoke into her phone, "I have a Sergeant Treavett from Recon and a WPC Bell here to see you." She nodded, then looked up at Lucy and Kirk, "You can go straight in."

Kirk opened the door, indicating that WPC Bell should enter first, "Sir." he nodded respectfully to the Chief Constable.

"Sir," Lucy did the same, handing the Chief a large file.

The Chief sat down, nodding at nothing in particular, "So is this complete?" his question was directed to both of them. Kirk smiled politely at Lucy and encouraged her with a nod.

Lucy's posture was perfect as she replied, "No, Sir, we're uncertain how we should proceed. We've heard unsubstantiated rumors that Mrs. Lutz has already left the country."

"There's also the issue of their unconfirmed diplomatic status," added Kirk.

"Quite right." Replied the Chief, who had stopped nodding, even though he was now in apparent agreement with them both. "I spoke with the Foreign and Commonwealth Office this morning. They've had confirmation that both Mr. and Mrs. Lutz left the UK, claiming the right to exercise their diplomatic immunity under the Vienna agreement of 1961." He looked up at his two officers, "However, the FCO hasn't as yet supplied me with anything which shows that either of the Lutzes had been properly listed as diplomats here in the UK." He threw the file onto his desk.

"Although I'm sure that's just a clerical issue, which will be resolved in due time. And that, I think, is what we're facing right now; time." Lucy and Kirk looked at each other.

The Chief Constable continued, "If the Lutzes had remained in the UK, our next step would have been to apply for an immunity waiver, which is now rather redundant. So we're looking at the possibility of an extradition request instead, but as I'm sure you can guess, we quickly get into murky waters."

Even the Chief didn't seem to fully know what would happen next, "I'd like you to complete your file, so that should we make a formal extradition request, we'll have the best possible supporting case. I'll have to talk with our friends at the Crown Prosecution Service, who I'm sure will be talked to about the ramifications of pressing charges by the FCO, the Home Office, and quite possibly the Prime Minister himself. As I said, now it's all about the time it may take."

As Lucy and Kirk walked back down the stairs from the Chief Constable's office, Kirk realized that the Chief's honest approach in his presentation of the huge obstacles ahead was in danger of demotivating anybody working this investigation. He chuckled; he'd only figured that out because he felt a slight case of *so what's the point* himself.

"Alright, Bell, we've heard about the obstacles facing the Chief Constable in such a complicated international case, but none of that changes our obligations. We're still building a solid case for the family of the dead boy."

He continued as he turned to descend the next flight of stairs, "The Chief just mentioned the possibility of an extradition request and if that's made, then our case needs to be the foundation that request is built on. The Government would only make an extradition request after pressing charges through the CPS. Now, if they make that extradition request and it's approved, then Mrs. Madyson Lutz will be shipped back to face our charges, so let's make them perfect."

Another turn in the stairs, "If their request is made and it's denied, then the relevant arrest warrant remains valid until an opportunity to use it arises." Skipping down the steps while talking was making him short of breath, "That means if Mrs. Lutz takes a trip to Canada, for example, then she'll suddenly find herself on a plane bound for the UK."

"Oh." Lucy was visibly energised by this news.

Kirk smiled back. He hadn't known it himself until the previous night when he'd stayed up late researching this grey area out of pure frustration. "So then WPC Bell, we still have a driving recreation to run, we have more statements to take, and we need to see if they've managed to unlock her mobile phone yet, meaning there is no time to hang about."

"On it, Sarge."

Part 2. Hope. New Realities, Loss.

30.

Madyson pulled herself together, stood back up, and picked up her bags. She waddled them to the front door, dropped them, and slid her key into the lock. Suddenly she had a worrying thought; what if the key didn't operate the door? She couldn't remember if she'd ever used it in the front one.

She turned the key and heard the lock click satisfyingly. Of course, one lock for all doors. It was America - the land of convenience.

As she walked into her home, the cold was the first thing to hit her. Jeff must have left the place barely warm enough to avoid frozen pipes. She left her bags by the door, walked over, and punched the little rubber button on the climate control, instantly hearing the gentle clinking of expansion created by the warm water flowing into the baseboard heaters.

Next, she pulled the carafe from the coffee machine, placed it into the sink, and started filling it with water. Seeing a normal flow of water was uplifting. She experienced the briefest moment of relief; maybe she could cope after all.

She started running through the problems again. Whatever the deal was with the car, it was better if it just stayed there, it's not like she'd ever want to drive it again. Whatever paperwork was involved, they'd complete it. Whatever money was required, they'd pay it. She just wanted that car gone. No matter what it had symbolized to her in the

UK, now it was. *Ugh, don't go there.* Maddy was in dire need of some positivity.

Pouring the water from the carafe into the top of the coffee maker, she picked up the remote and turned on the kitchen television. After the sharp, precise pronunciation she'd got so used to in the UK, the softly flowing American accent was soothing to her ears. Now she clicked the button on the coffee machine and as it illuminated in green, she smiled for the first time in twenty-four hours, just as she heard her name on the television.

She'd get through this. She was a coper; it was just a matter of...

Wait.

She flinched and looked at the television. No, these were different names, she must have misheard. They were talking about Damien and Tracey Rigg, now about Luke Rigg. There was a photo of a good-looking teenage boy, blonde, with a cheeky smile, but it sounded like something really bad had happened to him. Odd that they were showing the familiar gates of the UK Air Base, she fell backward onto the kitchen counter, her mouth wide open. It couldn't be, could it?

Oh please, no, she was shaking her head, "Please no, no. No." she was breathing too fast. Her head was suddenly out of adjustment as if she were debilitatingly drunk.

"Mrs. Madyson Lutz, the wife of an American intelligence officer based in the UK, has since left the UK," said the lovely TV voice. Madyson's eyes fluttered, she snatched at her breaths, her vision went dark, and she dropped, her head hitting the edge of the kitchen granite counter as she fell.

31.

Toby Miller sauntered down the corridor in the general direction of the Quartermaster. He needed some new kit as when he'd been re-attached, he'd binned some of his older, worn-out gear, and being back here amongst soldiers meant looking the part again.

"Oh, you have gotta be bleeding kidding with me, Staffy Miller? It can't be you? Is it really you?" the huge man started running toward Toby.

Toby beamed a huge smile, already knowing the Captain had been right. Being back here amongst the lads really was just what he needed, "Browny, you big ugly bugger." and before he could even finish the words, he'd been lifted off the floor by his old friend.

Browny immediately dropped him because hugging was strictly off-limits in this world. Toby had to quickly regain his balance as his feet hit the floor.

"Did you get RTU'd? I thought you'd gone for good." asked the giant.

Toby rolled his eyes and laughed, "No, I didn't get RTU'd, you idiot. I'm here short-term, like a holiday."

"Nice!" yelled the big man, "for how long, Staffy?"

Toby scrunched his face, laughing, "You know what? I don't even know. Until you lot deploy again, I'd guess."

"Nice!" The big guy did a little dance. "So why then,

man? What's the deal?"

Toby rolled his eyes, the answer to that question had emotion attached, and in this environment, he needed to be seen as the Sarge, the reliable one, a solid bloke who just got on with it. "My sister's lad got hit by a car and he didn't make it, so she's pretty broke up, and the brass decided I should be here, close by, to help them through it."

"Whoah." Browny's expression was transformed, "Not the lad on the news?"

"Yup." But as they started on the dreaded topic, Toby could already sense a change in his own emotions. The upset was gone, and now he wanted action. "So what have they been saying on the news then?"

"Um," Browny thought back, "that the boy was riding his bicycle, the driver was on the wrong side of the road. She was from the airbase, wife of somebody working there, both Americans."

Toby's expression hardened, "Did they say what he does? The husband?"

"No, mate, it didn't sound like they even knew. Why?"

Toby shook his head and shrugged, "Because they bailed, they've been flown back to America, saying they had diplomatic immunity."

"For running down a kid? I thought diplomatic immunity only covered incidents related to their duties?" Brown asked incredulously.

"So did I."

"Oh, that's messed up, man, well messed up." Browny wanted to give Staffy Miller a hug but wasn't about to do that, so he placed a huge hand on Toby's shoulder and gave it a gentle squeeze, "Let's go get a cuppa."

Toby let out half a smile and nodded.

"Who is that mutated civvy freak? And what's he doing in our barracks?"

Toby hadn't even walked fully through the canteen doorway and they'd already started.

"Ha! I don't bloody believe it. I thought you'd died in some shameful self-abuse accident." A different voice.

"I thought he'd become a nun." Another new contributor.

"You mean a priest ya pillock."

"No, I bloody don't! A nun's exactly what I meant."

Toby threw his arms in the air, "Well, it's nice to see you lot too!" He playfully jogged over to their table and started sharing some suitably casual love amongst his old mates, a fist bump here, an arm around the shoulder there, messing up the hair of the youngest ones.

"Staffy bloody Miller. I don't believe it," said the nun joke supplier, "It is so good to see you, Sarge, but you didn't get RTU'd, didya?"

Browny stepped in with a booming voice, "Look, you

rabble, Sergeant Miller here has been given a soft duty back with us. He has not been returned to the unit because he has never in his short and ugly life let anybody down."

The crew was laughing, "Alright, turn it down, boys, let's not turn this caff into a noisy rave. Sergeant Miller's nephew was just killed in a car accident and yes, it was the one from the news."

"What one on the news?" asked a young soldier with newly disheveled hair.

"Oh Moore, you pathetic boy, you really have got to start watching the news. Now zip it and listen. So the brass has brought Staffy Miller home to us for some compassion. So we're going to be compassionate, aren't we?"

"Yeah, right," replied another of the younger ones, before shrinking into his seat, "Sorry, Sarge, I didn't mean it to sound like that."

Toby glared at him. The crew turned silent, then Toby smirked, "I don't want any compassion from you; you might get funny ideas." Having got them all laughing again, he added, "But I'll take a cuppa."

Overcome with relief, the lad stood up, "On it, Sarge," and headed away in the direction of a big shiny metal tea cylinder.

Toby looked at the faces seated around the long table and he couldn't wipe the smile off his own face. These were his boys, his brothers. His new work had been exciting in a dangerous way. It had been intensely challenging, and once the challenges had been met, it had been unbelievably rewarding. But what hit Toby while looking at his friends' faces was how lonely it had been. Right now, there wasn't a place on earth he'd rather be.

32.

Maddy could hear voices, they had American accents, but without even opening her eyes, she could tell they weren't the voices of people who were present in the room; it must have been the television. She reluctantly opened her eyes and winced in pain, as apparently, the back of her head was throbbing now too. She caught her breath and closed them again.

She sat on the floor listening to what they were saying. Depressingly, it was all coming back to her, except for her head pain and how she'd ended up on the floor.

She let out a mock laugh; what did she care? She was on the floor, and so she'd stay there. Her head hurt, and it would just have to continue that way. She cautiously opened her eyes again and started watching the TV from where she sat.

As she sat on the floor listening to them explain her life story, she started to feel numb, emotionally numb. She'd done something, something awful admittedly, but it had been an accident, and now she was everybody's business. Why she hadn't expected this mess to follow her back home was beyond her. But with the manic speed at which everything had happened, it was inevitable that she'd eventually find herself playing catch up to what had happened in her own life.

It hurt, because to this news channel, she was just a stupid woman who'd screwed up. There was no attempt from them to switch their perspective, not even a little. Surely they couldn't all be looking at it in exactly the same way?

She rotated her shoulders and gently reached up to take the remote from the countertop, changing to another news channel. They were telling the same story, her damn story; they even showed a photo of her. Really? Was that necessary? It wasn't even a good one, and where had they even got it? She straightened her legs to be a little less uncomfortable, rested the remote on her lap, and gently felt around the back of her head. There was already a lump forming, so whatever she'd done had put her down here after whacking her head.

She stared at the screen, which now showed a different photo of the boy. The cheeky smile had gone, but it was still recognizably... My God, he was beautiful. She couldn't help but think it, then felt obliged to defend herself to Him, if there even was a God. She'd never been fully convinced by it, but it suddenly felt more important to consider the likelihood...*I never intended to, God I truly didn't.* Inevitably, some tears returned, but they no longer brought the shaking and trembling of before; previously, it had been shocking and traumatic. Now it all felt so completely and utterly hopeless.

She found herself looking down at her feet. Her head had started throbbing so badly it hurt to look at the TV. Should she get it looked at? *No,* she slumped further. She had no phone. She shook her head, laughing at how pathetic it was. But even if she had one, would she have called anyway? She curled down the corners of her mouth, thinking it through;

103

an ambulance would arrive and see that she was the stupid woman from the news. She didn't know what was wrong with her head, but she knew she wasn't ready for that. Concussion? Whatever. She probably deserved worse.

The tears were flowing harder now, but she remained silent. Her home felt like a sanctuary; this was the only place she could be.

33.

Damien lay in the dark room, wondering just how long he'd been evading sleep. He hadn't wanted to wake Tracey, so he'd stayed as still as possible. But he couldn't take it any longer, so moving his shoulders and hips as gently as he could, he inched his way toward the edge of their bed, where he paused, waiting for a sign of her having been disturbed.

Satisfied, he slowly raised his upper body, swiveled his hips, and gently stood up. With the room still silent, he turned to see how his poor wife looked, only to find her absent. His shoulders slumped; how had she managed that? Maybe he had napped a little after all.

He made his way out of their room, walking their short hallway to the top of the stairs, where he looked into Luke's room out of curiosity. There she was, sleeping with Frodo, his heart sank. *Every one of us is bloody broken.*

He leant on the door frame, considering whether to join them. Deciding it was better to let them rest, he tip-toed down the stairs into the living room, closed the door behind him, and turned on the TV. The only news coverage he'd watched was what had pushed his wife over the edge prior to the arrival of the Police. Now he wanted to see how they were presenting it in full.

As the TV came to life, he hurriedly pressed the down button for the volume, not wanting the device to sabotage his stealthy trip down the stairs. As the bright picture illuminated the room, his eyes struggled to adjust to what was being shown, but it quickly became apparent it was irrelevant, at least to him.

He stood up and walked into the kitchen, switching on the electric kettle before leaning back to take another look in the direction of the TV. Unsatisfied, he took down his favorite mug and dropped a tea bag into it, now he had to wait, so he leant on the kitchen door frame, staring into space.

His mind was on overload; he couldn't tame his thoughts at all. Why weren't they showing Luke on the news? His eyes welled up. Luke was more important than the European Community crap under current discussion. Why hadn't the Police stopped the stupid cow from leaving? Or the Government? Why had she been allowed to kill their boy and just leave? His intakes of air were getting snatchy. Why was she on the wrong side of the road? Why weren't they taught how to drive before being allowed on the roads here? Why wasn't she looking where she was bloody going? His face was distorted with anger; he swung around the frame into the living room, about to punch the wall, he pulled his right arm back, balling up his fist, breathing as if he'd just run a sprint. But he froze, shaking, as his breathing slowed. His blank stare returned, the wave of anger subsiding. Irrational anger wasn't going to help his boy; that's what he told himself.

Unfortunately, another voice in his head told him that nothing was going to help his boy, increasing his breathing rate once more. He stubbornly fought back. Calmness would help his beautiful Luke; he knew that. Calmness is what they'd need to....To what? He wasn't sure what they were going to do.

Sliding down the wall until his arse hit the floor, he focused on that question; what on earth were they going to do?

Tracey lay on her beautiful, sweet boy's bed, the side of her face soaking wet. Her presence had allowed Frodo to fall asleep; sadly, his presence hadn't reciprocated. She'd heard Damien walk toward the room and stop. Then she'd heard him go down the stairs. She'd definitely heard him turn the TV on; the whole town had heard him turn the TV on.

But she didn't want him to know she was awake. She didn't even want to be awake. She certainly didn't want to talk to him, not to anyone. She sobbed silently; how was she going to be able to carry on living?

What was the point now? She'd lost her baby boy, the perfect human being she'd created, carried, and lovingly raised. What a boy, he was smart; he'd got that from her. He was sweet, that was from his dad, and he was tough, he'd probably learned that from his uncle Toby. How many kids could compare with her son? He could have done anything he wanted in this world. She was furious. He should have been allowed to do anything he wanted in this world.

But he'd been taken from her. How could this much pain even exist? Every day of the rest of her life in this miserable world was going to be a continuation of this agony, a living hell. She already knew that.

What would ever be the point?

She just wanted to die.

34.

Maddy could hear the garage door opening. Jeff must have finally come home. She sniveled some of the tears back into her nose.

She made the tiniest hint of a movement, then changed her mind, uninterested in standing up. She changed back to the other news channel; maybe they'd use some new words.

A door closed loudly, making the TV harder to hear, so she turned the volume higher. The screen showed that same old photo of her; hadn't people gotten it already? She was quite sure her face had been etched into every human being's mind by now. The American woman who was a monster; enough already, they know what I look like. Say something new.

She was shivering with cold but had at least found an ability to blank out the throbbing inside her head.

Huh? It was the sound of Jeff speaking. *What*? She realized that she needed to say it out loud, "What?"

"What are you doing?" he asked.

I dunno, she thought. Again, *out loud*, "I dunno? What are you doing?" It sounded like she'd retaliated. Why did she do that? She had no idea.

Jeff looked at her, at the TV, at the coffee pot, and then back at the TV. He hadn't seen any televised news yet either, but he didn't want to. He leaned down, pulled the remote out from her tight clammy grip, and turned off the TV.

She looked up at him. Why did he do that? *Out loud.* But what was the point saying it out loud? She couldn't find one so just stared at him blankly.

Jeff looked down at her, a part of him wanted to ask her what was wrong, but that part just wasn't big enough. He looked at his wife; she looked terrible, absolutely terrible. Her eye makeup was all over her cheeks and the backs of her hands, and her expression was, he studied it more carefully, trying to figure it out. She looked vacant, dumb even.

The bigger part of him was driven to deal with what was going on, fixing whatever was in his power to fix. So the part which weighed most heavily on his mind came out first, "We'll probably need to move. House, I mean. CIA officers can't be in the news and they'll find our address really quickly. They're like bloodhounds, those reporters."

Her breathing started to falter again.

35.

Bill Addison had stopped the newsroom temporarily, "So regarding the diplomat story, we're gonna keep propping it up."

"How? We've got nothing new." asked one of his colleagues.

"I know, but if you look at the comments below every relevant piece we've run, you'll see this is getting more interest than any other story, fifty even a hundred times the amount of comments. Passionate comments, angry comments, but more and more, and more comments. This, and only this, is what people want to read about right now. It's what every Briton cares about. This Yank diplomat runs down an English kid and then runs off to escape justice, consequences too. And yes, they are two different things."

"So we need to find new stuff to write. Start harassing the Foreign Secretary. Let's get his take on why the woman was allowed to leave and who her husband is."

"He won't answer that." interjected another of his team.

"So then that's our story." Bill gestured as if it were obvious, "The British Foreign Secretary refuses to comment on the blah blah. If he won't identify the husband who supposedly carries the diplomatic status, then how do we know if this American and his wife even have legitimate diplomatic status? I mean, how do we even know they had the right to leave? You can guarantee the FCO already knows exactly who the bloke is. They just think this story will blow over and they'll get away without sharing such sensitive information. But they won't get away with it, not with the strength of feeling I'm seeing."

"We've gotta find some tangents too: Are we behaving like lapdogs to the Americans? Analyse. Are diplomatic immunity agreements being misinterpreted, abused, or are they just horribly out of date? Discuss."

"And another one, is there any comment from our American cousins yet? If not, then why bloody not? Don't they care that one of theirs ran down one of ours? If they don't, then why the hell are we inviting them to work over here?"

Noises of frantic scribbling came from all directions, "Bottom line, Joe Public ain't happy, and they want to know more. And that people, is what we are here for." Bill readied himself to leave but then had a last thought he wanted to share, "Look people, we all know we're not anybody's favourites, we're the dirtbags from the tabloids and all that crap. But sometimes," he was grinning enthusiastically, "we get a chance to push something that really needs pushing, and I mean push it bloody hard. So hard that it can't be ignored, and I tell you when we get to do that." He shimmied, "You don't feel so dirty, in fact, you feel quite righteous." he had a look of pride on his face like they'd never seen before, and it spread throughout the room.

"Now get on with it." and with a movement of his hands, he ushered them back to their desks.

36.

Toby hesitated in the corridor leading to the Sergeants' Mess, aka pub for soldiers. He'd been warned off his sister's house for the night by his mum, who'd just got back into town. He'd tried arguing, but his mum always won, so he'd finally agreed to a first night of beers with the lads.

"Sarge." the Lance Corporal greeted him as he walked by.

The passer-by was accompanied by a fresh new face, "Why were they calling him Staffy earlier?" Toby could hear the new boy ask, in a lowered voice, "His stripes say he's a sergeant, not a staff sergeant."

Toby grinned mischievously, waiting to see if he'd be able to hear the inevitable response.

"You know what a Staffordshire Bull Terrier is?" asked the Lance Corporal.

"Course I do, Corporal, it's a mean fighting dog."

Toby couldn't resist turning to see the newcomer's face. "That's our Staffy, you pillock, and God help you if you get on the wrong side of him." The young Private turned to take a last look at Toby, and his surprise at seeing Toby already looking back at him, resulted in an expression that looked he was undergoing a proctology examination.

Toby had to look away quickly to avoid bursting out laughing. He sighed. Was it wrong to laugh right now? He had no concept of mourning etiquette, as when his dad had died he'd been too young to mourn, while his mum and everyone else was still around. He shook his head and walked into the mess.

"Staffy." there were a handful of his friends by the bar, "What are you having, mate?"

Toby looked at what was currently on tap, pointing to an amber ale he enjoyed.

"I see you found your bag of uniforms, looking dapper." Browny complimented him, throwing Toby off guard. "Look, I hope it's okay, but we've got a surprise visitor for you." he nodded for Toby to turn around.

Surprise was right, Toby knew the man, had even liked him, but he wasn't ready for this. Toby was shaking his head, probably glaring too, though certainly not intentionally, "I just can't deal with an American right now."

The man wore a United States Air Force uniform with stripes signifying the master sergeant rank. "I'm sorry, Miller. I'm sorry for what happened and I'm sorry they left. If it makes any difference, I think it stinks. I'm a proud American, but I'm not proud of this. I just wanted you to know that." He waited, hoping for Toby to come back with something.

But Toby just stared into space, thinking. After an uncomfortable pause, the Master Sergeant turned to leave reluctantly, but Toby forced himself to reciprocate the gesture of friendship, "Wait. Wait, I'm sorry."

"Dude, you've got nothing to be sorry about."

"Apart from his bloody face." Browny felt it necessary to add.

The men chuckled and Toby, who was really starting to understand the significance of this gesture, took Master Sergeant Woydziak by the forearm and led him to the bar, "Beer, that's what we need. Friends and beer." For Toby, that was akin to a Shakespearian sonnet.

"I appreciate it, Staffy Miller." the man's face showed a level of sincerity like Toby had never seen before.

"I appreciate you coming here, Woydeezedyak." he opened his mouth and wiggled his tongue, "But I still can't say your name."

Master Sergeant Woydziak was already laughing, "Come on, say it with me, Woy."

"Woy." both Toby and Browny replicated the sound.

"dzee." he continued.

"Tsee." Toby copied.

"Bless you," said Browny.

"Thanks, mate," Toby said playfully, rubbing his nose. The other British soldiers were all listening in now.

Woydziak gave Browny a not amused type of amused look.

Sorry, I meant "Duzee." Browny played nice.

"Yak." the Master Sergeant finished."

"Yak," they both said in unison, "That one's easy," Toby said to Browny.

"Seriously, it's like a big cow innit."

Woydziak could only shake his head at the children, "Now put it together, woy-dzee-yak."

"Wozneedeekak." said Browny, as Toby simultaneously turned it into, "woznotcakyoudik."

"Oooh, bless you again," said Browny.

"It must be allergies," Toby replied.

"Why did I even come here? Seriously, I should just drive back to my own base."

"No, don't do that, Zodiak, have a beer. Come on." Toby was grinning.

"Ooh, that's it, Staffy. Well done, mate, that was perfectly pronounced." Browny again.

"It's easy, you big dumb lug, Zo, right? Zo then dee, then yak," said Toby

"I can remember the yak bit alright, but the rest's still a bit of a mystery."

"Guys, just Joe, enough already." the Master Sergeant could barely stop laughing.

"Alright, Zodiak, keep your hair on, mate." Toby grinned.

"It's just wrong. That's not what diplomatic immunity is

for." Browny was shaking his head.

The three friends had long since sat down at a table, but only just started on the inevitable subject.

Master Sergeant Woydziak was quiet, trying to formulate the right words. He knew that feelings were running high on the subject, and while he was in complete agreement, Miller's initial reaction had understandably been uncomfortable for all, "In my head, I'm comparing this to the way a cop applies the laws."

Toby and Browny were intrigued by where this was going.

"And I always think the best cops look at the intent behind the law."

Toby leant in closer, "Go on."

"I need an example," he drummed his fingers on the table, "what about turn signals? Let's say you're driving on the highway, it's deserted, and so you move over to another lane without signaling. A cop flies out from behind a bush and writes you a ticket. Good cop?"

"No." Toby needed no time to consider.

"Bit of a wanker." Browny upped the level of response.

"And why?" asked Woydziak.

"Yeah, I see where you're going." Toby nodded.

"Because that's not what the law was written for, is it? If you're driving on a really busy highway and you change lanes without signaling, you could cause a wreck. And so they made a law to prevent that wreck. But the cop who tickets for that same thing on a totally empty road, they're just not contemplating the point behind the law. That's bad policing, for me."

"Yeah, I agree." Browny was leaning in too.

"And I think this situation is comparable. Those diplomatic immunity treaties were created to protect real diplomats from trumped-up charges and harassment. Not so that the wife of a maybe real diplomat could play it as her get out of jail free card after running down some poor kid. You know what I mean?"

Toby felt a rise in his emotions because, for him, Zodiak was absolutely right in his opinion. "Well said, Joe."

Woydziak had noticed how Toby finally used his real name but wasn't ready to disrupt his flow with any more banter quite yet. "I just can't figure out if it makes this an intentional misuse of these old agreements or if the rules themselves are too open to interpretation."

Toby had been reading some of the applicable rules since the accident. He'd been struck by the same worrying uncertainty, "From what I've been looking at, the rules aren't clear enough, and I think my government is scared to push too hard with yours. But they've swung too far the other way, and now they're playing it too soft, coz like who is the guy, the husband? So far, nobody has said exactly what work he's doing here that would even qualify him as a diplomat."

Woydziak grimaced, "We've strayed onto something we've gotta be careful discussing." he looked around the room at all the British uniforms surrounding him.

Toby patted his arm, "I know mate, don't worry." The Master Sergeant lowered his voice, "We've got guys like him on our base too, civilian clothes, don't socialize with the rest of us."

Toby felt slightly fraudulent sitting there wearing a uniform he'd only just taken out of the bag.

Woydziak continued, "I'm damn sure those diplomatic immunity rules need a rethink though. Especially after this."

Toby leant back in his chair and exhaled slowly. He was really glad that Zodiak had made such an admirable gesture by coming to share his condolences and personal feelings. Holding back would have betrayed those feelings, so Toby smiled and gave the big American a shoulder hug, "I really appreciate you coming down tonight."

The American smiled, "I'm glad I came too, Staffy."

"So." Toby wanted to take the next logical step in the conversation, "What do the other guys on your base think of this situation?"

Joe didn't bother sanitizing his response, "We're here in your country, so there are plenty of people talking about it. The guys I hear are pissed, because in the pledge of allegiance we talk about liberty and justice for all. So the contradiction here isn't lost on us. Some of the guys are really ashamed of this, but quietly, of course."

"Hmm. That's interesting." Toby replied.

37.

"I have the Foreign Secretary holding for you." said the desk intercom. Foreign and Commonwealth Senior Officer Chris Watkins sighed, clicked a button, and picked up his phone, "Rupinder, how can I help you this morning?" He already knew exactly why she was calling.

"The American diplomat incident, I have to brief the PM on the situation, so you need to bring me fully up to speed."

"Everything? He asked suspiciously.

"Absolutely everything," she answered.

He shrugged, "Alright, well, I'm sure the Chief Constable is better equipped to fill you in on the specifics of the accident itself."

"Agreed."

"So then, the aftermath. Immediately after the accident, we were informed of their decision to fly Mr. and Mrs. Lutz back to the USA."

Rupinder Garcha interrupted, "Oh, so you knew they were leaving." She said it as if she'd caught him in a lie.

"Of course, we knew." his tone betrayed his emotions, "We already knew it would happen before they'd informed us. What else were they going to do? Have their people taken in for questioning by the humble British bobby?" Chris was shaking his head, wondering how she'd managed to climb so high. "Mister Lutz was cooperating with us on the Torch

121

Programme, so for the sake of both parties, he left."

Chris waited for a response and, in its absence, officially stamped home his point, "This is exactly why we agreed to cover them under the diplomatic umbrella in the first place."

It was Rupinder's turn to sigh. She'd always known the Torch Programme would bite them in the arse eventually.

"Crown Prosecution Service, how may I direct your call?"

"I have Chief Constable Geoffrey Palmer for the Attorney General."

"Patching you through."

Both ends of the phone went temporarily silent, but the Chief Constable picked up his handset, seeing that his line had started flashing. With his phone resting on his shoulder, he continued reading the finer details of the Vienna diplomatic agreement.

"Good morning Geoff, how are you?"

The Chief Constable adjusted his phone's position., "I'm very well, Tony. How are you?"

"Can't complain. How's Anne, the kids?" The polite formalities were expected.

"Everybody is just fine, thank you. Look, the reason I'm calling is we've had this incident land in our laps over here." said the Chief Constable.

"So I understand and what a complicated one it is."

"Hence my call, I've got some of my people building the case against the driver, a Mrs. Madyson Lutz, and well, we've never had one quite like this, and so I'm skipping my local Chief Crown Prosecutor and coming straight to you."

Attorney General Tony Mason had also put some time into refreshing his memory on the details of the Vienna diplomatic agreement, "I don't think anybody's had one quite like this before."

"Which is the problem. As you know, my officers would typically request CPS advice on charging decisions by phone or electronically, but we're so far beyond that level of help." He let his point hang in the air.

"Quite right, reaching out to me was the right thing to do. To be honest, I've already started my own research as I'm loathe to misadvise you myself."

The Chief Constable had expected as much, but where was it going to stop?

The Attorney General continued, "Look, I'm trying to set up a meeting with the Prime Minister and the Director of Public Prosecutions right now. We're all aware of the potential ramifications of doing anything which might upset the special relationship with our American cousins."

Chief Constable Geoff Palmer was accustomed to operating at the highest level within his Constabulary, a position which required him to see things from a complex perspective, making him too much of a politician in the eyes of most humble coppers. But something about this situation was awakening his youthful urge to fight for the underdog, "Let's not forget there's also a family who just lost their son. We need to be seen to supply some kind of justice for them." Realising how callow he'd just sounded, he quickly added, "Can you imagine what a field day the press will have otherwise?"

"Prime Minister, I have Foreign Secretary Rupinder Garcha for you."

The PM looked up from his desk, "Send her in, please."

"Prime Minister." she bowed her head reverently.

"Foreign Secretary. Please, take a seat. How are you?"

"Very well, thank you, Sir." she took her place. "You wanted to discuss the American diplomat incident."

"I did, Rupinder. I understand the basics; there was an accident, a young man died in hospital from the injuries sustained." He sighed, reading the summary notes on his desk, "and the driver, an American, left the UK shortly after. Can you fill me in on them, please? The information which isn't shown in my notes."

Rupinder straightened her posture before answering, "The driver was the wife of an American diplomat, which allowed them to exit due to our diplomatic immunity agreements."

Now the PM looked up, unimpressed, "I asked for what was not in my notes."

Rupinder caught her breath, knowing she'd deserved that one, "I'm sorry, Prime Minister, I meant to elaborate. The husband, Jeff Lutz, was cooperating in the Torch Programme, which is why they wanted to extricate him so quickly. And why we allowed it."

The PM looked back down at his desk. There was never a straightforward answer to anything. "Remind me, what is the Torch Programme?"

Rupinder fidgeted in her chair uncomfortably, "Under current UK law, Equipment Interference, that is to say, government hacking, falls into two categories; Targeted and Bulk. Targeted Equipment Interference requires a warrant obtained at the ministerial level. It is typically reserved for situations where we believe there's a valid terrorist threat."

The PM pushed back in his chair and crossed his legs, "I'm aware of targeted equipment interference."

"Yes, Sir, but bulk hacking, or Bulk Equipment Interference, is only performed by GCHQ and legally, it can only be used to monitor foreign targets."

The PM knew this too. He maintained eye contact with Mrs. Garcha, waiting as patiently as he could manage.

"The Torch Programme," she was starting to pick up on the PM's desire for her to get to the point, a point she'd have been much happier to evade, "is an agreement where we utilise a loophole in our own rules. You see, as we can't spy in bulk on our own people, the Americans do it for us." Ouch, she'd rushed that information out too clumsily. "Which means the information is given to us, but as we didn't actively engage in..."

"Bulk equipment interference." he was nodding, "I understand and presumably this torch agreement?"

"Torch Programme, yes, Prime Minister."

"This Torch Programme is reciprocal in some way?"

"Exactly, Sir, it was instated by your predecessor."

"And so the Lutz fellow was spying on Britons, for us, while based in the UK?"

Foreign Secretary Rupinder Garcha nodded apprehensively, "Exactly, Sir."

The Prime Minister rolled his eyes, "And Mrs. Lutz is, I assume, his wife, a woman with no involvement in, or knowledge of this?"

"Correct."

"And so she killed a British boy in a simple car accident, and we were not in any position to stop the Lutz couple from leaving." it was no longer a question.

Rupinder nodded, knowing she'd finally let the Prime Minister fully appreciate the steaming pile of disaster that had landed just on his plate. "Yes, Prime Minister." she frowned, "Although it may not have been a simple accident.

The primary police investigation shows her driving on the wrong side of the road."

"Oh Lord no." he shook his head, "So she was negligent."

"There doesn't seem to be any doubt."

It was a lot to consider, "And the press reaction?"

"All over it. They know exactly who to blame, and they're doing just that. Getting the general public onside has been easy because the victim and his family are very sympathetic. And so the press is now demanding justice, loudly."

"Justice?" he asked in disbelief. How could anybody take these disparate pieces and assemble them into something that could be presented as justice? He picked up his desk phone, "Would you please arrange an emergency cabinet meeting?"

38.

A thick drizzle blanketed the cemetery, silently attaching itself to everything, it beaded on the wool of Toby's dress uniform. He was glad the weather was foul; it was appropriate, a full-on rainstorm would have been better, but this would do.

Everyone wore black from head to toe. Toby's sister was in heeled shoes and a lightweight dress with a big padded coat worn on top. Damien wore an ill-fitting suit that Toby had borrowed from one of the other soldiers in the barracks.

Damien was shivering with the cold or emotion; Toby couldn't really tell which. Both Tracey and Damien were crying, but not the kind of crying he'd seen a couple of days ago. That stage had been violent sobbing, it had been hard to hold onto his sister with all of her convulsions and spasms. But now, there was a peculiar absence of movement, save for the shivering on Damien's part.

Toby wasn't sure which was worse: the first part had been disconcerting and uncomfortable to watch, but at least when Toby had held his sister, he'd felt her take something from their shared contact. But this new part was totally different, the energy had all gone, and both Tracey and Damien looked broken, empty.

What really hurt Toby was that holding his sister now achieved nothing, as if she wasn't really aware of his presence. How long would this part continue? And what followed it?

Toby refocused his attention on his mum, who was standing by his sister's side. She knew how to cope better; she was in control. But she was someone who'd navigated loss before; she knew the ropes.

Then Toby considered his own emotions, realising they hadn't changed much since the pathetic mugging attempt. He was upset, but his tears were done. He was angry, but not in a volatile way. He was disappointed, but at what? He scrunched his face in thought, at the world for creating a system that allowed this. And he was motivated; he just had nowhere to direct it.

Tracey's house had become the destination for the wake, and Toby was keeping a watchful eye on his sister from a discreet distance. "I'm worried about her mum."

"Toby, she just lost her only son. This is to be expected."

Toby huffed, "But how long does it take, to," his words tailed off.

Toby's mum took his hand, "Bless you, Toby, this never was your thing, was it? Emotions, I mean."

He merely rolled his eyes.

"Sweetheart, when did your dad die? Twenty years ago? And I still find myself having a little cry sometimes, for no reason other than I miss him."

Well, that certainly wasn't what he wanted to hear. His bum slumped onto the backrest of the couch.

"I've never seen you slouch in that uniform before. It usually has the opposite effect. Which reminds me, why are you back in uniform again? I thought you were attached to some plainclothes division now."

The plainclothes division of the British Army, that's how he'd sold it. "I'm on compassionate, and rather than getting full leave, I'm temporarily back with my unit." he paused, "It's a good thing, for now."

She squeezed his hand, nodding, "I'm sure it is. So have you found yourself a nice girlfriend yet?"

He raised his eyebrows in disbelief. Only a mother could do this, "Really, mum? Now?"

"Well, excuse me, Toby Miller, I lost your father and now my only grandson, and I'm too old to think that waiting in silence is the right approach. I'm not getting any younger, you know."

And they call me Staffy, he thought to himself. "Going back to what I originally asked, can she get through this, mum? I mean really, is she gonna be able to cope?"

As a mother, firstly, she would allow him that change of subject, considering the circumstances. And secondly, as she'd known all along, that was the big question. "Something like this haunts you for the rest of your life, it will never go away, and your poor sister will be fighting it right up until the day she dies. But if we're here to help, then yes, Toby, she will survive it. It will go from being the only thing in her life to a smaller manageable part. That's all we can hope for.

Does that make any sense?"

It did. It was the type of answer he'd been looking for.

"It's bloody disgusting, that's what it is." said an elderly lady friend of Toby's mum's.

"It might have made sense twenty years ago if you were sending an ambassador and his family to the Middle East, but what relevance does it have to a Yank's wife over here?" replied the lady's husband.

Toby had been standing to the edge of the group, arms crossed, scowling, "So what can we do about it?" he chipped in.

The man turned to Toby, "We can't do a thing, son. This is politics now, which is what's so bloody disgraceful, coz those shysters won't do anything unless there's something in it for them."

"Like what?" Toby so desperately wanted to be able to do something.

The elderly group sat and considered the question, "Well, firstly, it can't be allowed to become old news. They'd like it to blow over; oh yes, that would suit them. All of them, the Yanks and our lot of worthless liars."

"Ain't that the truth" was the grumbled response.

"You know, son, what you need is for somebody to keep pressure on those politicians." The old boy was still formulating his thoughts, "Either pressure to extradite the stupid cow, or pressure to prosecute her over there in America. Or at the very least to admit these diplomatic immunity laws are out of date."

"Bloody right, Albert," agreed another golden oldie who nodded passionately. "Diplomatic change is what's needed here. It won't bring back poor Luke, bless him the poor sweet lad, but it'd be a proper victory. In his honour, you could say."

A shiver ran down Toby's spine. If he could achieve something in Luke's honour, he could claw back something positive. "You know the Yanks aren't happy about this either?"

"Ay? What?" asked old Albert, turning his better ear toward Toby.

Toby couldn't help but smile, leaning further toward what he now knew was the working ear, "I said the Yanks aren't happy about this either. I know some of them, US Air Force guys from a stint I did in Afghanistan."

"Really?" asked the first elderly gent.

"Yeah, they were ashamed of the decision. That was how they put it. Ashamed." replied Toby.

"Well, good for them. I always thought they were a good bunch, at least the common man is. I served with some of them years ago. Good blokes, the lot of them. Sounds like you need a way of letting people know you're united because then it isn't us versus them; it's just an issue of slippery politicians."

"Shysters." Albert spat out, blissfully unaware of his own volume.

Toby was standing straight again. How could somebody as low ranking as him make a statement with his American friends that they were united in their anger? Talking only carried so far, and while complaining online would travel further, it could also get any one of them court-martialed. There needed to be something that triggered a conversation about diplomatic immunity face to face, something which showed their support for change, but something subtle that wouldn't drop them all in trouble.

"Lads." Toby stopped in front of the group of Luke's old school friends who'd assembled in the back garden.

"Shit," one of them spat out involuntarily.

"What the hell are you doing here?" Toby asked the first runner from the night he'd nearly been mugged.

"I'm sorry, Mister Miller, I mean," the kid tried to figure out Toby's rank from his uniform, but he didn't know a private from a field marshall and didn't want to risk getting it wrong, so went with, "Sir."

"Sir?" Toby laughed, "I'm not a Rupert. I work for a living. It's sergeant boy. Sergeant."

"I'm sorry, Sergeant Sir. I told him who you were, I ran. You know I wouldn't try anything like that, Sergeant Sir."

"Oh my God." this was painful, "just call me Mister Miller. Why are you here, boy? What's your name?"

"James, Mister Sergeant Miller Sir, and I'm a friend of Luke's." the kid's head dropped in sorrow, "I mean, I was a friend of Luke's."

"Okay." it was time for Toby to start over, "Lads."

"Yes, Mister Miller, Sir." replied one

"Yeah, Sergeant Miller, Sir." another.

"Mister Sir Miller." yet another one.

Were they having a laugh? Toby honestly couldn't tell. It seemed unlikely given the scenario. Maybe they were just that dopey. "Look, I remember Luke was artistic, and he talked about a friend who was even better. Do any of you know who that was?"

They returned with an anarchic assortment of affirmative responses, finalised by one boy saying "Him." while pointing at James.

"Oh fanks, Paul," James hissed at his friend.

"You." Toby pointed at James, then swivelled his finger and hooked it to signify James should follow him.

After summoning James and giving him his project, the herd of remaining boys had followed the lad to the dining room table, which was now covered in paper, pens, sparkling drinks, potato crisps, and mobile phones.

"Mister Miller."

Toby turned his head waiting for the latest unnecessary embellishment to his name; stunned when one didn't appear, he walked over to their table.

"Look, we could do one like this." James pointed.

Toby took a glance at it, but his eyes were drawn to a design he'd already spotted in the centre of the table, "What's this one mean?"

The boys looked at each other, concerned.

"It looks good, but what does it mean? If we could keep the way this one looks but use better initials, then that could work."

Silence.

Toby could see that viewing him as a Staffy wasn't helping them, "Boys, you're doing great work here. I'm really impressed. Who did this one?"

A boy silently raised his arm. "What's your name, mate?" Toby forced a smile.

"Blake." it was almost a whisper.

"What does four DC mean, Blake?" Toby had lowered his own voice to a comparable level.

"I thought the number four could mean for, as in for, not against. And the DC means diplomatic change."

"Ah," Toby smiled, "I thought DC meant Washington DC, like the American capital."

135

"Oh no, I meant; For Diplomatic Change. Just using 4DC." the boy pointed. Toby was really impressed, "Coz you'd said to design something that wasn't obvious."

"You could print stickers." said one of the others.

"You know what'd be really cool?" asked yet another one, "Reversed out, so the outline was black and the 4DC lettering was transparent, so you'd see the colour of what you'd stuck it to."

Toby beckoned to his mum and her friends. The boys at the table continued brainstorming, "We could do patches, like the stitched kind, and they could put them on their uniform." He looked over to Toby's uniform though not at Toby's face.

Toby knew he'd never get away with sewing that patch to his uniform, but he didn't want to stop them when they were on a roll, so he answered by suggesting a subtle tweak, "A patch with a velcro back would work."

The boy scrunched up his face, leant in, and lightly touched the sleeve of Toby's jacket, "Velcro wouldn't stick to that."

Toby smiled again, "It'd stick to my other uniform, though."

"You have more than one uniform? Man, that's mental."

Toby laughed out loud now, "On my combat uniform, I have a big velcro patch on the top of each arm, we all do, and if that was a small enough patch, in the same colour as my uniform, I reckon I could get away with wearing it. And the stickers, reversed out you said?" Toby looked at the appropriate boy, "That would be great. I might even get away with sticking a few on some of the Army vehicles."

The boy beamed proudly at his mates.

"I don't get it." Toby's mum had been waiting for a break in the conversation.

"Look, mum, 4DC means For Diplomatic Change." Toby pointed to each relevant character as he said the words. "And it's so subtle we might get away with wearing them."

"We'd wear it too if there were normal t-shirts." added another of the boys.

"Or hoodies." said another, receiving universal approval.

Toby shrugged, "Why not?"

39.

Every morning started the same way for Madyson. Sleep had become her only sanctuary, as yet uninvaded by the accident, so she fought for more of it. But it was a futile fight this morning, as it had been most other mornings. She sat up, growled and slammed her closed fists down on the mattress.

She looked around, no Jeff. That was another part of this new cycle. He'd probably got up quietly and headed to work early again, leaving her to deal with this huge mess unassisted. How long was this going to continue?

If the Maddy from a few days ago had told the current Maddy that her husband would isolate her like this, in her biggest time of need, the past Maddy would never have believed it possible. They were simply too close, too in love; they were best friends. But now she knew they weren't because he'd shunned her, instantly and comprehensively.

In their early days together, she'd prioritized him over everybody else, causing rifts in her family and distancing from her dearest friends. And for what? For this? It was unfathomable how badly everything had worked out. Her mom had at least taken her phone call if only to tell her "she'd made her own bed," etc. But there was still hope there because Maddy knew her dad; he would turn it around. He loved her.

Not so with some of her oldest friends. They'd just let her go to voicemail and seemingly hit delete on that voicemail. So far, the only friend she'd met with had been one of the coffee-drinking local wives. Maddy had opened up to her, gushing forth, probably in sheer relief. The woman had since blanked her out too. Maddy suspected the meet had only been arranged to get the inside scoop for the rest of the pack. What a total bitch.

So, now it was time to get out of bed again. She had to get up in order to do nothing and see no one. Maddy swung her legs to the side of the bed and considered what she could do with her morning.

Like an outdated computer, her brain had crashed, and after an unknown quantity of time, she'd found herself still sitting on the edge of her bed. On autopilot, Maddy finally stood herself up and walked to the bathroom.

Glancing in the mirror and seeing an unrecognizable Maddy jolted her back into reality. The day before, she'd ventured out reluctantly, bought a new cell phone, and then, in desperation, headed into a salon and turned herself from a blonde into a brunette, something that had since slipped her mind. She studied her new reflection, feeling only disappointment at what she saw. Typically a makeover was an invigorating indulgence, but a disguise adopted through necessity, less so.

Her hair was beautifully done, and it suited her, but it made her look more? She tilted her head in uncertainty; mousy?

Mousy? Maybe. Different? Very. So, good overall.

Her face still looked the same though, she frowned. Maybe she could go darker with the eye makeup and use bolder lipstick? No, that was makeup for going out at night and it always attracted attention. The thought of additional attention made her feel a rising sense of panic.

A different approach was needed. Barely any makeup and light lipstick would make more sense. Maddy dug through her makeup bag and started applying a look she'd never gone with before. As it came together on her face, she nodded; it was good. It wasn't really her anymore. She might even get away with participating in the human world with some kind of anonymity. She tried to smile in the mirror, but what came out was an utter failure. Still, she could go out without smiling.

It was time to get dressed.

Her attempts to get dressed had been as problematic as making up her face, so eventually, she'd dug through the recesses of her closet and taken her style back at least a decade. It had added to the overall transformative effect and lifted her spirits a little more.

Maddy walked down the staircase, cautiously optimistic about getting out and taking a tentative first step toward rejoining the world; then, a movement outside the front door caught her eye. Knowing it was probably a delivery driver, she continued toward the door, but the self-doubt kicked in again. Whoever it was, they could leave the package out front. Her new habit of avoiding human contact was going to be harder to break than she'd thought.

Only out of idle curiosity, she leaned toward the adjoining window to catch a furtive glimpse of whoever was there, snapping her head straight back in reaction to the sight which greeted her.

In disbelief, she took another look. No, she'd never even contemplated this, for things to get worse still hadn't even been a faint possibility, but it had gotten worse and dramatically. Frozen to the spot, she started to tremble as she took in the circus of logoed media vans parked outside her house and then one of the group noticed the movement she'd created. She watched in horror as this sole person broke into a jog, heading for her front door, the runner calling back to another person who tried in vain to catch up while carrying a huge camera.

Maddy leaped back out of sight then realized the futility of it. The whole front of her house was glazed and it was too late to close the blinds, at least anonymously. Instead, she double-locked the door and ran back up the stairs. She stood at the top of the staircase, there was an odd urge to go to one of the front windows, which overlooked the once decorative front street. She was baffled as to where such stupid ideas came from, what kind of self-destructive instinct was that?

As she stood, frozen by indecision, she could feel her morale had dropped to yet another new low. How many times could your sanity take these hits? With each new challenge, her old self and her old life felt ever more distant.

But this one, it was more than she could handle. She just wanted some help, some support. How had she gone, in less than a week, how had she gone from popular and loved to...?

She slowly slumped onto the floor; she'd become an outcast. That was what she was, despised, ridiculed, even hated in the country they'd just left behind. And the man she'd gone over there for? He was treating her the worst of them all.

Suddenly she was done, done with lying down and taking it, she'd given Jeff everything, and now she wanted some payback. She took out her new phone and pressed speed dial number one.

Ring. *Come on, you know it's me, hurry up and pick up, you jackass.* Ring, *the longer it rings, the ruder you look.* Ring, *I mean, are you kidding me?*

"Hi, this is Jeff Lutz. Leave a clear message."

Her heart started to pound, her eyes bulged, her nostrils flared, and she growled like an animal, "You son of a bitch, you send me to voicemail? Who the hell do you think you are, you slippery little freakin turd? Have you forgotten I could've had any man I wanted? Do you remember that? Or is your head so far up your own ass that you've forgotten? I was so far out of your league, I settled for you, you dorky little piece of crap, and mostly I did it because of all..." Beep.

"If you'd like to re-record your message, press one. If you're happy with your message, press two."

She didn't know whether to laugh or cry, but she was on a mission, so she chose button two, then redialed.

Crap, where was I? Oh yeah, "I did it because of what you said, all the promises of love and doing anything for me and dying for me. I mean, are you freakin kidding me? I follow you to another country, out of love. I have an accident, an accident, you jackass, and you just abandon me. What kind of a slimy worthless piece of human crap are you?" Beep.

God damn it, she pressed two again, then redialed.

Her breathing was calming, "You know what, Jeff Putz, you're gonna support me, you're gonna fulfil all of your lovesick promises or I'll fuck up your life even worse. I don't know how I'll do it, but I will. Listen to my voice, and you'll know I'm serious as cancer. Support me, Putz boy, or I'll find a way of really fucking up your career." she took the phone from her ear, then changed her mind, "Oh, and by the way, there are a hundred reporters camped outside the house. You're the important government guy, fix it." and hung up.

40.

Toby rolled down his car window to talk to the MP on the gate, "Yeah, I'm here to see..." Crap, he couldn't ask for Zodiak. Hang on, it'd come to him, it ended in yak. Then there was the bit where Browny sneezed, so atchoo? No, tsee, dzee that was it.

"Sir, are you alright?" the American MP looked concerned, patient, but definitely concerned.

"Woydziak!" Toby literally spat it out.

"Master Sergeant," they were now talking in unison, triggering laughter in the pair of them, "Woydziak." they both finished.

"Sorry." Toby was still grinning.

"It's okay, Sir." the MP smiled back, "Sergeant Miller is it?" he read it off Toby's uniform.

Toby nodded, finding it strange how he'd greeted him as sir, knowing full well he was a sergeant. He peered through his car's windscreen in the direction of the US Air Force base, even to a member of Her Majesty's Armed Forces this agreement where the UK Government leased out old RAF airbases to allied countries seemed odd.

"Can I see your ID real quick, Sir?"

Toby grinned again and felt obliged to share why, "It's weird being greeted as Sir, I'm an NCO."

The gate MP's smile grew now too, "Yeah, we greet all

144

strangers that way. But I understand, you're not a cake eater."

"A cake eater! What the hell is a cake eater?" Toby's expression was childlike.

"An officer, what do you guys call them?" he asked back.

"Ruperts," Toby said at a reduced volume, then wondered why he'd done it. "It's just an upper-class name, and they're all upper class. Or they were." he'd corrected himself as things were gradually changing.

"Ruperts?" the guy scrunched his face in confusion.

"Yeah, but cake eater is much better. I'll use that from now on."

The MP nodded and returned Toby's ID, "The Master Sergeant is coming out to meet you. If you just pull up your car over there, he'll be right out."

"Thanks, mate," Toby replied.

"You're welcome, and have a nice day." the MP stepped back from Toby's car door.

"You too," but Toby couldn't resist, "and would you like some fries with that?"

"You Brits." the MP walked back to his hut, chuckling and shaking his head.

"Staffy Miller, what can I do for you?" asked Zodiak.

"I brought something for you." Toby stepped out of his

car.

"But my birthday is months away. You shouldn't have." the Master Sergeant grinned.

"I didn't. I said brought not bought" Toby smirked, "Look." he opened the top of a plastic supermarket bag.

Woydziak took out a sticker. "I don't get it. What's 4DC?"

"For Diplomatic Change," Toby replied proudly.

"Dude, are you kidding me? You did this? You never struck me as the artistic type." Toby actually laughed out loud at the idea, "Yeah, No. Not me. It was a team effort. Some old soldiers from the First World War kick-started the idea, then I got some schoolkid friends of my nephew to do the designing." he shrugged.

"But these are good. They're even the right colour." Woydziak dug through the bag. "Oh no way, you've got velcro ones too? I can stick it straight to my fatigues." he was gushing.

"So, do you want to keep some?"

"Hell yeah."

"How many?" Toby pulled out a handful.

"This will do," replied Joe Woydziak taking the whole bag off Toby.

"Cheeky bugger! Are you serious?" Toby's eyes widened.

"Yeah. If that's okay."

Toby looked at the ratio of what Zodiak had to that in his own hand, "I tell you what, if you can put them to good use, then you can take them. But I need another handful for my boys." he leant in and took what he needed, "Then I'll get some more made."

The Master Sergeant had already stuck one of the Velcro patches to his upper left sleeve, "Say, Staffy?"

"Yeah?" Toby was stuffing what little he'd got left into the largest of uniform pockets.

"You like stirring shit up, don't you?"

Toby slid his jaw forward, biting his lip with his teeth as he briefly considered a denial. "Yeah, I guess I do, really." then, looking at Woydziak's new patch, "But hang on, are you allowed to wear that on your uniform?"

"No." Joe jiggled his head slightly, "Well, sometimes I can get away with it. But no, I shouldn't really be wearing it."

"So, you like stirring up shit too, then?"

Woydziak grinned back at Toby, "Yeah, guess I do too."

147

41.

The media circus had long since left, leaving Maddy alone with her thoughts, yet again. This time she was hung up on trying to decide how much of what she felt was due to the accident, and how much was simply due to having nobody to help her through it. There was no doubt that being alone, endlessly, was the most demoralizing experience of her life.

Her phone started ringing; finally, it was Jeff calling back. This would be no fun. She hit the green button.

"Maddy?"

She took a deep breath, "Yeah."

"Have they gone? The reporters?"

She smirked, so that was how he was going to play it? No acknowledgment of her voicemail, or to be more accurate, three voicemails. "They have."

"Okay, well, you need to know that it's only temporary, they will keep coming back, and there's only so much we can do to force them away."

More good news, she was so glad he'd called.

But he wasn't done, "The real problem is now they know where we live, so we need to get away properly. You understand?"

Putz. She shook her head at him, "You mean on vacation, like Cabo or somewhere." It was sarcasm, but would he get it?

A pause, "No, I mean we need to relocate."

"Back to the UK? Or maybe Iran this time? I'd probably have been executed there. There's that, I guess."

Another pause, a possible sign that he was getting it?

He continued, "No, relocate stateside. The agency can help us with that. We'll get set up somewhere new, and we can rent our own house out for now. But you should pack some things quickly. The things you can't live without."

She looked around her; that would be everything. It was beyond her comprehension. Now she was losing her home too? Part of her wanted to make a joke; admittedly, it was only a tiny, tiny part of her.

Instead, there was a drawn-out silence. Eventually followed by another "Maddy?"

"Yeah."

"Did I lose you there?"

"No, I heard you. You've told me I'm losing my house too and I've got to pack my bags. Now it's my turn."

A shorter pause, "Okay."

"I need a car, right now. So you can give me yours and either borrow one from work or buy another one."

"But..."

"No!" she snapped. "I asked you to help me get a car

before, and you did nothing, absolutely nothing because you're only thinking about yourself now. So your car is mine, and maybe you'll be more motivated now that you're the one without a car."

The only response was a faint sigh.

"And you need to start wrapping your head around the fact that I had an accident. I didn't take a gun out of that base and go on a shooting spree; I had a car accident. They happen every day; you've had one. No, you've had more than one, and I didn't just throw you out with the trash in reaction. You made vows at the altar, and you've treated me like shit since."

"You killed a kid, Maddy! You didn't have a fender bender going to the mall. You killed a British kid, in Britain. They're our strongest ally, and you took one of theirs."

"It was a goddamn accident. Why don't you get that?"

"It doesn't matter. You still killed him, and now we don't even know how they're taking it. Are they pissed? We don't even know. This is a shitstorm, Maddy!"

"Yeah, and that's all you care about, the politics, not the people, certainly not me. If you're that cold, then you should never have got married in the first place, not to anyone, and especially not to me. I could've done so much better."

Another long pause, "Just pack your bags, Maddy."

42.

"This is good work." The Chief Constable turned another page, "Very good work."

"Thank you, Sir," replied WPC Bell. Having never been noticed by anybody of such high rank before, this was going to be a day for the diary.

Sergeant Treavett nodded to the Chief and then smiled at Bell, quietly impressed by how she'd stepped up on her first serious case.

The Chief closed the bulging folder, "There's just one thing missing."

"The driver's statement." Treavett was already nodding, his smile gone. "We were aware of that, Sir, but due to the reach of this case, it was the one thing we needed to run by you."

"Quite right." The Chief nodded, "So this doesn't happen very often, thankfully. But the protocol in this type of situation is to send a pair of officers to interview the relevant party in their home country." The Chief turned his focus to the WPC, "A jolly is the term you'll typically hear WPC Bell, even though the circumstances are far from jolly, the trip is known amongst the officers as a jolly."

WPC Bell tried unsuccessfully to hide her smile, "I have heard the term, Sir."

He rolled his eyes and smiled knowingly, "Of course you have. So, now that we have a complete case file, bar this one statement, I'm going to need to talk to the head of the CPS again. Then I will get back to you both regarding this jolly over to America."

He looked down at the file, then back up at the two investigators, "So that will be all for now. But again, I must congratulate you both on putting together such a thorough case file. You're the type of officers this Constabulary can be proud of. Excellent work, the pair of you." The Chief reached out and gave both Bell and Treavett a hearty handshake.

"Wow," said Lucy Bell, still gobsmacked as she headed back down the stairs toward the more familiar lower levels.

Kirk laughed, "I can't argue. Wow, indeed."

WPC Bell literally had tingles running through her body; to be on the edge of closing such a big case was more invigorating than she'd ever imagined possible, "Sarge?"

"Yes, Bell."

"Thank you." she stopped walking to emphasize her point, "For bringing me in, I mean."

Kirk looked bemused, "WPC Bell, I'm the one who should be thanking you. You've done great work on this case."

"I've enjoyed myself too." she was beaming.

"Good. I'm glad to hear that because I wanted to talk to

you about your plans."

Bell's excitement levels raised a level further, "My plans, Sir?" she played it coy.

"Yes, Bell, and come on, you already know what I'm going to ask you. Do you intend staying a local bobby, or are you ready to move up to a specialist squad?"

"Oh, Sarge, I'd love to work on your team. I really would."

Police Sergeant Treavett was just as certain as she was, because from his perspective, he'd just been given an opportunity to poach the best of the new talent, "Good, then I'll start the transfer process. Now, going back to the diplomat case and the sombre jolly which the Chief Constable referred to."

"Yes, Sarge?"

"Everybody wants to do a long-distance jolly, so suddenly all of the higher-ranking officers want involvement in a case they know nothing about."

"I can imagine that, Sarge."

"But for credibility, they'll usually understand the need to take one of the original case officers, which means one of us."

Lucy Bell smiled, "Then have a nice trip, Sarge."

He chuckled, "I think you'd be right in most cases as these trips involve pulling rank. But I would prefer to send you, that's if you want to go."

"To America?"

"Yes, WPC Bell, to America to interview the Lutz woman. Remember, we still want justice for our local lad, so there's work to be done. I think as the first responder, you'd be the better one for the job because you have an existing rapport. Mind you, it will probably mean sitting next to the Chief Constable on a plane for nine hours, coz I think he's already booked himself a ticket, in his head at least."

Now Bell laughed, "I think so too, but I'd be on my best behaviour, Sarge."

"I don't doubt it, and as you'd be representing my squad, I'd expect nothing less."

"You can count on me, Sarge."

"Yes, Bell, I have no doubt I can."

43.

"Good Morning, this is Chief Constable Geoffrey Palmer. I'd like to talk to Attorney General Tony Mason, please."

"Putting you through now, Chief Constable."

"Geoff, how are you?" asked the Attorney General.

"I'm well, thank you, Tony, the family are too." the Chief Constable was in more of a hurry than usual to get through the formalities.

"Glad to hear it. I assume this is about the diplomat case?"

"It is, so Tony, our case file is complete with just one exception. The interview with the accused. But I don't want to send two of my officers to America unless I'm certain we're going to pursue the case on their return, hence my call."

. "Understood. Well, the powers that be have decided that we will bring charges of death by dangerous driving against Mrs. Lutz. Now, may I be honest with you, Geoffrey?"

"Of course, you can." replied the Chief Constable.

"Good, then I'd like to make it clear, the fact that we're pressing charges does not necessarily mean we expect them to be successful. This may be a case of going through the motions."

"Oh." that was genuinely disheartening news and would probably be best kept to himself.

"It's not to say we don't want them to be successful, but

we must be realistic. The Americans are highly unlikely to agree to an extradition request for Mrs. Lutz, and let's face it; after we bring charges, an extradition request is the next logical step."

"I see." and he did. The Chief Constable already knew they couldn't make their American friends send her back, only ask them politely.

"Another option is not to bring charges at all, but the press would have a field day with that. They don't seem to want to let this one go."

The Chief Constable bristled, then struggled to come up with a suitable response. Was there another route he hadn't considered? Bringing charges against somebody in a friendly foreign country, with no likely prospect of them sending their accused back to the UK, seemed like an exercise in futility. The press though; it was a valid consideration. This was a level of politics too far.

"Geoffrey? Are you still there?"

"I am. I'm sorry about that, Tony. I was just looking at the case file again." the Chief rolled his eyes; his case file wasn't even open.

"I'm glad you understand the pickle we're in. So yes, send some of your people to America, have them take their interview, and who knows? We might get lucky."

44.

"How are you doing, mate?" Toby was genuinely concerned about Damien's appearance.

Damien shrugged, went to talk, and then lost interest in his own reply.

"I'm gonna put the kettle on for you. Where's Tracey?" Toby figured Damien couldn't dodge that question, not without appearing rude.

"Um, she went to meet your mum." His answer was lacklustre, to say the least.

"Sorry, I forget; how do you take your tea?" Toby hadn't forgotten. He wanted to draw Damien back out.

"Milk, one and a half sugars."

"Please, you forgot to say please." Toby looked back at Damien with a stern, frightening glare.

Damien looked terrified, truly terrified, "Sorry, Tobe, please, I meant please."

Toby felt like absolute crap, "I'm sorry, Damien, I was just playing around. What's up with you? Come on, talk to me, pal" Toby put his arm around Damien's shoulder for the first time since? Probably since Damien and Tracey had first got married.

"It's just, it's been nearly a month." Damien's eyes were welling up.

"I know." It had been one of the slowest passing months

of their lives. Toby could feel his eyes filling too, and fought it hard. Toby kept his arm wrapped around his brother-in-law's shoulder and slowed his breathing down. This emotion was a very unwelcome return. "I know."

Toby really didn't know what other words he could add. Every option running around inside his head was useless: Luke wasn't coming back, nothing tangible had happened since his death, and what they'd read in the newspapers didn't make it seem like the woman would ever be returned. It was like the shit had hit the fan and totally stopped it from turning.

"I know." Toby had nothing else, so he held on to Damien's shoulders as the man's emotions took over, and yet again, Toby fought to control his own.

The worst wave seemed to have passed, so Toby reboiled the kettle and made the tea he'd initially promised his brother-in-law. He'd also put a teabag into a mug for himself but decided to put that on hold for now.

His sister's house was modest, but it was loved. They paid their mortgage, took pride in their home, and it showed in the way they cared for it, or at least it had done. What Toby was looking at now was unrecognisable; the sink was full of dirty plates, tea mugs, and empty beer bottles, the first milk carton he'd found in the fridge had nearly made him gag, and the second one he'd used for Damien's tea wasn't far behind.

This was his family and it was falling apart, so Toby

rolled up his sleeves, and set to sorting the place out. As a military man, he knew that the best therapy for Damien would have been to make him participate, but Toby just didn't have the heart. Not after that breakdown.

Toby methodically worked through one task at a time and undertook every single one with army precision and cleanliness. Once the sink was clean enough to eat off, he restored the fridge to the same level. Then the kitchen bin and finally the floor.

With the kitchen fit for inspection, he went upstairs, leaning his head to look into Luke's old room out of morbid curiosity. And another wave of unwelcome emotion washed over him because there was Frodo, still sitting on Luke's bed waiting for the lad to come home.

This wave was a big one and much harder to fight. But why? It was just a dopey dog, so what made that summon such a massive wave of grief? Toby sat down next to the dog again, "A month." he whispered, the end of Frodo's tail skipping around in response.

"Come on, you silly mutt, let's take you out for a walk, then when we get back, we can see what state the bloody toilet's in."

"I'm sorry." it was a young voice.

Toby gently pulled back on Frodo's leash and turned to see the familiar face of the country's most incompetent

159

mugger. Coming to a complete stop, Toby could only manage a sigh. He'd barely come to terms with the state of his broken brother-in-law, and now this?

The lad looked down at the floor, "Really, I'm sorry, Sir."

What was it with these kids all calling him sir? "I'm a sergeant boy, a sergeant." Toby snarled.

The boy looked like he was going to cry, "I'm sorry, Sergeant, I'm sorry for trying to steal your phone, and I'm sorry for Luke."

The mention of Luke's name made Toby's breathing quicken involuntarily, "I'm sorry too." Although getting his breathing back under control was getting quicker each time. "Thanks, kid. It was Jay, wasn't it?"

"Yes, Sergeant."

"Look, Jay," he huffed again. "You know what, come on, take a walk with me."

"Yes, Sergeant."

"Sarge or Toby. Pick one."

"Yes, Sarge."

Toby rolled his eyes.

"I'm sorry for Luke; he was nice, like when we moved here, even when some of the other kids were wankers. He was nice to me."

"Language Jay."

"Sorry, Sarge."

"But I know, he was a good lad." Toby frowned, "Wait. Luke welcomed you to the neighborhood, and to thank him, you thought you'd teach him how to mug people?"

The kid clearly couldn't reply with yes, so he locked his eyes back onto the pavement in embarrassment.

Young Jay changed the topic, "I wanted to talk to you about the Army, Sarge. You know, after what you said the last time." He walked more like an uncoordinated puppy than even Frodo did.

"You mean that time you tried mugging me, and I punched you in the throat?" It was simply too good to miss. Toby felt no guilt.

"I am sorry, you know."

"Bloody should be." Toby grinned mischievously, "How's your throat?"

"Fine." the delivery made it sound like the boy had rediscovered some of his fight, Toby liked that.

"So what do you want to know then, kid?"

"Well, everything really. Like do you get paid well, is it a good job, it is dangerous, do you get to see all the world and stuff, do you get to shoot the really big guns and tanks, and like helicopters and? Huh." Jay knew there was more but was struggling to remember what.

"Wow." Toby took a deep breath, "Not really, yes, yes,

only the worst places, yes, only if you join a Tank Regiment, and yes."

Jay stopped walking, "What?" he looked baffled.

"I answered your questions." Toby paused with him.

"Bloody hell, are you kiddin me? You remembered all of them?"

"No, not kidding you. Look, kid, the Army is dangerous, especially right now, and too many good people are coming home with broken bodies or broken heads."

They were walking again now, "Okay." replied Jay.

"But." Toby grinned again, "I was a screw-up, a bit like you. I was doing all the wrong things, making stupid decisions, and I can't think of anything else, apart from the Army, that could've turned me into what I am now."

"A proper man."

"Ha! You cheeky little bugger, I should sock you in the throat again."

But Jay hadn't been joking. He looked at Toby, trying to hide his hurt feelings, poorly.

"Oh, I'm sorry, mate, I thought you were taking another dig," Toby replied, wide-eyed.

"No." is all Jay could say. He wasn't going to say the nice bit again. No way.

"So, where's your Dad then, Jay?" Toby asked him in a more matey way.

162

"He left; never see him."

"Mine died. Never see him either." Toby winked, Jay sniggered. Toby continued, "And let me guess, your Mum's ready to kill you?"

Jay's eyes widened as he nodded enthusiastically, "Oh yeah."

"But still, if you're good at something else in school, you should think about that before getting too serious about the Army. So what are you good at?"

"I'm not good at nothing."

"Everybody's good at something. Your mugging skills need some fine-tuning, though."

"Was going fine 'til you came along."

"I'll pretend I never heard that. Look, kid, go home, stop being a pain in everyone's arse, let people keep their bloody mobile phones, and if you're serious about joining up." Toby huffed, "Send your Mum over to talk to me."

"Cool, man."

"Yeah, I guess. Now buzz off." and just as Jay turned to leave, Toby stopped him with his hand, "and call me Staffy."

"Okay, Staffy, later." and just like the first time, Jay the mugger ran off as fast as his legs could carry him.

"Hey, Tobe." Damien had already opened the front door before Toby reached it.

"Hey Damien, how's it going?" Toby already knew that was a better sign.

"Good. Look, you didn't need to do all that work in the kitchen."

What Toby wanted to say was, *Oh yes, I did*. But while that level of directness was appropriate in the forces, it seemed to upset people in civvy street. "I just thought it'd be nice to help a bit."

"I feel rotten, making you do our cleaning up. It's only coz I've been so busy with work, and Tracey." Damien stopped dead.

Toby waited for him to complete his sentence, eventually giving him a nudge, "Yeah? Tracey..."

"She's not doing very well, Tobe." Damien shook his head as if in minor disappointment.

"How do you mean?" asked Toby.

Damien searched for words, "If she'd just lost Luke," he caught his breath, "then it would have been hard enough. Too hard, really, just coping with that. I mean, how do you do it?"

Toby held his eye contact. He really had no response.

"But she'd put so much hope into seeing some punishment dished out to the woman. We know it won't make Luke come home, but somehow it's what we've been holding on to. I mean, you mess up, and you pay the price. But she's not going to have to pay for what she's done, is she?"

Toby looked into Damien's despairing eyes, felt rising anger, looked away, found himself thinking bad thoughts, and finally looked back at Damien, unable to console him.

45.

"WPC Bell?" the Chief Constable gave her elbow a gentle nudge.

Lucy took the earbuds out from her ears, "Yes, Sir?" she touched the screen of the tiny television recessed into the headrest of the seat in front. She was hoping to pause the movie she'd just begun but seeing that wasn't an option, she turned to her boss.

"About the interview." The Chief Constable had been mulling it over since their plane had taken off but still hadn't quite figured out how to say what he needed to say.

"Sir?" They'd maintained silence since meeting at the gate inside Heathrow Airport, and only now that she'd finally found something to occupy her time did he want to talk shop.

He still had no idea how to broach the subject, meaning there was no option but to start the discussion and fix whatever came out wrong. "Typically, we have expectations of our officers when conducting suspect interviews, certain standards of professionalism."

"I understand, Sir. This is a very high profile case; I will be at my most professional." Lucy respectfully assured him.

Oh dear, she'd totally got the wrong end of the stick. He needed to veer her in a different direction, "I don't doubt that, Bell. However, it's not exactly what I meant."

Lucy tried reading between the lines, and while certain intended possibilities sprung to mind, she wanted clarification instead of potential misinterpretation, "Then I'm not sure I understand, Sir."

Oh dear, thought the Chief, "Well, firstly, follow my lead when we start the interview. It will become apparent, I'm sure, but what I'm trying to say is that, our suspect, Mrs. Madyson Lutz."

There seemed no reason for Lucy to keep saying 'Yes Sir,' so she just maintained eye contact.

"This is a very unusual case due to the circumstances."

Lucy could only repeat the same thoughts inside her head.

"And therefore, we must be realistic, which may be disheartening."

Okay, now there was a glimmer of understanding about where he was trying to go with this conversation.

"So we may have to step over some lines which would typically be frowned upon."

Ooh, this had just got more interesting, Lucy nodded.

"What I mean to say is, we may be required to push slightly harder."

So what the Chief Constable meant was to try and get a rise out of Mrs. Lutz.

"You see, there is an unfortunate possibility that regardless of how strong our case is, she may never be returned to the UK to see justice served."

That depressing possibility had been on Lucy's mind

since the Lutz woman had first boarded her transport plane home. "I know, Sir. So what are we hoping to achieve, other than completing our case to the CPS' satisfaction?"

"That is the question WPC Bell, and there may not be a straightforward answer." he paused, still deep in thought, "May I be honest?"

I wish you would, Lucy thought before answering with slightly more tact, "Please do, Sir. I understand that such an unusual case might require a modified approach."

Excellent, that's what he'd wanted to hear, "Look, Bell, Madyson Lutz left the UK knowing she'd done something very wrong. You were the first responder, and so you know that better than most. In your report, didn't you write that she admitted fault in the hospital?"

Lucy thought back, firstly to Mrs. Lutz falling out of her SUV, having already puked all over herself. Then her terror and shame when they'd met at the hospital shortly afterward, "Oh yes Sir, she certainly did."

"Doesn't it appear to you that there's been a change? Since you took that hospital statement."

It was a good question and Lucy had felt the same way, "I've wondered the same thing, but we've heard nothing since then and..." Even in such a noisy environment, Lucy was concerned about talking too openly as half of the people on board were probably American, "the American authorities seem to have kept her shut away from all outside contact."

The Chief leant in too, "Exactly Bell, and so we have no idea of her current state of mind. Does she still admit to culpability, or has her mind changed? Has she simply realised the gravity of her situation? Because since she ran from the UK, she must have been briefed on the workings of our justice system. Therefore, she must also understand that this charge could see her sentenced for up to fourteen years. What I mean is, do we have a potential situation where she has been persuaded, either by her own sense of self-preservation or by what may be countless external influences, that she's simply not at fault?"

Lucy turned her head away from the Chief, staring blankly into space. She knew exactly where he was going now, "So we may be the last chance. No, the last people?" she couldn't verbalise her thoughts.

The Chief stepped in to finish her sentence, "To get into her head and remind her about what she's actually done. After six weeks in America, I doubt she has any remaining sense of perspective, other than denying fault and avoiding prison at whatever cost."

"And we can't do that if we're worried about 'Significantly harming her mental state'." Lucy nodded as she spoke.

"Exactly Bell." the Chief felt uplifted. WPC Bell was quoting from the Police Conduct Codes, this young officer had genuine potential, "I'm not saying we should disregard her mental state, because I am adamant that we will return to the UK knowing that the Crown Prosecution Service will be satisfied with every single aspect of our case file. But often, our officers are hampered by their own interpretations of that particular quote from the PACE codes. And what will we have achieved if we choose the softest possible route of questioning, out of an excess of caution, only to find an extradition request is flatly denied regardless?"

"Very little. And we might never find ourselves in a British court, with her brief attempting to criticize the way she was questioned anyway." Lucy replied.

"Quite right. So we have two options, we could interpret our own PACE codes in the most overly cautious way and stop any lines of questioning that make her appear agitated. Or we could interpret the same PACE codes in a way that allows us to be considerably more direct. That's not to say we will achieve anything more, but I can't help but think we are looking at the UK's very last opportunity to remind Madyson Lutz of what she's actually done."

46.

Lucy Bell and the Chief Constable parked their rental car in the parking lot of the agreed-upon Police Precinct. They popped the trunk and removed a couple of cumbersome bags.

"Hats too, Sir?" asked Bell.

"Yes, Bell, hats too." He took his, "Today we represent our country."

They each used one of the car's side windows to check their headgear was straight, picked up their bags, and headed toward the front doors.

"How's it going?" A local uniformed officer greeted them as he exited the building.

"Good. Good Morning." Chief Constable Palmer replied.

Another officer held the door open for them from the inside, "Hi, we've been expecting you. How was your trip? Did you find us okay?" The officer greeting them had a warm, welcoming manner. Simple gestures like this went a long way, and Lucy felt her nerves start to settle.

"Good, thank you," Lucy replied, "we used a sat-nav, so we had no problems. Where can we set up?"

The American police officer smiled, gesturing for Lucy to follow. The Chief Constable waved her away, having already stated his intention to meet with his local counterpart quickly.

"Officer Tupuola, let me know if I can help you in any way." He flashed Lucy another sincere smile, "And call me Ross." Ross Tupuola stopped outside an interview room, unlocked the door, and gestured that it was their destination.

Lucy rolled her bag into the room, then turned and finally shook his hand, "Thanks. WPC Lucy Bell, it's nice to meet you, Ross." Lucy had been nervous all morning, firstly about the importance of finishing this case file, which would no doubt be one of the biggest of her career.

But she'd also been nervous about the reaction from their counterparts in US Law Enforcement. Local opinion was an unknown quantity, and she'd not known whether to expect the cold shoulder or even open hostility. This American cop had taken her by surprise, in the most welcome way.

Lucy smiled, her relief evident, "I need to set up a voice recorder. I've got an adaptor for the plug socket; where can I?"

"Here you go," he pointed at some unfamiliar-looking electrical outlets, "but you won't need to use your tape recorder, this room is fully set up for recording interviews, and we can give you the master DVD when you're done."

"Oh." Lucy hadn't given any thought to procedural differences. "That sounds great, but um," As much as she appreciated the offer, she knew she had to play it safe, "I really do need to set mine up too. It records two audio channels. One has the time into the tape, it shows the timeline hasn't been tampered with, and we're required to have it. I also need to bag them in a specific way as sealed evidence. But I'll happily take your DVDs too; can't have too much, can you?"

"Sure, of course. I guess we've both got our different rules." Ross Tupuola smiled again, he had a calming manner, and Lucy already liked him.

"I'll be in the next room down if you need me." Ross headed toward the doorway, then had a change of heart and took a couple of steps back toward Lucy, "Can I just say something, only as an American and not as a cop?"

"Um, yes, of course." Lucy's confusion was apparent.

"I'm glad you guys are here, in the US I mean, and our department too. But I really hope you guys can get something useful out of this."

Lucy's eyes widened. An open gesture of support was more than she'd imagined possible. "Thanks," she said, slightly dumbstruck.

"If this situation were reversed, we'd want you guys to waive the diplomatic status, so this, it just isn't..." he'd made his point and seemed reluctant to say too much more.

The main thing Lucy had taken from his response was the word 'we.' She lowered her voice, "You said we'd want it waived? Is that how people feel?" she really was taken aback.

"Pretty much, yeah." he'd turned his volume down too.

Wow. She really couldn't have asked for a better way to

start the day. She'd assumed they'd be unwelcome visitors or viewed as anti-American or something equally ridiculous. The wave of relief was immense.

"Thanks for saying that, Ross. That means a lot, really." Her relief was evident.

He smiled that warm smile again, "Like I said, if I can do anything, anything at all, don't hesitate."

"Well, if you're serious, there is one thing," Lucy whispered.

47.

Lucy was confident she'd set up perfectly. Her voice recorder had been tested and double-tested. She'd got everything laid out on the large interview table with the copy of their huge case file taking center stage. Local cop Ross had helped her bring in enough chairs and had since returned to give her a 'heads up' that Madyson Lutz was already in the building, accompanied by an attorney as everyone had expected.

"Sir." Lucy greeted the Chief Constable as he finally entered the room, "A word, quickly, before she arrives."

"Yes, Bell." the Chief accelerated to Bell's side.

"Firstly, the Americans are on our side, or at least they sympathize with us. I was surprised, but they're not necessarily in agreement with the way this situation has been handled. I only mention it because it might change how we can do things, Sir. Prior to my arrival, I'd considered we might be unwelcome here. The truth is far from it."

"I got the same feeling from the Police Chief, but no actual statement of it. Did you just assume this, or?"

"No, Sir, I was told by one of the local officers."

The Chief took his seat, "Well, that is interesting. What else? You said firstly."

"Well, she's got a brief, as we'd expected, but that leads to the other thing, the local cop also explained their interview rules, and they're different from ours."

"WPC Bell, if you talk about a brief over here, nobody is going to know what you're talking about."

"Right, sorry, Sir. I mean her lawyer, or attorney." Lucy wasn't sure of the difference.

"Any way Bell, I'm not sure that differences in interview regs will help us. We've still got to consider the PACE codes of conduct for the British courts."

"I know that Sir, but her brief, sorry attorney, they won't know that. I mean that what might trigger a brief in the UK to complain, won't over here." Lucy could already see that altering her jargon wasn't going to be easy. She just hoped her boss would see past it and understand her point.

The Chief was dubious, "I'm still not sure how that will help us, WPC Bell."

Now Lucy was the one pussy footing around, and she was running out of time, "I understand, Sir. I only say this in relation to your comments on the flight about reminding Mrs. Lutz of what she's done, because while those differences in interview regulations might not help us achieve anything useful for the court case, they might give us the extra wiggle room we need to get under her skin."

"For the sake of the recording, this interview is being conducted by Chief Constable Geoffrey Palmer." Geoff Palmer leaned back in his chair.

"And WPC Lucy Bell," Lucy added for the tape.

"Please state your name for the recording." The Chief had directed the request to Maddy.

She huffed, looking down at the table as she'd done since first entering the room.

The Chief didn't look amused, "Mrs. Lutz, this interview has been organized by both the British Foreign and Commonwealth Office and the US State Department. We were informed that you would be attending this interview with cooperation in mind. If you do not cooperate with these simple questions, then my next course of action will be to complain in the strongest possible terms to your State Department and use your non-compliance in support of our extradition request. I will ask you again to state your name for the recording."

Maddy's attorney nudged her and whispered something inaudible in her ear. "Madyson Lutz." she answered without looking up.

Both Lucy and Geoff Palmer looked over at the attorney who understood what the foreigners required, "Lilly Hart, council for Mrs. Lutz."

"Thank you." Geoff Palmer opened the large case file. "Can you confirm you were the driver of this car," the Chief slid a photo toward Maddy, "which was involved in a road traffic collision on the eleventh of March?"

Her poor car looked awful, Maddy nodded.

"Can you please respond for the benefit of the tape?"

"Uh-huh." Maddy slid the photo back and continued avoiding all eye contact.

"What was the reason for your presence in the United Kingdom at the time of the accident?"

"My husband was working there."

"And what was the nature of your husband's work in the United Kingdom." Geoff was pushing his luck with that one, it was motivated by personal curiosity as much as professional.

"You know that subject is off-limits, Chief Constable." Maddy's attorney intervened, "Her husband holds diplomatic status, and that is the only point of relevance on that matter."

As WPC Lucy Bell listened to her superior fire off question after question, she studied Maddy intently, curious at the reason for her reluctance to answer. Madyson Lutz could have said she'd run down Luke Rigg because she didn't like his haircut, and it wouldn't have got Lucy or her boss any closer to securing a conviction, making her reticence seem redundant.

Lucy also knew that her own personal involvement in this interview would be minimal and so what little she contributed would need to really count. Part of that was getting into Madyson's head.

There was a pause as the Chief Constable consulted the file, in search of his next question. Lucy used it as an opportunity to locate the photo of Madyson Lutz's recovered mobile phone, which she slid over toward her boss without saying a word.

"What exactly were you doing at the time of the incident Mrs. Lutz?" The Chief had clearly understood.

Maddy, who'd never faltered in her downward gaze, didn't look at the relevant photo.

"I was driving." she delivered the response in a surprisingly juvenile, almost antagonistic manner.

Neither Lucy nor Geoff appreciated it, but it was Geoff who had the stage, "Was that all you were doing?"

"Of course, it was all I was doing." her attitude was unchanged.

Lucy Bell watched Madyson, baffled. In her profession, it always surprised her that people didn't consider the consequences of treating the Police in such a combative manner. As a cop, when somebody argued with her, Lucy relished the moment when she could knock them down for it, as she knew the Chief was about to do.

"Do you recognize the mobile phone in this image?" The photo was finally slid into Maddy's line of sight.

Lucy was examining her so intently that she noticed a quick widening of the eyes when Maddy saw the photo of her phone. That was guilt, and it was as good as an admission for Lucy. Any remaining sympathy she may have had for the mess Mrs. Lutz had got herself into was evaporating rapidly.

"I don't know. It looks like one I had, but they're not

179

exactly rare, you know."

Again with the attitude, Lucy shook her head so gently as to be barely visible.

"This particular phone is registered in your name, and we have call logs of your usage on this phone whilst in the UK."

"It's mine then." Madyson just couldn't believe she'd been made to do this. She rolled her eyes in irritation.

The Chief clenched his jaw, then barked his next question, "Were you using this phone at the time of the accident?"

"No." She knew she might have been, but what did it matter now? She'd lost that old phone and that old car, then her friends and her house, but she still had diplomatic immunity. It had been made clear to her that she was the evidence to all other serving US diplomats, that their country would never hang them out to dry. It had taken her so long to see it, but that knowledge had become her only positive because, without it, these people would undoubtedly be taking her to some terrifying British women's prison.

"Mrs. Lutz?" Chief Palmer used more volume to regain her wayward attention.

"Uh-huh." she looked at him for the briefest of moments.

What was she just thinking about? Lucy wondered,

"I will ask you again. If you were not using your phone at the time of the accident, then how do you explain that your phone has a stored photograph, which is time and date stamped at that exact moment?"

"I don't know." she'd been told to cooperate in this sham of an interview, but as the questions grew more accusatory, her enthusiasm waned. "Maybe the time was wrong?"

"But as you'll see here, we have your phone records," Geoff slid another sheet of paper toward her, "And if we choose this call here, for example, we can cross-check against the receiving phone number and use that to prove the accuracy of the time and date displayed on your own phone, as recorded in the call logs on your handset. Therefore the time and date on the photograph are perfectly accurate." Geoff felt powerful delivering that shot.

"Oh." she hadn't expected them to be able to do that, "But my phone was locked." It seemed like a slight change of subject, but it was suddenly important to Maddy. She felt violated at the idea of these people going through her personal phone information.

"It was, and our technical team unlocked it," Geoff answered.

It was your birth date woman, any one could have unlocked it. Lucy was glaring at Maddy now.

"So, I will ask you again, were you using your phone at the time of the accident?"

Maddy was done cooperating. It was time to give as little back as possible, "I don't remember. I blacked out."

The Chief Constable was aware that there had been some mention of her losing consciousness but wasn't ready for that to stop his flow. "Were you driving on the wrong side of the carriageway?"

The what? She was lost. "The carriageway?" she asked, finally looking up properly.

"The road Mrs. Lutz, were you driving on the wrong side of the road? The wrong side would be the right-hand lane, so which side of the road were you driving on?"

Maddy winced and looked back down, "I don't remember."

Geoff Palmer came back quicker. "But our scene reconstruction shows your car came to a stop here," he stabbed at the large accident map, "that you started to lose traction here," he stabbed again, "which means you were driving on the wrong side of the road Mrs. Lutz. The wrong side when you started braking, the wrong side when you lost control, the wrong side when you hit young Luke Rigg, and the wrong side of the road when you finally came to a stop. Mrs. Lutz you were always on the wrong side of the road. The reconstruction shows it clearly."

Now Maddy's attorney stepped in, "What is this reconstruction?"

The Chief looked straight at the attorney, he was at full speed ahead now, "It is an accident reconstruction. It takes into account every part of the accident scene. We measure the tire marks, gouge marks in the road surface, calculate angles of direction, calculate speeds, we drive reconstructions of the accident to prove the speed at which the vehicle was traveling. This," he stabbed at the map again, "is damning evidence in a Court of Law."

"In a British Court of Law? Now I don't mean to be disrespectful, but my client is the wife of a US diplomat, and his diplomatic status applies to her." Maddy's attorney's relaxed manner was in sharp contrast to the Chief's. "So my client will not be tried in a British Court of Law."

"That remains to be seen." The Chief Constable was clearly not amused.

"As you stated at the beginning of this interview, we are all here by agreement, an agreement made by people way above our pay grade. Now I believe that my client has been very cooperative, so are there any other questions?" She quickly corrected herself, "Any new questions?" she looked at the Chief Constable before finally settling on Lucy, who could no longer hold back.

"I have a question." Lucy feigned an unthreatening manner. "Your memory of the incident is clearly patchy." she smiled at Maddy, "but do you remember me Mrs. Lutz?"

Maddy looked up, she hadn't paid any attention to Lucy until now, but yes, she did remember her. It started coming back; she'd been kind, helpful, caring, "I do." Maddy nodded. "We spoke in the hospital. You were with another cop, a man."

Maddy's attorney sighed impatiently and slumped back into her chair.

"Exactly," Lucy's smile grew, "I'm glad you remember me from the hospital, but do you remember me from the scene of the accident?

A wave of some strange emotion started welling within Madyson.

"I can help your remember." Lucy's tone was hypnotic, her smile added to the effect. "I held you as you vomited after getting out of your car. Do you remember that?" Lucy was absolutely sure that would be the trigger, because she'd wanted to vomit at the scene too.

Maddy's mouth slowly opened. It all started coming back, fear, panic, the taste of vomit.

"Do you remember why," Lucy paused awkwardly, "why you vomited Mrs. Lutz? Do you remember what caused you to vomit?"

Maddy's mind started automatically following Lucy's triggers. It conjured up the face, a few inches from hers, separated by a blood-spattered windshield, the face, its lifeless eyes staring away from her. Everything that Maddy's subconscious had so successfully suppressed suddenly came flooding back. Maddy swallowed and then caught her breath. She could see it all again perfectly. Her breathing was quickening; her eyes started flitting from side to side, the gray sky, the road, the trees, the face, the smell, the blood, her phone, the face, the panic, suddenly Maddy stood up, rocked her head backward, took in a huge breath and vomited, moaning in pain as the bile gushed out from both

184

mouth and nose.

The attorney flew back from the table, "Uhh, a trash can for my client."

Bell whipped the case file off the table as Maddy took in another lungful of air, now leaning even further forward before vomiting all over the table again.

With an expression of sheer horror, Madyson Lutz looked at Lucy Bell, turned, and then ran from the room, her attorney giving Lucy a furious glare as she took off after her client.

Lucy corrected her posture and turned toward the tape recorder, "This is WPC Lucy Bell. For the benefit of the recording, Mrs. Madyson Lutz has left the interview room. She was immediately followed by her attorney..." Lucy looked back down at her notes to locate the right name, "Lilly Hart."

The Chief Constable had Madyson's vomit splattered over the lower part of his jacket, but he wasn't angry or outraged, he was smiling, and it was directed at Lucy.

"Interview terminated," he consulted his watch, "at exactly eleven seventeen am." Chief Constable Geoffrey Palmer pressed the stop button, turned back to Lucy, and shook her hand. "Skillfully done, WPC Bell." He shook his head in disbelief, "I don't think I've ever seen anything quite like it."

A quick knock on the interview room door was followed

by Officer Tupuola, "Uh," self-doubt had accompanied him. "Can I get you guys anything?" Ross Tupuola was beginning to realize his quick entry could only be attributed to him having watched the whole interview.

The Chief looked suspiciously at the local cop, while Lucy just smirked.

"I hope you don't mind, but I was watching your interview." he bowed apologetically and paused to better formulate his words, "It's a big case. Sir." he now nodded to the Chief Constable.

"That's no problem, officer, so what did you make of it?" the Chief was uncomfortable due to the vomit, which was already soaking through the material of his uniform trousers, making the skin of his legs feel cold and greasy, but he still managed to project a kind, friendly manner to the local.

Ross Tupuola was gently nudged into the room from behind, making room for another two cops who must have seen the show too, "Wow." he tried to control his smile, failing disastrously, "You guys do intense interviews."

"Seriously." said the stockier of the two cops who'd followed him in, his expression more serious. "It's good to meet you guys."

"You too, Officer, actually I should say Officers." The Chief raised himself from his chair, with the intention of shaking their hands but pulled it back after realizing the vomit had even found its way there.

"Hey, let me run and get you some stuff to clean up with." said the third officer, who spun on his heels and left the room.

"When I met Officer Bell this morning, I thought she seemed... efficient. But." Ross shook his head in appreciation, directing his comment and embellishment toward the Chief Constable, who couldn't resist rolling with it.

"When we started our interview, Mrs. Lutz didn't seem to be taking it very seriously, but WPC Bell gave her quite the wake-up call."

"Did she ever." Ross beamed at Lucy and nodded in appreciation once more.

"As you said, it's a big case, but a messy one too." it was Lucy now, "We can go back and finally bring charges against Mrs. Lutz, but we can't control what happens after that."

Ross' smile faded, "Isn't that the truth."

"Tsh, it's always the truth. But with this case, you guys have it even harder. I'm Mark, by the way." the stocky cop raised his hand in greeting, "I hope you can get some kind of justice for the boy. We all read about the story here. And you know what, if it would help any, tell the boy's family that we're sorry for their loss. Really, all of us."

"It's the truth," added Ross.

The man's comment took the Chief Constable back in time. He was a young Policeman again, and his younger self had been emotionally invested in the job. Mark's words held power and the Chief had to show his appreciation in some way, "Thank you, I wish I could shake your hand, both of you," he raised his filthy arms in explanation, "but know that when we leave, your words will travel with us, that your gesture will be shared, and appreciated, sincerely."

Lucy decided to throw caution to the wind, "Maybe the politics of this will get in the way of justice. But if we just managed to remind her of what she's done, and triggered some guilt or shame, then speaking personally, I won't feel like we totally let down the boy's family. It won't feel like Madyson Lutz totally got away with it."

"Amen to that sister." Mark stood proud and straight, and Ross smiled that kind smile one last time.

48.

"Just here on the right, Sir," Lucy pointed to the house while stabbing at the passenger footwell, wishing she had her own brake pedal. "I'm sure you can park in their driveway."

"Thank you, WPC Bell." replied the Chief Constable as he pulled on the handbrake and unfastened his seat belt.

They stepped out of the marked car and this time, Lucy waited to follow the Chief's lead regarding hat etiquette. Watching her boss grab his, she knew they were expected to be formal and made sure hers was suitably straight before taking the lead in the direction of the front door.

She pressed the tiny doorbell button and was still straightening her uniform when the door opened.

"Good Morning, it was Lucy, wasn't it?" asked Damien.

"Yes," Lucy was flustered, knowing that the Chief wanted formal, "It's WPC Bell." she replied awkwardly, "And this is Chief Constable Geoffrey Palmer."

Damien's eyebrows raised on hearing the high rank, "Chief Constable." they shook hands.

Damien ushered them into the family living room, "This is my wife, Tracey," he turned to his wife to properly introduce her to the top man, "this is Chief Constable Palmer."

"Oh," her eyebrows raised in the same manner as Damien's had, then she turned to greet Lucy, "Lucy, wasn't

189

it?"

Lucy squirmed once more, "Yes, WPC Lucy Bell."

Toby watched the introductions, frowning slightly as Lucy repeatedly corrected his family.

"And finally, this is my wife's brother Toby." Damien stepped aside to allow Toby the space to exchange handshakes.

"Chief Constable." Toby shook his hand firmly.

"Pleased to meet you, Toby." the Chief Constable nodded.

"Toby." Lucy Bell reached in to shake his hand.

A smartly uniformed Toby, always one for confrontation, couldn't hold himself back from correcting her, "It's Sergeant Miller."

"Of course, Sergeant Miller." Lucy squirmed in discomfort.

"I think we can drop the formalities, don't you?" the Chief was looking at Lucy.

"Of course, Sir." *Why hadn't he led with that?* Her smile was embarrassingly awkward.

"Call me Geoff, please." the Chief's smile was much more practiced, which isn't to say sincere. "So, we're here today to fill you in on what's been happening with your son's case."

Tracey had been waiting for this day since the accident. It had been close to two months of torture. Luke had gone, taken before his time by a dangerous driver; she knew that,

190

everyone in the country knew that, but nobody knew what was going on. Inevitably she'd convinced herself nothing was going on, and that sense of betrayal and impotence had multiplied her pain.

To finally have somebody arrive with the promise of answers and the top man no less, it was overwhelming. It wasn't the time and she fought the welling emotions as hard as she could, but they were overpowering, and with no warning discernible to anybody else in the room, she started wailing. The noise was embarrassing, but she couldn't stop it. It had taken on its own life, she had to just ride it out and wait for it to pass, and so the noise, her noise, filled the room.

"So after the interview had been transcribed, the case file was complete, and it's now been handed over to the Crown Prosecution Service." the Chief Constable concluded.

But neither Tracey, Damien, or Toby felt any sense of conclusion. Since recovering from her emotional release Tracey had said very little, and now she looked at both Police Officers with a look of confusion, then did the same to both Toby and Damien.

Toby took a deep breath and spoke for them, "I guess I should start by thanking you, but then I think we'd all like to know what happens next. Because it sounds like you've got a strong case, but a case against a runner with diplomatic immunity, so what are we looking at?"

The Chief knew his explanation would culminate in this

question and had to return to playing the politically adept Chief Constable to handle it. "Well, the CPS will almost certainly liaise with the FCO and the Home Secretary to apply for the extradition of Mrs. Madyson Lutz."

Tracey gasped in hope, "That means we're asking them to send her back, doesn't it?"

Toby didn't share his sister's faith, he'd known the whole time it would come down to this. He'd played it all out in his head, going right back to the way Captain Bowyer had told him at the airport that the diplomats had already gone home. His old Captain had known that before the Police and before the newspapers, and then Toby had recognized the suit from GCHQ the following morning. Obviously, he, or one of his GCHQ colleagues, had been the ones who told the Captain. And for them to have known that so early, it simply couldn't mean anything positive. If they'd known all along that the American couple would leave, it implied they were part of an agreement to let them, and now his poor sister was energized with hope. Toby shook his head, knowing another crash would follow, maybe not for a while, but why file an extradition request for somebody who'd been mutually and quietly allowed to leave?

While he knew this, he also knew that calling the coppers on it now would only hurt his sister. So while he wanted to confront them on the percentage chance of the request being successful, he altered his approach, "So if the extradition request is successful, she'll be returned to the UK, tried in a court of law, and be sentenced for death by dangerous driving?"

"Correct," replied Geoffrey Palmer.

"Assuming that your case is strong enough to ensure a conviction, which it sounds like it is." this was all for his sister's benefit.

The next question needed more tact, not a quality he'd needed to use very often in the military, "And if the extradition request is denied..."

Tracey's arms shot out in front of her as if in some form of primitive instinct to protect herself.

"Wait, Tracey," Toby held his arm out too, attempting to reassure her with a calming movement of his hand, "if it is denied, then we still have hope, isn't that right?" Toby already knew the answer. He also knew that hearing the next piece of information would be more reassuring coming from their region's top cop.

"That's true, Toby." The Chief was glad the soldier had brought the conversation around to that point, "Because a denial of an extradition request can be altered by any subsequent American administrations."

Tracey looked baffled, and Damien wasn't far behind, so Geoff continued, "basically, that means when this President loses an election, the following American President could choose to extradite Mrs. Lutz, which is a likely scenario. It's very similar to here. If the Conservative party loses an election, the Labour party will usually try and reverse any of their controversial decisions as soon as they get into a position of power."

"And this is about as controversial as they get." Toby chipped in.

"Also very true." the Chief nodded appreciatively toward Toby. "Additionally, a denied extradition request would only apply to Mrs. Lutz while on American soil."

As Toby waited for the next inevitable point, he studied his sister, trying to get a read on how she was coping with all this new information.

The Chief elaborated, "So let's say Mrs. Lutz takes a holiday, or vacation as they'd put it, and that holiday is in Canada, well Canada would honour our extradition request without hesitation. It would strengthen their relationship with us in the UK, without damaging relations with their US neighbors. Because the US government won't feel any sense of obligation in protecting Mrs. Lutz, once she's left their borders."

Tracey seemed to have taken that point well. Toby breathed a small sigh of relief.

"And so unless Mrs. Madyson Lutz is willing to spend the rest of her life on American soil," The Chief Constable allowed the Riggs to end the sentence in their own heads, "And since there's an American election not far away. There's also still the possibility they may approve our extradition request."

Yeah, right. Toby rolled his eyes cautiously.

The Chief sat up straight as if he were drawing to a close, "Moving forwards, I give you my word that we will inform you of any updates the moment we have them." He stood up and leant forward to shake Tracey's hand, then remembered something, "I'd also like to share something else with you. Whilst we were in America, we were asked by the local law enforcement officers to extend their sincerest condolences,"

A wave of disbelief shot across Tracey's face, everyone in the room spotted it. The Chief made sure to nullify it without delay, "They were heartfelt wishes, I assure you, it was a touching moment."

Tracey's head tensed up, her breathing faltered again, and the tears leaked once more, but a smile struggled to break through, "Really?" she shook gently.

Lucy leant forward and took Tracey's hand, "Really, Mrs. Rigg, it was an emotional moment for us all."

Tracey's shaking amplified, "Oh bless them." she wiped her cheeks dry, "thank you," she reached out to hold the Chief Constable's hand too, "thank you so much."

"Wait, WPC Bell," Toby called out as Lucy opened the marked police car's door.

"One moment Sir."

The Chief nodded, "Of course, Bell, go ahead."

Lucy walked back toward Toby, meeting him halfway between house and car. "Please, just call me Lucy. I should have stuck with Lucy all along."

Good for her, Toby appreciated that. "Lucy." he flashed a quick grin, "There's just one thing I'd like to know."

"And what's that?" asked Bell.

"Did she show any signs of remorse? You're the only people who've seen her since it happened, so?" Toby was no longer confrontational, just businesslike.

Lucy allowed a little laugh to escape. Toby frowned, "What was that? What's so funny?"

She couldn't help but feel taken aback when this man had that look on his face. He was genuinely intimidating, "I just flashed back to how our interview ended in the States."

Toby's face was granite, unchanged and disconcerting, but Lucy was determined to let it wash over her, "She showed plenty of emotion."

Toby liked the sound of this, "Look, Lucy, we probably got off on the wrong foot, but I'm starting to see you might not be so bad after all. Please, tell me everything you can get away with. Please." he reiterated.

Lucy considered looking back at her boss, but realising it would only serve to attract his attention, she stopped herself, instead closing in on Toby, "Only if I know it can stay between you and me."

Toby nodded firmly, "It will. Only be between you and

me."

She couldn't remember anybody who'd made their words sound like such an unbreakable bond before, "Alright, so she was a bitch. An absolute bitch, I couldn't tell if she was feeling sorry for herself, in the most selfish inhuman way possible. Or if she was just in total denial. And I tried reading her."

Toby wanted more. What was Bell pausing for? "Okay, come on."

Lucy's interpretation of Toby's manner was starting to alter too. It wasn't intentional rudeness. It was just a brutal directness. Maybe he wasn't such an arse. "So when I attended the original accident scene, with your nephew," her training made her feel obliged to interject with a customary sorry for your loss type comment, but Toby had already read it.

"I've seen death. Don't worry, go on."

That comment felt even darker, Lucy put it aside to continue, "She was fully aware of what had happened, she was freaked out, Luke's blood was all over her car," again, she hesitated, and again Toby kick-started her.

"My nephew bled, I get it, go on."

"She was so affected by it all that she puked on herself getting out of her car. Then once she'd got out, I handled her, and my partner tried to help your nephew." Lucy knew not to get hung up again, so she pushed onward. "And then she puked again, outside, while I calmed her. She was repulsed, panicked, she was shaking and in shock."

After two months of nothing, Toby was riveted by these new details, "Got it."

"But when we arrived in the States, she was different. In denial is how it struck me. I think she'd blanked it all out. She'd put it into a box somewhere, at the back of her mind."

Toby was nodding, listening intently.

"On the plane, the boss," Lucy's eyeballs pivoted toward the Chief for clarification, "said we should use that last opportunity to make her remember what she'd done."

Now Toby smiled a dark but appreciative smile.

"So, right at the end of our interview, I went for it."

"Good." his smile grew.

"I asked her if she could remember me from the incident, and she did, but she had to think back to do it. I could see her really searching for that memory, and once she thought back, the box opened, that one in her mind. And it was like..."

"What?" Toby's grin was really freaking Lucy out.

"She couldn't close it again, the box opened, and all of the darkness came flooding out."

Toby liked what he heard, that bitch needed to feel some remorse, but he wanted to be certain, "How do you know? What makes you sure it was remorse?"

Lucy laughed with the same laugh she'd used at the start

of their conversation, "Because she reacted in exactly the same way she had at the original scene, back when your poor nephew was lying on her bonnet."

Toby leaned in even closer.

"She stood up, rocked her head backward, filled her lungs with air, and then puked all over the place, groaning in pain as if she were right back there, on the side of the road."

Toby's ominous smile faded, and for a second, his face was blank, then another smile took its place, a kinder one.

"Thank you, Lucy." Toby took a small step, filling the gap between the couple, and then threw his arms around her, giving her a completely unexpected hug, "You're alright, Lucy Bell."

The hug triggered an understanding in Lucy, a true sense of perspective for the victim's family, her eyes welled up, catching her totally off guard. She wanted to blot them away with a hand, but his hug was so strong she couldn't move her arms. It was unbelievable how powerful it was, he only had a couple of inches in height on Lucy, but this guy was immovable, "Um, thanks." She didn't know how to make him stop.

Toby had misjudged her, he'd categorized her as an unremarkable plod, a rules-loving jobsworth who enjoyed their meagre allowance of power over others, but she'd just proven him wrong, and he loved her for it. What she'd done in America showed she cared; about Luke, about fighting for some justice, and about Madyson Lutz's infuriating persistence at evading it.

Clearly, Bell had made Madyson Lutz relive the trauma, and it sounded like the woman had really suffered whilst doing it; Toby beamed in pride at the thought. But he also knew Lucy had completely misread that as remorse.

It was an easy mistake to make. He'd seen the same dramatic reaction in young soldiers, the sweating, puking, and temporary incapacitation. The problem was they didn't just do that after their first kill. You could be on patrol in a hostile area, turn a corner and find a body, somebody you hadn't even shot, and it would still have the same effect on the greenest young men. It was merely a reaction to death, to the gore, and the shock of what it triggered within you, or not, in some cases. Toby's typical lack of remorse had been seen as a useful quality by his superiors, but now, thinking about Madyson Lutz's lack of the same quality, he felt ashamed of its absence in him.

I'm not her; he ostracized himself. Their similarities had just struck him, but the differences told more. A sweet innocent teenage boy versus the pieces of filth who'd fallen at his hands. He shook his head, gently relaxed his grip, and asked Lucy, "Did she say sorry though? Or talk about Luke?" he stepped back to resume their original spacing.

Lucy cast her mind back to the interview, "No, she just ran off. Again." Then she realized Toby had made it worse by letting her go because now all she could think of was her teary eyes betraying her. She quickly needed to provide another focus, choosing, "And that was when the American

200

Police walked in. It's when they told us to share their deepest sympathies with the family, with you."

Toby's stiff manner returned, "About that."

Lucy was slightly thrown off guard by the sudden change, "Yes?"

"Do you remember their names?"

"Yeah, why?"

"Well." Toby considered the implications and then, happy with his calculations, continued, "I'd like to send them some stuff. We've made some badges and stickers. It's something we've called 4DC, and it's about trying to force a change to these old diplomatic immunity rules."

Now it was Lucy's turn to smile, "Oh yes... tell me more."

49.

Her lungs snatched at the air.

For God's sake, gotta stop the damn car!

No, no. "No!" she squealed.

The face, again the face.

Her stomach contracted violently, and the fowl fluid started gushing up into her mouth.

Madyson's right leg was locked outward, pushing on the absentee brake pedal with everything her muscles could give. She kicked her other leg in protest, threw off the sheets with her hands, and shook with disgust as she swallowed the sour stuff which had made it up into her mouth.

Then Maddy started to sob like she'd never sobbed before. Her body undulated as she lay in bed, her pajamas moist with sweat and her hair stuck to the side of her face.

It had been fine before, she'd never been so wrong in her whole life. Really, even with all the losses: the possessions, the people, her home, it had still been fine until that bitch cop had summoned the ghosts with her dirty parlor tricks.

Now what? Did she need a priest for an exorcism? A shrink? Pills? Hundreds of pills; all the pills in the world. She snatched at the sheets and yanked them back up over her shoulders, wriggling herself into a cocoon inside them, only her head exposed to the darkness of the unfamiliar room.

Where was she now? She couldn't even remember. What

did she care?

She didn't dare sleep again. He kept finding her; he knew exactly where she was, and he didn't need extradition to make her pay. He just arrived whenever she was at her most vulnerable. The daylight world already hated her for what she'd done. Her husband especially so, he'd even bailed on sleeping in the same bed, but he'd timed his absence ruthlessly, just when she needed protection, a guardian for the dark hours. Now her sleep had been taken too. There was nothing left to give.

50.

"Good morning, this is Attorney General Tony Mason. I'd like to speak to the Home Secretary, please."

"One moment, please, Mister Mason," there was a faint crackle on the line, followed by, "Putting you through now."

"Good Morning Tony, how are you?"

"I'm very well Christine, how are you?"

"Busy, as I'm sure you are."

Oh good, we can get right to it then, "Listen, Christine, I've just had word about the Police file for the case with the American diplomat. It's finally been handed to the CPS, and our next step is to apply for extradition of the wife; Lutz is the woman's name. Obviously, such sensitive extradition can't go through until we're absolutely sure that everyone is on board."

"I understand."

"Now, I've spoken to Rupinder at the FCO, and she's of the same opinion as myself, that you have the PM's ear."

"Loud and clear, Tony, I'll see when I can raise this with the PM. Give me a little time, and I'll get back to you once I've got something solid."

"Understood, thank you, Christine."

51.

Bill Addison stood up, pierced the din with his trademark whistle, and waited for the newsroom to settle.

"Do we remember the American woman who ran? That diplomat immunity bollocks?" Silence. "Yes? Do we? Or no?"

It was as if he were a headmaster in a room full of sixth-form school kids who were playing dumb while waiting for the final bell.

"I don't want any cardiacs through over-excitement. What is wrong with you lot?" he really wasn't amused.

"Yes, Bill, remember it." replied his closest colleague, which triggered an uninterested chorus of agreement.

Bill scowled, which gradually silenced the room as one after another the news hacks looked up in search of the reason for such an unexpected drop in noise. Instead of yelling, Bill slowly looked around the room, studying the faces he knew so well, he was disgusted with them, and they felt it.

"Stop what you're doing." He spoke quietly, but the whole room froze. "Talk to me. What's your deal? Come on. Somebody?" he challenged them, his volume unchanged.

There was a reluctance to speak as replying would imply the speaker represented the whole room, and in a workplace where they argued about everything, they all knew better.

"Somebody with a backbone, explain to me your lack of interest."

The same woman positioned to his side stepped up, "The story is old. It's dead."

Bill glared at the woman, "The boy is dead. The story is alive."

Ouch, that one hurt, the woman sunk into her chair, "I didn't mean it that way, Bill. But that story has gone as far as it can go; she hit the boy and ran."

As the woman spoke, Bill looked around, gauging the mood of the room. Most people played it safe and avoided eye contact with him, either by looking at the lady speaker or staring into space.

"And I think we all know, that's gonna be the end of it. Look, Bill, we did our research, and we all know the route ahead. Our nut-less government won't push the Yanks too hard coz they're too worried about trade deals with them. And the Yanks wouldn't extradite the stupid cow anyway. Nobody would ever admit it, but why would they extradite her? It would be suicide for them if one of theirs was sent back to face the music in Britain. Why would any of their people risk a posting somewhere really dangerous? It's shit Bill, but the story is dea... it's over." People either nodded or murmured in agreement.

Bill had never experienced this before. It wasn't a mutiny; if it were that, there wouldn't be any attempt to play it so civil. But they all clearly thought the same thing. What irked

Bill was they were all so wrong. He continued to look at the faces he worked with every day, considering his approach.

Eventually, he looked down at his neighboring colleague and gave her a subtle nod, "Thank you, Joyce."

She smiled, then Bill looked back at the remainder of the room, "Do we know who the husband was yet?"

"Yeah, Jeff Lutz." replied a young woman diagonally opposite Bill's location.

"Okay, and what does Jeff Lutz do? For the American Government, I mean?" the silence continued.

Bill maintained his gentle, unhurried manner, "And doesn't that strike you as odd?" he looked down at the table, running his fingers up through his hair and scratching his scalp. Bill walked to the centre of the newsroom and started nodding, "I understand you. I do, and usually, you would be absolutely right, but..." He pursed his lips as he started shaking his head, "Not this time. Sorry guys, but there are a couple of perspectives." He decided to take the thorough approach as he'd already got the room's undivided attention, something that happened annually, at best.

"I've got three kids," he chuckled, "It's a bloody newsroom, and I bet that's news to most of you, isn't it?" When everybody smiled or sniggered, Bill knew he'd already reclaimed his team. "Who else has kids? How many of us?" There were too many people trying to reply, so Bill adapted, "Stick your hand up if you've got a kid, and both hands up if you've got two, I don't even know what to say if you've got more than two of 'em." Hands starting rising around the room, one guy leaned back in his wheelie chair and lifted both his legs too.

"You've got four kids?" Bill pointed his colleague out to the rest of the room, "Actually, I do know what to say. Sorry!" He paused for his audience, "I mean... four kids! What were you thinking, Jimmy?" The laughter level raised another notch.

"Personally, I've got two girls and a boy. The boy is more manic, but the girls are harder. For a dad, they are anyway." More knowing laughter. "A couple of years back, my little boy was running around, you know how they are, it's like they're on crack, but at least they're made of rubber." Much louder laughter now, "So when they fall, they just bounce back up onto their daft little feet and start running all over again."

He'd finally got them into the right mindset, one of regular people, outside of a newsroom environment.

"So my daft little one is running, down the stairs, with his sweaty little paws clutching at handfuls of toy cars, doing the whole rmm rmm revving sound." He could see the expressions change in anticipation, "And he fell." Bill inhaled slowly, and it wasn't acting. The memory triggered some unwelcome emotions.

"So we were talking in the kitchen, me and the missus, when we heard the thud thud bang and a chilling squeal and," Bill shuddered, "I've never felt anything like it. I ran to him and look at me," Bill massaged his ample gut, "I don't do running."

A flurry of laughter was replaced by an uncomfortable silence. Eventually, one man spoke up, "Was he alright?"

Bill looked over at the speaker, at the sincerity on his face, and then pointed at him, "Do you see?"

The room turned to look.

"He's a callous journalist, supposedly, too cynical to care. But he did care. We do care, don't kid yourself, people." he let his words linger before turning back to the colleague who'd asked after his boy, realising that the act of asking had made Bill like him more.

"To answer you, no, at the time, he wasn't. When I got to the bottom of the stairs, he was screaming, and blood was spewing out of his mouth. For a moment, I was just totally out of my depth; panic was all I could feel, I was useless. It was bloody horrible, and I hope I never, ever have to experience that again." The room remained silent.

"Anyway, we ran him to hospital, they stitched up his tongue, and he's got no permanent damage. We were lucky. But what if he'd got hit by a car? What if he'd died? What if that was your son, your daughter? What if the driver fucking ran off and even the law couldn't make them come back?"

You could have heard a pin drop in the newsroom, "I'm not manipulating you lot with emotion; honestly, I'm not. I know it's a news story, but please let's not forget how truly fucked up this situation is."

"Sorry, Bill."

"I get you mate."

Multiple similar responses sounded around the room, "And I know that hasn't altered what dear Joyce here just said. But if we look at it from that perspective now, who the hell is this wanker? And why was our own government so keen to let him fly home? That rings alarm bells for me." Bill looked around the room again, he still had their full attention, but the slumped heads had been raised in concentration once more. "For me, this story is nowhere near dead. I'm sorry, Joyce, but I strongly disagree. What have we got that's unresolved?" he was clearly asking himself, "This Jeff Lutz bloke, there's something being hidden, and it's being hidden really well. I think we need to reach out to any American contacts that we have. I'm happy to give them whatever is required, money, credit, or even anonymity. But we need to get to the bottom of this bloke's identity." He paused as he was losing his flow.

"Oh yeah, the reason for all this, I just got told the Police have presented their completed case file to the CPS and only two months after the day of the accident."

"Jesus Christ."

"What did they do, send it by donkey?"

"Ass more like," Bill grinned mischievously, "But think about the reasons for that. I can agree with our good friend

Joyce on at least one of her points. Our government doesn't want to push the Americans too hard. But let's face it, it's also in their interests to slow everything down, then hopefully the story blows over. How long do you think we're looking at before they have the balls to even ask the Americans for extradition? Imagine it; the Police have to ask the CPS, who asks the Attorney General, who asks the FCO, who asks the Home Secretary, who asks the Prime Minister. It'll be Christmas before that lot agree to anything."

Bill paused again, "And the whole time, that kid's family is in limbo. I don't envy them."

"So we could do a reminder piece, culminating in the details of the newly completed police case." somebody chipped in.

Bill nodded and pointed at the speaker. "Yes, and especially because he used the word culminating, did you just swallow a dictionary, David?" The chuckling resumed.

"And something showing the timelines of the extradition process, so people can see exactly how it would pan out, for both the approval or denial scenario," added another.

"Love it." Bill pointed his finger again.

"What about looking at previous extradition cases, which ones were a success and which ones failed?" A third new contributor.

Bill put his hands together, "That's a great one because I've seen a few of these over the years, and eventually, you see a pattern of abuse. You'll need to highlight similar cases where the immunity rules were twisted just to dodge repercussions. We really need to go for it on this one."

"Seriously, we're going all out?" Asked the man with four kids.

Bill nodded.

"Like Brexit level all out?" The man seemed shocked.

"Close to it, yeah." A couple of the newer faces looked out of their depth, Bill didn't miss things like that, "Before we get back to it, a quick explanation for you new kids, we in the British press hold power, formidable power."

One of the younger faces bust out an appreciative laugh, only to realize Bill and the whole newsroom already knew it to be serious. "Oh, sorry. I thought you were messing around."

"It's alright, kid, understandable really, but we do. I have a question for you; were you old enough to vote in the UK's decision to leave or remain in the European Union?"

"If you were a remain voter, you might wanna keep yer mouth shut in here." Another interjected.

Full of trepidation, the new kid chose to play it safe, "Yeah, I voted."

"And you voted based on your own unbiased knowledge?" Bill asked. A few others in the room laughed, further throwing the new kid's understanding of what was and wasn't funny.

"Yeah." his self-doubt was evident.

"And nobody altered your opinion in any way?" Asked Bill, still disconcertingly calm in his manner.

"No, I make my own decisions; I'm not a child."

"And that young man is the beauty of it. Most people don't notice what we do, not even while we're doing it."

The kid rocked back in his chair, his nerves replaced by a restoration in the confidence that his decisions were always unfettered by external influence. He shook his head at Bill, smirking as he did it.

"I've got to ask him, you know I've gotta do it." Bill grinned cheekily, his head panning the room.

"No, not this; it could take all day." The Brexit vote had divided Britain like nothing else in decades, possibly centuries, pitting family members against each other in unresolvable disagreement.

"Don't do it!" a girl put her hands on her head, dreading what would come next.

"Young man, which way did you vote?" Bill raised a finger in hope of steadying the room, "It's okay, nobody will judge you." Now the whole room erupted in laughter.

The young man's confidence was faltering. He'd stumbled into an in-joke that he didn't even know existed and was now faced with being cast out if his answer fell on the wrong side of the room's majority vote. But he knew he couldn't dodge the answer, "Leave, I voted to leave."

A raucous cheer filled the room, drowning out the undertone of disappointed groans.

"Good for you, son." Bill was smiling. The whole team was having fun. "And why did you vote to leave?"

Various sarcastic options for a reply were offered in lowered tones.

"Because of the way the EU was taking from us but giving nothing back. Because of the way they were more concerned with imposing stupid rules, while they couldn't fix anything important."

"Like what?" Bill already knew the answer. He leant in, mocking curiosity.

"Like immigration."

"Ka-ching. There we have it, and where did you learn about the problems with the EU? Regarding all the points you just made." Bill was playing to the room but made sure to retain the appropriate respect for his young colleague, smiling and nodding him on in encouragement.

The young man looked down in thought, then around the room, before sighing as the realization hit him, "In the newspapers."

"Formidable power, my young friend, and that power now lies at your fingertips. Thanks for being a good sport." Bill wanted to personalize his thanks, "What's your name, kid? We've not spent any time together yet."

"Andy," he replied, his smile restored.

"As you know Andy, the results came out at fifty-one percent voting to leave the EU and forty-nine percent voting to remain. Those votes came after years of us finding reasons to criticize EU decisions in our newspaper. This means that before you were lucky enough to get into the world of tabloid reporting, you'd read stories about the EU worrying more about how we measure the weight of our fresh produce than doing anything to stem the rampant immigration into our country. You read stories about them trying to control what ingredients were allowed in the humble British sausage, whilst still ignoring things like the massive unemployment in the south of Europe which drove their young people north to France, Germany, or here. I could go on."

"Please don't." Added funny guy Jimmy.

"I don't want to!" Bill didn't hesitate, "Because he gets the idea. Would the ratio of leave versus remain voters have changed, without the reporters of Fleet Street waging our own campaign against the EU?"

"Bloody hell." Andy was mulling over thoughts he'd never previously entertained.

"And did the British Government have more or less power than us in swaying popular opinion?" Bill smiled warmly at Andy once again.

"That's crazy." Andy was shaking his head in respect.

Bill knew he had to let his crew get back to work as this had taken longer than anticipated. He chose how to finish up, "We left the EU to see a return to Britain making her own decisions, which she'd be free to do with her own best interests at heart."

"For better or for worse." Some comic inserted.

"In sickness and in health," Added another, to more chuckles.

"Finally going back to the diplomat." Bill resumed, "Here we are again. Britain is hand-tied again, because of decisions made somewhere else, again. And if we, the press, held that much sway with Brexit, one of the biggest decisions in our country's history, then shouldn't we have a little go at pushing for an improvement to this diplomatic immunity farce?"

52.

Madyson walked along the row of kennels, each dog reacting differently to her presence. She had no idea of what she wanted, just why she wanted it. She longed for willing company, and now that people had bailed on her, the job would have to fall to a dog.

Too yappy, she continued slowly. *Too ugly*, onward. *Too small*, another step. A large dog tried pushing his nose through the cage, his paw raised as he did it.

"Are you trying to give me your paw?"

Ruff! Maddy leaped back instinctively. *Whoah! What a huge bark*, but then realizing he was still wagging his tail, she moved forward again. The big animal altered its approach and slumped to the floor, spreading his back legs wide.

"Oh, you're trying to say sorry, aren't you? You silly thing, I don't mind, you've got a good bark, a big strong one." He sprang to his feet, his tail resuming its frantic speed and tried giving her his paw again, unsuccessfully due to the cage separating them.

Maddy turned her head away from the dog, "Scuse me!" she called out. Then, "Is anyone there?" much louder.

"Hi, did you find one you liked?" a teenage boy approached, wearing a t-shirt emblazoned with the rescue center's logo.

Maddy looked back at the dog and smiled, it made her

face feel strange. She hadn't done it in so long, her cheeks felt pudgy as she did it, "Even better, I think I found one that liked me."

"He's a big boy this one, let's see, what's his name?" The teenager looked at the information plate attached to the kennel's side, "I guess we don't know his name, so he'll need a new one. They adapt really quickly you know, they can learn a new name in no time."

Maddy was rubbing his whiskers with her finger through the small holes, "I thought you couldn't teach an old dog new tricks?"

"That's not my experience. Dogs form habits and yeah that's easier when they're young, but they're smart too, and so it's just whether they've got an incentive to do whatever it is you want them to do. The dogs who end up in here usually turn out to be real pleasers, coz they've lived without love, and so they value it."

Maddy knew it would be a perfect match.

53.

"Good morning, Mister President."

"Good morning to you, Prime Minister. How are you this morning?"

"Actually, it's a beautiful afternoon over here," replied the Prime Minister.

"Of course. I'm sorry, Thomas, I'm usually more in tune with those time differences. It's already turning out to be a challenging day here. But it's a beautiful day there, you say?"

"It is. The sun is shining, and the sky is the brightest blue."

"Say, how quick could I get there? I've never seen London on a dry day." the President laughed at his own joke.

"I've only seen a couple myself." The Prime Minister laughed at both the original and his own retort, "I'm sure it will be umbrellas at the ready tomorrow."

They shared some more polite laughter.

"Anyway, Christopher, I don't want to be too much of a drain on your time." The Prime Minister walked as he spoke. It sharpened his reactions.

"Talking to you is never a drain on my time. How can I help you this morning, or afternoon?" The President had cleared the oval office and was reclined in his office chair, his feet up on the desk.

"I wanted to inform you of a change in that diplomatic

219

immunity matter." The Prime Minister smiled, hoping the gesture would somehow be infectious over a phone line.

"Oh, of course, that's a tricky one. So what's the news then, Thomas?"

"As I'm sure you know, some of my Police Officers travelled to your country to perform an interview with the driver."

"Yes, yes, I was informed."

"Which means they were able to complete their case, that is for the prosecution of the driver."

There was a pause, "Who has diplomatic immunity."

The Prime Minister's pace quickened, "She does, Christopher."

"So there's no change there then?"

Now the pause came from the English end of the phone line, "No, no change. No change in her status. It's just that the next step required, legally, is to apply for extradition of the driver."

Another US pause, "I see." The President sounded dubious.

"Therefore, I wanted to let you know, personally, that one of my departments will be requesting the extradition of the driver in this matter."

Yet another US pause, "Wasn't she the wife of one of my operatives helping you guys out on that secret program of yours?"

"As I understand it, yes, her husband was part of the Torch Programme."

The President nodded, "Yeah, Torch Program, that was the name." He wanted to say more, and if this had been a discussion with his own staff, he'd have sure as hell said more. But he didn't want to clumsily upset the special friendship, so he was happy enough to let the call play out.

The Prime Minister knew what he wanted to say too, but had to get his point across without dealing in specifics; he continued to walk, "Since the incident happened, the tabloid press over here have made quite a lot of noise about it."

The President hated those bastards, even from another country, they could be a thorn in his side.

The Prime Minister went on, "And as the next required step is to request extradition, we will shortly be requesting her extradition. If your State Department then denies our request, you will be seen to have done what is expected of you according to the Vienna Convention. Also, we will have done exactly what we are expected to do."

Finally the call was starting to make sense, the President nodded, "That seems clear to me, Thomas."

"And, should your State Department agree to extradite the driver involved in the incident, then I can assure you she will receive a fair trial."

"Oh, I don't doubt that." The President took his feet off

his desk and sat back up in his chair, "I appreciate your call, Thomas."

"And I appreciate you making some time to talk during a busy day Christopher."

"It was a welcome distraction. Oh, and Thomas, let me know if anything else changes on this matter."

"I certainly will, although I think changes are quite unlikely."

54.

Toby was running his fifth lap of the Army base's perimeter fence. It was jacket weather, not parka level, but certainly worthy of a rain jacket with some added warmth. The fact that it was June was disappointing but not remarkable. After all, it was England, and some years the summer could just go awol.

Undeterred by the weather, Toby was in the sweet spot. The stiffness of the early stages of his run had already passed, but the fatigue hadn't yet set in. The rain was an irritant, the droplets forcing him to hold his head at an uncomfortably low angle and narrow his eyes as he pounded the tarmac, but it was also refreshing and wonderfully uncomfortable.

The Army was all about uncomfortable, something they made crystal clear from the very first day for all new recruits, and those who struggled to cope were shoved toward the exit. Of those who remained, the majority were the soldiers who could handle discomfort, while there were a precious few who actually embraced it. Toby had embraced it and more; he'd gone on to flourish. The higher the level of hardship, the stronger was his resolve to overcome it. It had been the strength which earned him the respect of his fellow soldiers and the rare quality which had caught the eye of his superiors.

The downside to Toby's freakish ability to cope with all manner of hardship was the struggle to cope with tedium, and base life was growing more tedious by the day. He took in a couple of deep lungfuls to fuel an increase in speed. He then forced himself to sprint to the furthest vehicle building, his pack flying wildly around on his back due to the amplified arm movements.

Reaching his destination, his lungs begged him to stop and recover, but he ignored the messages, slowing only to his original jogging pace.

"Staffy," called a familiar voice.

Maybe his lungs would get their way just this once, "Browny," all the resolve in the world didn't alter the fact he couldn't get his breath back to talk though, "how's it going mate?" Toby came to a stop and forced himself to stand straight, knowing he'd better recover if his lungs could fully inhale the fresh stuff.

"I'm great. I'm dry; I'm warm; I'm not running around in the bloody rain."

Toby's pained breathing was interrupted only slightly by a quick laugh.

"What are you doing, Staffy? Why would you run in this?" Browny shook his head in disbelief.

Toby forced out another chuckle, his breathing quickly returning to normal, "Better than hot sun."

Browny shook his head, "And in boots and a pack? What have you got in there?"

Another embarrassed chuckle, "A twenty-pound weight

from the gym, wrapped in a blanket."

There was no point in asking Toby why, as the reason never made sense. Browny decided to change the subject, "Word just came down from above; we're deploying."

"Oh." Toby's smile evaporated. News of deployment always brought forth conflicting emotions. There was an element of excitement because, as a soldier, you lived to serve in conflict zones. It was why you'd joined up. But the news of deployment reminded you of your own sense of mortality, of the real risk you may not make it home and that even if you did, one of your mates might not. "Where?"

Browny folded his arms and leaned back onto the wall of the building, "Afghanistan."

Toby nodded. Currently, it was the most dangerous destination, and they both knew it, "How are the men taking the news?"

Browny shrugged, "I haven't told them yet. I just went for a walk, so I could absorb it on my own first."

And you ended up out here, Toby thought to himself, realising that his old friend must have known exactly where to find him and wanted to do so, pressingly enough to postpone notifying his own men. "You'll be alright, mate. We're the best regiment in the British Army."

"Yeah, I know." Browny nodded unconvincingly. "So, have they told you what's going on with you yet?"

Toby knew what his friend was really asking, but he didn't

know the answer himself.

Browny continued, "Coz the lads would feel pretty indestructible if they knew their Staffy was coming out there with them."

There was a time when Toby would have taken the news in his stride. He'd have immediately started working on getting the men into the right frame of mind, one which would make them formidable to the enemy while simultaneously maximizing their chances of getting home in one piece. But in his heart, he already knew he wouldn't be deploying.

When the Captain had brought him back to the barracks, it had been presented as a temporary measure, supposedly a compassionate gesture. But Toby wasn't stupid; while there had been an element of truth in that, he knew it was also better to keep him under observation while dealing with his loss. The suits at GCHQ must have decided that the risk of Toby seeking retribution was sufficiently high to completely take him out of the field.

Toby would have gladly deployed with his old regiment and diligently watched their backs in their time of need, but to be deployed would mean that his move back into uniform was permanent, and he'd given the bosses no reason to deem that move necessary.

"I've heard nothing, but no matter which way things turn out for me, I'll get those lads ready with you. Nothing is gonna stop me doing that." Toby patted Browny's shoulder.

Toby's resolve triggered a warm smile on Browny's face, "How is your sister doing now? I haven't heard anything in a while."

The implications of every response had to be considered, because Toby's frame of mind would still be under scrutiny, and while Browny would never willingly report back to any of the Ruperts, he could easily be manipulated into doing so unwittingly. Toby chose his words carefully but delivered them with a casual shrug, "Since they requested extradition of the American driver, she's been better; it gave her some hope." *False hope,* Toby thought to himself.

Browny frowned, "Will she be alright if they deny the request?"

That likelihood had been keeping Toby awake at night, but again it was better downplayed, "She'd be disappointed, of course, but in the last four months, she's learned how to cope." She'd improved, that much was true, but the idea of her coping was a farce. Toby still had a lot of work to do and with the regiment being deployed, his stay at the barracks would surely be drawing to a close; therefore, the clock was suddenly ticking. "Look, I'm going to finish up my run, then we need to go and let the lads know the news. I'll meet you back here in thirty minutes, alright?"

"Yeah, and thanks, Staffy."

"You got it mate, see you in a bit." Toby tightened the straps on his bergen and mentally committed himself to one more lap of the base. It would give him time to think everything over.

The greater probability was that his men would be deployed without him, and with Browny instead as their most senior sergeant. Browny was junior to Toby but held the same visible rank, and Toby had absolute faith in the big man's abilities. Still, Toby loved his men and wanted to send them on their way, secure in the knowledge that he couldn't have prepared them any better. They needed to be able to use and field strip every weapon in current use, from sub, through light and general-purpose machine guns, right up to the vehicle-mounted fifty caliber weapons. The boys needed to be at one with them all. Their first aid training needed to be refreshed too, and most importantly, their confidence needed to be raised. It was a lot to do, especially considering they could be gone in as little as a week.

Toby's bergen felt heavier since he'd stopped for his chat. The pause must have allowed his muscles to start cooling down, and pushing himself along through the rain suddenly felt much harder. But he had to grit his teeth, push himself onward and concentrate on what lay ahead.

The second consideration was his own status regarding deployment. The idea of him deploying with the regiment seemed unlikely, as it would contradict what Captain Bowyer had originally stated, but it was still a possibility. On the one hand, it would be a huge disappointment as it would also mean the end of his new plain-clothed duties. He'd be officially returned to unit and would have to live with the slight scent of dishonor that accompanied it. But if that's what they chose for him, the bright side is that he'd be able to better look out for his men in Afghanistan. There was no point dwelling on that aspect any longer. It was out of his control.

Then there was his sister to consider. Her fragility since the loss really worried him, Damien was struggling too, but he had a job to go to and workmates to distract him, while Tracey had been a stay-at-home mom for years. But now, staying at home only served to prevent her emotional wounds from healing. Added to that, Toby's mum had made it clear that her stay in the local area couldn't be permanent and so he was convinced he needed to raise his sister's ability to be self-sufficient as much as possible, and as quickly as possible. Because even if he wasn't deployed, a return to his 'under the radar' duties could still see him heading out of the country just as quickly as his uniformed brothers, leaving his sister without any family support. But what could he do that would empower his sister? What could he create which would give her a sense of purpose?

He had nothing, and as the rain continued to spatter his face, he knew that he had to find something, and quick.

55.

Toby walked up the front path toward his sister's house. He peeked through the side window of their garage before swinging right toward their front door.

"Hi, Tobe." Tracey had opened the door before he'd even had time to knock.

"Hey Sis, is Damien not here?" the garage had been empty, but the person could be present without the car.

"No, he had to work late. Come in, I'll make you a cuppa."

"Thanks, and what about the gang? Did you ask Luke's old mates to come over, like I asked you to?" He took off his beret and carefully flattened it before setting it down on the table.

"Yeah, I did, but why do we need them here? What's the big secret?" She walked into the kitchen and started the ritual of filling the kettle and placing tea bags in mugs.

"It's not really a secret. I've just been thinking about a few things. Let's talk about that before I get on to why we need that rabble here."

"Well, let's hear it."

"I will, but how are you doing? You seem to have more of a spring in your step today."

Tracey looked at him and shrugged, "Umm," she hadn't considered her own mood, "I suppose I'm dying to hear news about the extradition. It's the first good news since it

230

happened." she faked a smile.

As he'd expected, she was putting all her hopes into the extradition. Toby faked a smile in return.

She started stirring Toby's tea, "I'd started to think she was going to get away with it, you know?"

He did, but unlike his sister he still believed that things were on track for her to do just that. His next question had been lingering in the back of his mind for some time, but with the clock ticking, it could no longer be put off, "Thanks, sis." he took a deep breath, "But what happens if they don't approve it?"

"Oh, come on, Tobe, how likely is that? If they didn't approve it, there would be no justice, and that's not how life works. I don't know what they'll do, but they'll come up with some way of making her face consequences. You don't get to kill somebody and then get off scot-free. That's just not how it works." She actually shook her head at him in disdain.

Toby felt a sinking sensation in his stomach, her trust in justice was admirable but hopelessly blind. It was time for him to get things moving, "So then, you know the newspapers have been harassing you for an interview?"

"They still are. They don't stop."

Toby placed his hand on her forearm and gave it a gentle squeeze, "I want you to say yes, Trace."

"But we talked about it, I don't want to. I'll just be the hysterical mom, bawling my eyes out. They'll only use me to put on an embarrassing show, to help sell more papers."

Toby kept his hold on her arm, "I know that's how it was, but it's not like that anymore Tracey, you're more together now. I know you could do an interview; a calm impressive inspiring one."

"But why?" she slumped. It wasn't something she wanted.

"Because it will help you get what you want, in the long term. When they talk to you, you need to tell them that you've started a campaign to change the diplomatic immunity system. That way we can use them back, coz when they print that, it'll be the best advertising possible and it's free. Everyone will know about it after one simple chat."

Toby lowered his head to meet his sister's glassy stare, "And if the whole country knows about it and they feel for you, that's a whole movement, Tracey. It's a big deal, and that's why Luke's old gang are coming round."

She sighed, "I don't get it."

"They're teenagers. They live online; one of them will know how to build a website for you, for Luke. Something people can find after they've read your interview in the newspaper."

Tracey finally looked up and showed some interest, "Oh." she raised her eyebrows, "Okay, I see." She walked back over to the kettle and filled it to the very top, "I'll need to make more tea then."

Toby could only chuckle, "And the rest! They're

232

teenagers, Tracey. They'll eat you out of house and home."

Toby made it to the front door before his sister could. He knew it was the teenagers, but as he swung it open, the endless line of teenagers that entered the house still took him by surprise, "Hey, you," he recognized some of them, "it was James, wasn't it?"

"Yeah, hi, Mister Sergeant Miller."

Then he spotted a face he wasn't expecting, "Jay? What are you doing here?"

"I came to help Staffy. I heard we were coming to do sumfin for Luke."

Toby frowned, "If you take anything from this house," Toby leaned in close to make his point quietly, "I'll bury you in the woods. Somewhere really remote, you understand me?"

"Alright, Sarge, I already said I'm sorry, jeez man, I won't, okay?"

As Jay protested against Toby's unfair character judgement, a pair of girls entered the living room, "There are girls now too?" Toby asked.

Jay looked insulted, "That's not girls, man, that's my sisters."

They still looked like girls to Toby, and the word sisters only seemed to confirm that point, but teenage boys couldn't be argued with. Toby shook his head, then leant to check there weren't more of them on the driveway before closing the front door.

"So then, guys!" Toby quietened the room with an authoritative voice, "Thanks for coming. Luke would be really touched." Oh no, he couldn't use that word around teenagers, any smart-arse response would be his own fault.

Having waited for a second and dodged that bullet, Toby resolved to choose his words more carefully, "You probably all know that during Luke's wake, some of the people in this room did a stand-up job of creating a logo, which we've used on merchandise that promotes diplomatic change. For those of you who don't understand that, diplomatic immunity is why the driver who ran down Luke hasn't been sent to jail, so I think you can see why that crap needs changing."

A rumble of agreement spread around the room, "What I'm hoping we can do now is make a website for the same cause, and…" he tried to scan the room and make eye contact with them all, "I'm paying you for it."

"Fucking sweet man."

"And again, language Jay." Toby threw him a dirty look.

"Sorry, Staffy."

"So I'll give each one of you fifty quid. Who knows what that will add up to?"

"I do, Sir." One of Jay's non-girl sisters was clearly a quick mathematician.

234

"Great, but don't tell me, coz I don't wanna know how much this is gonna cost me."

The kids laughed in response, and then knowing they were in the right frame of mind, Toby continued, "So what we want is a site that looks good and works properly. It doesn't have to be complicated, it just has to get the point across, and I think all of the 4DC gear that you guys designed before needs to be on there, for sale." What they were going to do with the proceeds needed discussion, but that would have to be between just the family members.

He smiled to the room, then took a quick look over at his sister to see she was as engrossed as the teenagers. "So what ideas have we got then?"

It was Jay the retired mugger's other sister, who was the first to respond, "You could have a petition, so that every visitor could sign saying they support that change and let them post a comment saying why."

Toby smiled. This was a step in the right direction.

The last of the teenagers had scraped even the tiniest remnants of potato chips from the big-serving bowls before finally leaving. "So what do you think then?" Toby asked his sister as he helped her carry dirty tea mugs into the kitchen.

"I'll do it if you're there with me," she replied.

Toby shook his head in disappointment, "You know I can't do that, Tracey."

"It won't hurt just this once."

"It will! This once would be the worst possible time. I have to be in the background Tracey, always, or my career is over." He hated saying no to her when it was so important, but it wasn't a negotiable point, "I cannot have my photo appearing in public like that. I'm really sorry."

While his professional life depended on privacy, that didn't necessarily mean he had to leave her to it, "Would it work if Mum was with you?"

"But she's gone home, Tobe, you know that."

"Then I'll get her back again." Having lost their father while so young, Toby and his sister had been inseparable as kids. They'd depended on each other more than most. Even in adulthood, their bond was unbreakable, he flashed one of the grins that were reserved just for her.

Tracey appreciated how much he was trying, so she felt like she had very little choice, "I guess I have to."

She did, of that he was certain. If consequences were what his sister sought, then he'd at least opened up another potential route.

56.

So she'd finally agreed to an interview, Bill Addison had started to doubt she'd ever cave in. That new development had proven him right in his decision to hold back the photos which had finally been supplied by an American contributor. Now Bill had to decide on his approach.

He also had to prepare himself, as while the diplomatic hit and run case had been a big one, it was just one story of dozens that ran by his desk every day. It was time to refresh his memory, so he ran the appropriate search term, and his screen showed links to each finished piece they'd run.

What a mess it was; his reporters had done good work, they'd constantly found ways to resuscitate the story using every excuse in the book, but Bill could see through the garnish, and what lay below was a whole lot of nothing. The police file had been handed over to the CPS, they'd requested extradition, and nothing had been heard since. Bill had made a few of his staff research relevant cases and use them as comparisons, and it had only served to show how full of crap the comments from both governments had been. The American driver was really abusing the system by running, although trying to guess the outcome of the extradition request had been harder than expected. With sufficient digging, they had found cases involving different circumstances, but involving crimes of similar gravity, and the relevant government had surprisingly chosen to extradite one of their own. Presumably, they'd decided to prioritize keeping good relations with the foreign government filing the request. Essentially, there was still a chance the Americans might send Madyson Lutz back.

Then there was the driver's husband, who was as good as a ghost, meaning they couldn't dig up any employment or personal history since he'd been in his early twenties. So he must have been posted to the UK, either with the CIA, the National Security Administration, or the US Department of Homeland Security, but every relevant agency had shut out all contact with the press. And knowing that Jeff Lutz was a spook but having no evidence and no evocative story to tell, made for a ridiculously weak news piece.

Which brought him to Tracey Rigg's unexpected agreement to an interview, the new photos of Madyson Lutz, and how to best work the interview for the sake of the story.

He had genuine sympathy for the family of Luke Rigg but took an even bigger pride in his work, and this was an opportunity. What he really wanted was to interview the mother and find a way to show her those photos mid-interview. That way, he'd be on scene to record her reaction and run it in print in the next edition. The tricky part was how to do it without being a total heartless bastard.

Police Sergeant Kirk Treavett put down the phone and lifted the bright uniform jacket off the back of his chair. "Come on, Bell, we've got an accident scene on the A-one-eleven, a joyrider lost control and clipped another car, and

238

we need to catalog the whole mess."

"On it, Sarge." Lucy whipped her jacket off her chair and was with him in an instant. In the couple of months since handing over the Madyson Lutz case, she'd become a permanent member of the Accident Reconstruction Team and thoroughly enjoyed her new role. The only negativity encountered in the new position had been the lack of a conviction in that first case.

"So, Sarge?"

"So, Bell." Kirk grinned.

She couldn't help but smirk back, "I've been thinking about the Lutz case, the diplomatic immunity one."

Kirk chuckled as the reminder seemed redundant, "I think everybody has been thinking about that one Lucy."

She nodded, "Probably, but what's been bothering me is the lack of a conclusion. Have you ever had that before? Because it seems like normally we present the case and either it wins in court, or it loses, but the idea that this one might just, I dunno? Float around in limbo, endlessly."

It bothered Kirk too. He'd become a cop for the sense of achievement, to be an asset to society and clearly Lucy shared the same drive. He sighed, "I can't feed you some crap, Lucy. I have to admit that it might. Have you been following it in the papers?"

"I have, but even that's odd 'cause they seem to know much more than we do. Isn't it usually the other way around?"

That was true enough, "Of course, but that's only because they've got all the time in the world to research similar incidents from the distant past, while we're straight onto our next case. Did you read about that one where it took them more than two years to deny the request?"

Kirk tossed Lucy the keys for the Recon Squad car, triggering a smile as he'd hoped it would. "Yeah, I couldn't believe that. Imagine if we dragged our feet for that long, we'd be out of a job!"

Kirk smiled and nodded. There was certainly no arguing that point. Lucy started the engine and then continued, "But did you hear what the family have done? To try and give justice a shove?"

"No?" Although he was intrigued.

"They've started making gear with this logo that says 4DC. It means for diplomatic change."

"Have they now?" Kirk's smile grew.

"Yup, and they've got shirts and hoodies, and stickers, and all sorts of stuff. I suppose it's just a way of trying to bring attention to the whole problem and to show support for the family."

Kirk nodded. It wasn't lost on him that Lucy was gushing in a way he'd not seen before. "And um, how do you know about this WPC Bell?"

Oh, busted. She'd not seen that coming, "Well..." she

accelerated the car, "You see, the uncle, the soldier, he told me and then sent me a couple of things in the post."

"Okay." Kirk's smile grew constantly.

"What's really nice is that all of the designing was done by Luke's old school-friends."

"Oh." Kirk was genuinely touched, "That's actually heartwarming."

"I thought the same thing. One of the things was a tiny little pin badge, which would fit on my uniform, so I was wondering."

It was time to interrupt her, "No, you can't wear something like that on your police uniform."

"Oh." Lucy slumped at the wheel in disappointment.

"Officially." Kirk continued. "Not if any of your superiors noticed it. Personally, I'm not sure I pay that much attention."

That was funny coming from him, considering the Sarge had an eye for detail like she'd never known before. Lucy grinned and sat up straight again.

"For all I know, you could be wearing it now. Are you wearing it now?"

"No, Sarge." She really wasn't.

"Good, because as I say, I don't notice things like that as well as I should. Even the Chief Constable, who you know well now. I don't think he'd notice that either, as long as he knew what it stood for."

Lucy's smile had grown to the same size as Kirk's, "I'll bear that in mind, Sarge."

57.

"Thank you for finally agreeing to this interview Mrs. Rigg." Bill smiled sincerely at Tracey.

Tracey tried to smile back, but the place where they came from was long gone, "Please, call me Tracey, and this is my mother."

"Thanks, Tracey. It's nice to finally meet you." Bill leant over to shake hands with both women, "I don't know if you remember my name from our phone call Tracey, but I'm Bill Addison, and I'm the Editor in Chief at the paper."

Tracey knew nothing of hierarchy in the world of news publishing, but he sounded high up. At least they'd decided Luke was worthy of somebody who knew what they were doing; she nodded to Bill.

"I'd like to start by saying how sorry I am, sincerely. I'm a father myself, and I don't know how I'd cope with this."

Tracey swallowed hard. This had been a mistake, a huge mistake, they were one sentence into this thing, and her eyes were filling. "You don't cope," was all she could come up with; it was the hard, ugly truth.

Bill studied the grieving mother and what he saw was distressing. She looked consumed by pain and utterly exhausted by it, "I am so sorry." He truly was. He was also doubting the wisdom of showing her the photos he'd brought. Bill sat back and took a deep breath of his own. He looked over at the grandmother and could read the suspicion

243

on her face. This wasn't going to be easy, "Can I tell you something?" He asked.

Tracey looked at him blankly, "Sure."

"I've had us run this story repeatedly because I think you deserved it."

Tracey didn't understand; she'd deserved to keep reliving it week after week? A scowl formed on her pale, drawn face.

Bill could see her reaction, but he'd meant it differently, "What I mean is that if we'd written just the one news story when the accident happened, then it would have faded into obscurity." He couldn't allow either of them to interrupt, he had to quickly make them understand his good intentions, "Which would have suited both governments, it would have allowed them to do nothing."

Her jaw retreated toward her slim neck, "But they have done nothing." Tracey instantly started sobbing.

"No." Bill insisted, "They've felt guilty because the story keeps coming back. It means they can't forget it. They can't forget what they've done, what she's done. What they've allowed to happen." He found himself pleading with her.

Tracey fought her breathing and wiped her eyes. She'd left the door unlocked after welcoming Bill, but now another man entered carrying a camera, which he raised and pointed straight toward her. A feeling of terror ran through Tracey's body; she started snatching at her breaths.

"No! Out!" Bill spat out at his colleague. The man

retreated testily, apparently unaccustomed to being talked to like that. Bill looked straight back at her, "I'm sorry, Tracey."

Tracey took another long breath, using the pause to try to make sense of it all. Bill Addison couldn't be all bad because he'd made the photographer piss off. She looked unsure of what to do, only managing to contribute another limp nod.

"I chose to keep the story alive," that word 'alive' again, it seemed to be welded to this damned story. Bill slumped in his chair now too, "I wanted to do something to stop this tragedy fading into obscurity, to do something to stop it from happening again." He looked into Tracey's eyes, "I wanted to stop another set of parents from having to go through what you've gone through."

Tracey's head was pounding; she was focused on his eyes too. Tracey's mum stood up and broke the silence, "Can I make you a cup of tea, Bill?" She'd seen enough to decide he deserved the simple gesture.

Bill looked up at her, "I'd really appreciate that, Mrs. Rigg."

She nodded, "Joyce, you can call me Joyce." Then smiled sympathetically and left for the kitchen.

The interruption had allowed the chaos inside Tracey's head to subside, "I think I understand you."

Thank God, Bill thought to himself, "Good." He nodded to her.

"On that subject, my bro.." she corrected herself, "We

came up with something, I'm not really sure what you'd call it though. My son's friends," she still found it very hard to say Luke's name, "did most of the work, they're just kids, but they called it 4DC, and it means For Diplomatic Change." She felt exhausted talking so much, so she took a 4DC badge off the coffee table and handed it to Bill.

His mouth opened, then closed again to form a smile, "This is," he shook his head in disbelief, "this is bloody great, and you say some schoolkids did it?"

She nodded limply, "His friends."

This was huge, "Can I put it in the news story? Please? It would really bring attention to it."

You'd better, she thought, then nodded again.

"I mean, this is absolutely bloody fantastic."

Now Joyce walked back into the room and handed him a t-shirt, "We've got everything, shirts, badges, hats, all of that stuff."

"Oh ladies, I'm so happy that you'll let me write about this. This is exactly what I've been talking about. This is the kind of thing that keeps the pressure on the politicians. I'm sorry, I know this is hard," he took out a notepad, "but please, start from the beginning, tell me how this came about."

Joyce sat down, figuring the tea could wait and proceeded to tell him the whole story. She included every little detail— everything except Toby.

"Okay, this is the last one, I promise." The photographer, who had been unexpectedly patient and courteous toward Tracey and her mother, framed and shot his last photo of the ladies reluctantly holding up some 4DC gear for the camera.

"So we're done?" Joyce preemptively placed the t-shirt she'd been holding back down onto the coffee table.

The photographer had no choice but to nod, before turning to Bill Addison, "I'll be outside when you're done."

"Alright, thanks, mate." Bill's time was up, and he could procrastinate no longer. He reached into his computer bag and pulled out a laptop. "There's something I need to show you before I leave. I'd prefer for you to see it this way rather than on the front page of the paper tomorrow." He opened up the computer and took a moment to find what he was looking for.

"We just received these images from a photographer we use in America." Bill swiveled the computer to face Tracey and her Mum.

Joyce leaned in to better see the images, her face quickly betraying the anger boiling inside her. Meanwhile, Tracey slapped her hand over her mouth and tried to suppress the howling noise which seemed to be emanating involuntarily from her lungs.

Bill winced and clicked the forward button to slowly scroll through the images. Tracey continued with her pained animal sound while Joyce calmly started to shake her head, "That's her, obviously. When were they taken? Are they old or recent?"

"They were taken a few days ago." Bill quietly replied.

Tracey fought to stop the bizarre noise and finally managed to turn the wail into words, "Why is she smiling?"

Joyce put her arm around her daughter's shoulder and pulled her in supportively. The ladies took in the details of the photo; Madyson Lutz, having run down Luke, had apparently undergone a makeover and was now glamorously dark-haired and adorned with expensive-looking dark glasses. The photo seemed to have been taken in a public place and showed Madyson playing happily with an energetic dog. The pair seemingly lost in the moment, with not a care in the world.

Joyce continued to shake her head in disgust, "A few days ago?" She felt obligated to confirm that Madyson's happiness was so recent.

"Yes." Bill nodded.

"Well, it's nice to see she's not losing any sleep over things." Joyce added acidly, "At least it's just the one family that has to suffer the consequences of her actions."

"Why is she smiling?" Tracey was trembling and still hung up on the only thing she'd taken from the image.

"Tracey?" Joyce spoke in an authoritative voice, "Don't let her do this to you, love. She's done too much hurting already, don't let her do anymore." Tracey continued to stare and tremble, "Tracey!" Joyce raised her voice, finally breaking the image's spell.

Tracey turned toward her mother, who immediately used the opportunity to lean inward and slam Bill Addison's computer shut.

"What did you hope to achieve with this?" Joyce snarled at the reporter, "Did we put on a nice show for you? Are you happy now?"

Bill opened his mouth to reply, but Joyce silenced him with a hand and "Out! Now. Get out of this house."

As Bill hurriedly gathered his belongings, he tried to talk over the top of Joyce's orders for him to leave. "We're going to run these images because they prove she's remorseless, and it's what people need to see. The politicians will see this, and maybe they'll realize what kind of a person they're protecting."

"Out!" Joyce snarled.

"These photos will demonize her and make people support you even more. You must see that."

"Get out!"

"Please, understand the photos will help your cause." Bill pled with Joyce as she pushed him out of the front door.

58.

"Good morning Miller, how are you doing today?" Captain Bowyer sat down opposite Toby, setting down a mug of tea and a plate containing a big fat bacon and egg sandwich.

"I'm doing fine, Sir. How about you?" Toby smiled.

"Not bad, Miller, not bad." As the Captain settled into his seat, he pulled a folded newspaper out of one of his uniform trouser's cargo pockets. "At the risk of being the bearer of bad news, I wanted to check if you'd seen this yet." He unfolded the paper and set it down on the table in front of Toby.

Use your poker face, Toby thought it the instant he recognized the face of the driver who'd taken his nephew's life. Her face had been in the news multiple times since the accident, but always the same outdated photo, and this one was decidedly new. "No, Sir, I haven't seen this yet." Although he'd been forewarned of its arrival by his mother.

Captain Bowyer studied Toby Miller's expression as he read the headline, "It must be upsetting." The Captain tried to keep his tone light.

Toby could read the Captain like a book, "Not really, Sir. Disappointing, I suppose, but it's not upsetting." What a lie. Toby was absolutely furious. This woman was clearly loving life while his sister struggled to find a reason to exist. *Poker face,* he reminded himself. "Everybody's come to terms with it all, Sir, and truth be told, it was only ever my sister who'd really struggled." This would be the ultimate test of his ability to lie.

"Really, Miller?" The Captain looked dubious.

In place of a psychiatrist, the bosses at GCHQ had clearly tasked the Captain with reporting back on Toby's mental state. It fitted. After all, they'd trained Toby how to misdirect people as needed to fulfill his task. So sitting him down with a shrink would have only served to confirm the efficiency of their own training. The Captain was a good choice because he'd known Toby prior to any of his specialist training and was undoubtedly the most trusted authority figure in Toby's life. Other than Toby's blood family or Browny, the Captain was the only choice, which is why Toby had to be so vigilant around him. "Yes, Sir and the 4DC website has finally given her some hope. It's changed her."

The regiment was shipping out in thirty-six hours, leaving Toby in a deserted barracks. It was vital the Captain bought into Toby's narrative, or he'd be stuck there shuffling papers and polishing boots for an eternity.

"In the early days after the accident, my sister's mental health was too closely tied to the consequences for the driver. Whether she was charged or not, then it turned into whether she was extradited or not, and potentially it could have continued with whether she was convicted or not. The 4DC cause has given my sister something to pin her hopes to, but it's something that can't be undone so easily." It had sounded like a good argument to Toby; he really needed that clean bill of health from the Captain.

Captain Bowyer took a bite from his greasy sandwich and considered Sergeant Miller's response, eventually nodding in appreciation, "Well, good for you, Miller, that's excellent news." The Captain adjusted his collar with his cleaner hand, exposing his own 4DC badge, "I show my own support actually, in a discreet manner."

Toby flashed a confident toothy smile, "Thanks, Sir, it's always nice to see somebody wearing one, but it's especially touching when it's you." He considered adding how keen he was to return to his previous role, but the risk of it exposing his previous words as manipulation stopped him. He needed another route, which came to him in a flash, "I don't suppose they mention 4DC in that story, do they?"

"Actually, Miller, they do. They give it a good write-up, although you're not mentioned."

"Nor should I be, Sir," Toby replied knowingly.

"Quite right, Miller, quite right."

"If they've written about 4DC in that paper, then my sister will be swamped with contact from people showing their support. She'll be kept busy from now on." That was the comment that should seal the deal.

The Captain raised his eyebrows in appreciation, "Very true, Miller. I must say, that was quite a clever way of dealing with things."

"Thank you, Sir." Now it was time for a redirect, so Toby

chose the subject most pressing for everyone else, "The boys are all shipping out in thirty-six hours. I really do wish I was going with you all."

"I imagine you do, but there are other plans for you." The Captain took another large bite.

Yes! Toby fought to maintain the poker face.

The Captain took a moment to swallow his mouthful before adding, "Anyway, you've done a superb job of preparing the lads; you can feel proud of that."

"Thank you, Sir." Toby did feel proud, but he was also terrified of how much this news story was going to set his sister back.

"How's she doing, Mum?"

"Oh Toby, she's gone backward again, and I don't know what to do. I've spent so long here looking after her, and there's no improvement, even after all this time. And how long has it been?" She barely took a breath before continuing. Clearly, Toby was not expected to participate, "Months, and I know I'm only working part-time now, but they've told me they won't keep my position for me any longer. Not if I can't be there. It's such a mess."

The phone line fell silent. Toby hadn't expected it and hesitated too long to get in a reply.

"Well? Haven't you got anything to say for yourself, Toby Miller?"

The one person in the world he couldn't shout at was the one who needed it the most.

"I don't know what to say. It's like I'm alone in this world." Clearly, he'd missed his opportunity to talk yet again. He squeezed the phone between his shoulder and ear so he could carry on looking at the newspaper the Captain had left him while she continued. "And I can't do everything myself. I don't know what your father would say. Really, I don't."

Toby glared on hearing that little verbal stab, "Mum? Can I talk now?"

"Well, thank you, now you imply you can't get a word in when I'm talking? That's harsh, don't you think? Especially considering everything that's going on."

He slumped, accidentally allowing the phone to slip out from under his ear. He panicked as it hit the floor and bounced, all the while with his mother's distant voice audible. "Bollocks!" he snatched the phone off the floor and put it back to his ear.

"Excuse me? Is that how you talk to your mother?" She was properly pissed off now.

"Sorry, Mum, I dropped the phone, I wasn't swearing at you."

"Well, I should hope not." Slightly calmer. "So what was I saying?"

He slumped again but had a better grip on the phone now, "You were saying you don't know what to do about Tracey."

"No, I wasn't."

Now Toby was totally confused, and considering he'd just told her he'd dropped the phone, he didn't want to risk repeating himself to her. Not with her already pissed off. He opted for silence, again.

"I was saying that I could take her home with me for a little while. That way, I can keep an eye on her until she's a bit more self-sufficient."

So that's what she was saying when the phone bounced off the floor. As an idea, it had its merits, "Oh." He continued to consider the implications.

"Is that it? The word 'Oh'? That's what you have to offer? I don't know Toby Miller. I don't know what to say. Look, I'm going to take her back home with me until I see some improvement, so you'll need to help Damien, at least by keeping an eye on the dog, if nothing else. The stupid animal is still spending half of its life on Luke's bed. All that does is upset your sister even more. That house is no good for her right now, and since she saw those bloody photographs..."

Toby winced. The photos had triggered rage in him, so his sister must have been distraught at the sight of that woman happily going about her life.

"That crushed her, and I think it's clear that that woman is never going to get what she deserves. The world is a hard, unfair place sometimes, Toby Miller." His mother paused for a second, then started again, "So you need to stop by the house asap and pick up your sister's spare key. Then I expect you to keep an eye on dingo or mojo or whatever the dog's name is."

"Okay, Mum."

"Anyway, I've got a lot to do, so bye for now." he could hear her growl before continuing, "I could kill that bloody woman, so help me, God, I really could."

Toby hung up, slammed his phone onto the mess hall table, and covered his face with his hands, vigorously rubbing it before facing the world again. "She could kill her?" He grumbled under his breath before picking up his dirty tea mug to leave.

59.

"Any idea what this is about?" Asked WPC Bell.

Sergeant Treavett had noticed that Lucy's lack of experience in dealing with the higher ranks brought on a fear of reprimand almost every time she encountered one. "Not really. It could be related to any of our open cases. It's nothing to be concerned about, I'm sure."

The two officers turned the corner from the stairway. They entered through the door into the Chief Constable's outer office, "Sergeant Treavett and WPC Bell for the Chief Constable."

"He's expecting you. You can go straight in." The Chief's personal secretary gestured toward the door.

"Sir." Kirk greeted the Chief.

"Sir." Lucy fulfilled her obligation too.

"Good morning both, please take a seat." The Chief Constable sat back down himself, "Some news has come through during the night."

The Lutz case was the only open case that could see a change happen outside of UK business hours. Lucy leant forward in anticipation.

"Not very good news, I'm afraid, they've denied our extradition request for Madyson Lutz." The Chief looked very stern. "The FCO received the news early this morning, and the information just came down the chain to me."

Lucy looked from the Chief to Kirk, and seeing nothing which helped, she was the first to speak, "What does this mean for us?"

"Essentially, it derails our case of death by dangerous driving." the Chief leaned back in his chair, "And now the only hope of her seeing justice is if something unexpected happens. Meaning the scenarios we discussed before, such as a new US administration overturning this decision, or another country extraditing Mrs. Madyson Lutz if she happens to leave America. Which she'll have been made aware of, the same as we have. It's all rather hopeless, I'm afraid."

Kirk shook his head, knowing full well what this meant. Lucy wasn't quite there, "So she won't see any punishment for what she's done? Or will the Americans try her for a comparable offense over there?" Lucy had read in the newspapers of that being a slight possibility.

The Chief just shook his head apologetically, "Unfortunately, I think that's probably the end of it for us."

No bloody way, I didn't join the Police for this; Lucy shook her head in disgust. "What about the chance of diplomatic change?" She was clutching at straws now.

The Chief inhaled deeply. News like this was damagingly demoralizing for the officers involved. He had another meeting on hold, but young Lucy Bell deserved more of his time, and he felt obliged to give it. "That is a possibility WPC Bell and one that's certainly worth pursuing, but do bear in mind change like that is very slow to come." He studied Bell's face and could see she needed more, "I've been considering instating a requirement that any Americans serving on our local bases, and their family members, would be required to undertake some driver training on arrival in the UK."

Lucy seemed encouraged by his words, so he went on, "I have already spoken with the Base Commander, and he seems to agree, in principle, but again, these things can take time to implement." *But it's better than nothing*, he thought to himself.

"Yes, Sir, that sounds like a very good idea, Sir." Lucy nodded her approval.

"And just for the record," the Chief stood up and removed his overcoat from the wooden stand behind his chair. "I support the cause, as you do." He lifted the oversized collar of his coat, revealing a silver-coloured 4DC badge on the reverse side.

Lucy smiled, "Luke's family would be touched, Sir."

She'd referred to the victim using his first name. The implications weren't lost on the Chief Constable, "And on that subject, I think we owe it to the poor family to inform them off this news, asap. Those animals in the tabloids seem to get news like this very quickly, and I would hate for them to know about this before the boy's parents have been informed."

Kirk decided it was time to let the Chief get on with his

day and stood up to shake his hand, "I agree, Sir, we'll do that immediately."

The Chief leant forwards to shake Kirk's hand, then Lucy's. Finally, the pair of them left the Chief Constable's office to undertake their final task on the Madyson Lutz case.

Everybody had gone, leaving Toby alone and in a foul mood.

Toby had watched his fellow men slowly board the two coaches. They'd all said their goodbyes and waved, leaving him standing alone outside the barracks. It had felt emasculating.

Those men needed Toby where they were going, and he'd been left behind, like a regimental bloody mascot. Toby, the regiment's pet pony.

In Her Majesty's Armed Forces, it was common knowledge that during the Second World War, most young RAF fighter pilots didn't make it through their first dogfight simply because they lacked the experience required to enable them to survive. Toby had just watched a dozen or so young soldiers board those buses, and he knew the problem was the same. They lacked the necessary experience, which is why they needed the Tobys and the Brownys of the Army to get them through those first, disproportionately dangerous firefights.

But instead of steadying them, directing them, and

inspiring them, he was waiting in line at the barracks canteen, the only remaining soldier of his entire regiment. Sure most of the engineers from the REME Regiment were nice enough people, as were the various other regiments stationed inside the same base, but he didn't know them, he didn't understand their roles, and they weren't his men. How many of his new men weren't going to make it back from Afghanistan? And how would that number change if he were there? He hated those thoughts.

Captain Bowyer had said that Toby was about to be pulled back into his GCHQ role, but didn't know exactly when that call would come. Toby wanted to be with the men of the regiment until the call came and had argued that point with the Captain, but no, for now, he was the regimental donkey, the ass. This wasn't what he'd signed up for.

"Did you miss your bus?"

Toby was aware of the words, but their significance took a moment to click. It was another sergeant, but this man was from the Royal Electrical and Mechanical Engineers, and he was talking to Toby. *What the hell?* Was this idiot for real? "What did you fucking say?" Toby glared at the man.

"I asked if you'd missed your bus." The man stood his ground.

The fury welled inside Toby. For a brief moment, he considered an uppercut into the man's jaw, knowing it would take him out in one blow. It would almost certainly break some teeth and send him to the medics. It would also undermine all of the work he'd put into persuading the Captain, and therefore his other superiors, that he was unaffected by the recent dramas and therefore ready to go back to work with a calm, unemotional head.

Toby closed the gap between him and the other Sergeant and lowered his voice to a whisper to reply, "You're not getting a rise out of me in here, but if you're really looking for it, we can leave our stuff here and go find somewhere private." He maintained the uncomfortably close quarters.

The REME Sergeant's confidence drained from his face. He was clearly unsure of what to do. He'd put on a show for his mates but hadn't reckoned on Toby being quite so intense and ready to go. He moved his head away from Toby's, and then all he could come up with was, "Don't take it so seriously, mate, I was just messing around with you."

The man had a coarse Northern accent, so thick that Toby struggled to understand the words. He wasn't interested in getting drawn into a conversation with this man, so he repositioned his face an inch or so away from the other Sergeant's once again, and waited.

The man backed up a step and turned to his two friends, "Come on, lads, we've got work to do, get your breakfasts in you, quick time." as he walked away.

The civilian contractor working behind the canteen's food counter looked at Toby cautiously and asked, "What can I get for you?"

Toby's anger just wasn't going away, he knew what his

face must have looked like, but it needed a few seconds to relax. In reaction, the man took a step backward. "Sorry about that," Toby finally replied, snapping out of it, then continued, "Bacon, sausage, eggs, mushrooms, fried bread, tomatoes, and what else have you got?"

"Uhh," the man looked unsure of everything, "I think that's the lot."

"Then I'll have it all and make that two cups of tea." *Coz I've got nothing else to do.*

"That's the husband leaving, Sarge." Lucy pointed toward Damien's car, "Stop behind him so I can talk to him before he leaves."

Sergeant Treavett pulled the police car to a stop, blocking the exit for Damien Rigg.

"Mister Rigg?" Lucy called as she swung open the car door. "Can I just have a word with you before you leave?"

Damien heard Lucy, looked into his mirror to see the police car had blocked him in, and turned off his car engine before stepping out of his car, "WPC Bell, isn't it? What can I do for you?"

"We'd like to have a word with you and your wife if she's home." Lucy smiled politely at Damien as Kirk walked up the driveway to join them.

"She's not here right now, she's with her mother, so it'll have to be just me." Damien tried to read the situation,

263

uncertain about what was important enough to justify blocking him in.

"We've had some news come through regarding your son's case." Lucy looked at Kirk, then back at Damien, "Maybe it would be better if we go back inside the house?"

Now Damien looked at both officers before replying, "I'm already running late for work, so if it's all the same to you, I'd rather not."

Again Lucy looked over at Kirk, who decided to take the lead, "I'm sorry to have to be the bearer of bad news, Mister Rigg, but during the early hours of this morning, the Foreign and Commonwealth Office received a communication from the US State Department, denying Britain's request for the extradition of Mrs. Madyson Lutz."

Damien visibly flinched, paused, then replied, "I understand." Another awkward pause, "So is that all?"

Lucy was visibly taken aback, while Kirk managed to hide his surprise better, but he was still unsure of whether the man was going to be capable of sharing this important news with his wife, "Should we reach out to Mrs. Rigg?" he asked cautiously.

Damien moved his arms a few inches out from his body then allowed them to drop back to their original position in a bizarre-looking shrug before adding, "Can you just let me out, please?"

Now Lucy and Kirk looked at each other and realising

they didn't know what else to do, they walked back to their police car and moved it out of his way, as requested. Damien had already restarted his car and was backing it out of his driveway with just inches to spare before they'd even had time to properly clear him a path. His car was accelerating down the street and out of sight within seconds.

The two officers paused in the dodgy road position they'd taken up, in order to make him enough room, and for a second, they remained silent. Eventually, it was Lucy who spoke, "Uhh, what the hell was that all about?"

"I have absolutely no idea, WPC Bell," Kirk replied.

Toby's phone rang. What a welcome distraction, "Hello. This is Miller."

"Good morning Mister Miller. This is WPC Bell."

The law, a slightly less welcome distraction. "Morning." he looked at his watch. It seemed unusually early for them to be calling, "What can I do for you?"

What order do I go in? She thought to herself, deciding on presenting the news first, "We just received word from the FCO that the US State Department has denied the extradition request for Mrs. Lutz."

He'd prepared himself for this eventuality, but it still hit with some power. Toby closed his eyes and rubbed his forehead. Alone in his office, he could relax his reaction. He was glad she hadn't driven to the base to deliver this news in person, "I understand." Toby knew he had to continue projecting the calm manner that he'd been required to use on base, so he added, "It's to be expected, really."

Lucy shrugged before answering, "I suppose so, but I'd still like to add how sorry I am."

That was sweet of her, "Thank you, WPC Bell."

"That's only part of the reason for my call, though."

"Oh yeah?"

"Yes, we actually drove to your sister's house to deliver the news in person, out of respect."

"Thank you, you'd promised you would, so I do appreciate it."

"It's the least we could do, but anyway, your sister wasn't there."

"I know. She's with my mother right now." Toby put his feet up onto his desk. There was no need to stand on ceremony whilst so alone.

"Yes, your bother-in-law told us, we managed to catch him on his way out of the house."

"Okay." Toby shrugged. This seemed to be going nowhere, slowly.

"Um." Lucy went silent, "I called because," another silence on the line, "He took the news very strangely."

Now Toby was interested, "How so?"

Toby could hear Lucy sigh, "I don't really know Toby, maybe I shouldn't have called you, but he didn't show any emotion at all, and it struck me. Actually, it struck both of us as very odd."

It certainly sounded odd, not at all like Damien.

"And so before we left, we asked if he'd let Mrs. Rigg, that is your sister, if he'd let her know, and I'm not convinced in that frame of mind that he will. On top of that, I don't have her mobile phone number, only yours, and it's not the kind of news I'd feel comfortable sharing over the phone."

Toby dropped his feet back to the floor and sat up straight again, "I understand. I'll call my Mum's phone and let her know, so that she can tell Tracey face to face."

"That sounds much better. Thank you, Toby. Did you have any questions for me? About the extradition denial, I mean."

"Nope." Toby found himself clenching his fists involuntarily. In his heart, he'd known this was coming, but he hadn't known such anger would accompany it. He took a breath and continued painting the picture of somebody at ease with it all, "I'm relieved we started the 4DC site. It means there's still hope that something can be achieved." What a load of bullshit. Thoughts were flying around inside his mind. He wanted to find the REME Sergeant from this morning and force him to fight, to make the passive-aggressive tosser eat his words and all of his smarmy smiling teeth. He also wanted to board a plane on his own, arrive at

267

the gates of the British forward operating base in Afghanistan, and join his comrades, where hopefully he could shoot some cowardly roadside bomb-making terrorist. But even more than that, he wanted to go to the USA, rent a car and accelerate it into that Lutz bitch, breaking every bone in her body. He wanted to recreate exactly what she'd done to poor young Luke.

Toby started to shake. He felt impotent; he could feel his eyes welling, but the anger was rising even faster; he just didn't know where to direct it.

"Mum?"

"Hi, sweety," she replied.

"Are you with Tracey?" Toby was in no mood to chat.

"I am. What's wrong?" His mother could sense it.

"Control your emotions, Mum, don't let Tracey see your face until you've had time to absorb what I'm about to tell you. Understood?"

Oh dear, Joyce didn't like it when her son sounded like this. She turned away from her daughter, as casually as she could muster, "I understand."

"They denied the extradition."

Joyce felt a shudder run through her body, "Okay." her voice was weak.

"You have to let Tracey know, and it has to be face to

face."

"Okay." Her voice was unchanged.

"And I've gotta go and figure out what's going on with Damien. The Old Bill just called me, said they'd informed him in person, that he'd reacted oddly. Now he's not picking up his phone."

Oh dear, Toby's mother felt slightly light-headed, "Okay."

"I'm on the way now. I'll fill you in later. Can I let you handle Tracey for now?"

"Of course, sweetheart." Joyce was trembling gently but committed to doing her job.

"Alright, bye for now." and Toby was gone.

Instincts. What a funny thing they are. Toby's had been screaming at him since Lucy Bell's call. He'd driven his car like a joyrider, slamming on the brakes to drop a few miles-per-hour as he approached each one of Britain's automated speed detection cameras, before dropping a couple of gears to wind up his speed once more. Worrying about getting stopped by the real-life variety of police was moot, as they'd long since allowed those damned cameras to completely take over that part of their work.

He drifted the back end of his car as he turned into Tracey and Damien's street, then floored the accelerator again, coming up on their house in an instant. He then squealed the tyres sideways one last time entering their driveway, before lunging to a violent stop in front of their garage.

He jumped out of his car, running toward their front door through sheer habit, before those same instincts redirected him back to the garage. Only then did he realize he could hear an engine running. A shudder ran through his body, but it didn't slow him. He tried turning the handle of the garage's side door, finding it locked. Without even taking the time to look through the window, he stepped back and used his leg muscles to strike directly at the door handle, which gave way instantly.

He leapt into the garage, and the fumes hit him hard. Toby started choking, so he pulled his shirt up over his mouth, using it as an improvised filter. He hauled on the cable to open the large front garage door, which illuminated the building's interior structure. He then turned to see Damien in the car's driver's seat, his head rolled back and eyes half-closed.

"No!" Toby bellowed, "I am not fucking losing another one." He swung open the car's door, leant in, placed his hands under Damien's armpits, and hauled him out from the car, initially turning him toward the larger front door opening before having second thoughts and shuffling backward as fast as he could manage, now heading toward the much closer side door.

Out in the open air, Toby leant down and placed his head on Damien's chest, his ear pressed down hard. Hearing nothing, Toby smacked Damien's cheek hard, "Wake up, now!" he smacked his other cheek even harder, "Do as you're told, Damien, wake the hell up."

With no reaction, Toby placed his hands on Damien's chest and started compressions, "One, two, three, four," each number was accompanied by a hard shove to the middle of his ribcage, "sixteen, seventeen," nothing was happening, "Eighteen!" Toby yelled right into Damien's face, then "nineteen, twenty." and on.

Reaching thirty with no change, he tilted Damien's head backward, opened his jaw, and squeezed Damien's nostrils shut, yelling "Come on!" before placing his mouth over Damien's and exhaling as he watched Damien's chest rise, then another long breath before repositioning his hands back on Damien's chest, all the while yelling at him, "If you don't wake up I'll bloody kill you." It was the most nonsensical thing to ever leave Toby's mouth, but he continued regardless, "Seven and eight, wake up, you stupid bastard! And ten and eleven."

The adrenaline rush which had kicked in as Toby approached the scene was starting to fade, and the realisation that Damien had already gone was starting to rise. "Thirteen and fourteen," Toby's eyes were filling, "not another one, please God not another, it's not bloody fair," he pulled the top hand off Damien's chest and wiped the moisture out from his eyes, "fifteen, sixteen. Just take me, let him live, and take me, please. Please!" The volume was back with a vengeance.

"Hhhhhhh." A wheezing noise emanated from Damien's chest. Toby froze, staring down at his brother-in-law.

271

"Hhhhh," there it was again. Toby started with the compressions again but then felt the chest move on its own. He raised his hands, held them in the air, and took a deep breath of his own. Toby carefully dried his eyes with his shirt sleeves to have no evidence of his weakness on show and finally stood up as Damien started to wheeze and cough.

For a moment, Toby couldn't stand the sight of Damien and walked back around to where he'd abandoned his own car, only to see a woman standing on his driveway, "Oh dear, what's going on," asked the elderly lady.

"Nothing." Toby's voice was calm, but his inflexibility apparent. He turned his back on the lady and returned to Damien, who was now becoming aware of his surroundings. Toby sat his arse down on the floor next to Damien and stared daggers, "Why? Why the hell would you do that, you fucking inconsiderate piece of crap."

Damien started crying, and Toby didn't care. "Answer me, Damien. Now."

It took a moment for Damien to find his words, "Because I've lost her too." He covered his eyes in shame.

Toby didn't understand, "What do you bloody mean?"

Damien continued but couldn't stop the crying. It was horrible to watch. Damien may have had a gentle manner, but he towered over Toby, and this behaviour seemed at odds with his stature, "I mean that since Luke was taken, Tracey has gone, she's drifted away, it's like I lost her too and now she's properly left me. I've gone from a perfect happy family

272

to nothing."

No. Toby had thought his Mum's idea was good, "She's not left you. She's just gone so that Mum can help her."

"Nobody can help her, Toby." He finally met Toby's stare. "Is the plan that she'll come home when she's fixed? Don't you see, she's gone, I've lost her, she hasn't properly talked to me once in the months since..."

"Oh my God, are you kidding me?" Toby jumped to his feet and ran back to his car, returning with his mobile phone at his ear, "Mum? Get Tracey. I'm putting her on speaker."

"What?" His Mum asked, then realised it'd be better just to do it. "Hello?" it was Tracey's voice.

"Tracey." Toby started.

"Yes?" she sounded confused.

"I'm done with you both. Do you understand me?" He sounded furious.

"What? I don't understand." Tracey sounded scared.

"Don't you love Damien anymore?" He knew it wasn't how people handled things, but he didn't have any remaining patience to do it their way.

"What?" she sounded part confused, and part offended, "I do love him."

"Well, I guess it doesn't feel that way to him, as he just tried killing himself." Toby's voice was still filled with rage.

"What?" For the third time in a row was her reply.

"He, just, tried, killing, himself." Toby knew how heartless and sarcastic he sounded, but it was the only remaining tactic he could try; everything else had been exhausted, "I just pulled him out of his car, dead. And by some miracle, he was not so far gone that he couldn't be brought back."

Damien looked utterly ashamed.

"So why would he do that, Tracey?" Toby so badly needed this one part of life to be less broken.

Instead of a reply, he could hear gentle crying, "I'll tell you why Tracey, because since we all lost Luke, you've shut down, and you've shut him out. And it's shameful Tracey, you guys, even after all you've been through, you guys are so lucky to have each other. But instead of appreciating that, all I see is you pushing each other away. How does that make any sense? Tell me, please coz I don't understand. For the life of me, I don't."

The sound of crying on the tiny speaker of Toby's phone had grown louder. "No, Tracey, I'm sick of all the crying. It releases all of your emotions, but it doesn't fix anything, and you need to fix this. Damien, do you love Tracey?"

Now Damien's tears started to flow harder, "Of course I do, I can't face life without her, that's why..."

"Do you bloody hear that, Tracey? That's how much he loves you, so why aren't you two helping each other through this? Instead of pushing each other away and wallowing in selfish pity? I mean, what the hell?"

"I'm sorry, Damien, I'm really so sorry, darling," said Tracey's voice softly.

"Listen to me, all of you." Toby interrupted, "You've got a choice. You either help each other through this and really truly remind yourselves of how much you appreciate that you've still got each other, or you go your separate ways. But decide and then do it like you mean it. And until you commit to a course of action, I'm bloody done with you both." He turned to leave, then hesitated, "I'm sorry guys, and I really do understand. It's the worse loss imaginable, but what would Luke think of this?" Toby pressed the red button on his phone and walked off, leaving Damien sitting on the concrete floor outside his house.

60.

"The Lieutenant Colonel will see you now, Sergeant Miller."

Toby quickly marched into the lavishly wood-paneled office, then continued marching on the spot before coming to attention with a sharp salute, "Colonel."

"Sergeant Miller, at ease." the grey-haired officer looked up from his desk. "How can I help you?"

"My Officer in Command just deployed, Sir, and so I must make any requests to you."

"I understand, Sergeant." The Colonel looked down, still fascinated by the unusual content of Miller's personnel record. "You have an interesting record, Sergeant, very interesting indeed." The Colonel hesitated, deciding on whether he wanted to say more, finally deciding to, "I must say I'm quite glad to meet you. Off the parade ground, that is. I feel I must also say that I'm sorry for your recent loss."

"Thank you, Sir."

"And from what I see here, we may be losing you again soon."

"I'm awaiting orders regarding that, Sir. I'm happy to serve in whatever way is deemed best."

"Very good, Miller, we could do with a battalion of men like you." The Colonel looked up at Toby and smiled very genuinely, "So what is it that I can do for you, Sergeant?"

"I seem to have a period where I'm of little use here Sir, considering my regiment have deployed and I'm awaiting new orders. I also have some personal time due. So I was wondering, Sir, if I might take my personal time now when it is of the least inconvenience."

"Hmm, I see no reason why not. Is there something in particular you plan on doing, a holiday perhaps?"

"Yes Sir, a holiday is exactly what I had in mind."

"Splendid, I'll happily approve that for you Sergeant Miller, going anywhere nice?"

"America Sir, I've always wanted to see New York City, the city that never sleeps, or so they say, Sir."

The Lieutenant Colonel smiled again, "I've heard that myself, Miller. Well, don't come back home too worn out. We'll need you ready for work on your return."

"Wouldn't dream of it, Sir," Toby replied with a cheeky grin.

Part 3. Forcing A Conclusion.

61.

Toby was different from most people; he knew it and always had. He was confident in his abilities, both physically and mentally, but never over confident or, God forbid, cocky. He was usually quite at peace with himself and from what he saw in others, that wasn't such a common quality.

He was also uncommonly pragmatic, which, combined with his self-confidence, created a barrier between him and almost everyone else. It was an endless source of frustration to him, but the only way to remove that barrier was to pretend he was a totally different person. Of course, he could manage that, but it got old.

He looked around the aircraft cabin at his fellow passengers, something that was easily done while sandwiched in the middlemost seat of five. The lady in front of him had asked for the lower calorie version of everything she'd been offered by the cabin crew, with the exception of soda, which she'd been knocking back in bulk for the last four hours. The lady was large enough to have been a burden on the passengers on either side of her, and judging by the amount of apologizing she'd done each time she'd needed the restroom, it was something she was painfully aware of.

The man seated to her right hadn't hidden his irritation at her repeated requests to get out, but even more insensitively, he'd also subtly shook his head while listening to her requests for the lighter foods on offer.

In contrast, the first thing that had come to Toby's mind

was that he could help her. But he knew how ridiculous that was. Once, an old girlfriend of Browny's had been talking over a round of beers about how she'd do "Anything to lose about twenty-five pounds." Toby had explained how she could do it in just a couple of months, finding some variations of exercise she seemed comfortable with and telling her she'd need to mentally block out the hunger for that relatively short period of time. She'd looked at Toby like he'd been spouting Nazi hatred, and after the fact, Browny had told Toby not to worry, as it's "Just not what people want to hear."

Two seats to the left of Toby was a woman in her early twenties. He'd listened as she told the man seated in-between them about how she "wanted to learn Italian more than anything in the world."

There was a time when Toby would have explained how he'd do it and guaranteed her she'd have been reasonably fluent in around six months, but he didn't make those mistakes anymore. It seemed to him that people didn't want solutions for their problems; they wanted sympathy.

Then Toby was distracted from his thoughts by the man two seats to his right, getting up to allow his wife back in. So Toby caught their attention and took the opportunity to finally get out of the middle seat and make his own bathroom visit.

Standing in the aisle, Toby looked fore and aft, finding toilet facilities in each direction. Out of habit, he chose the rear ones, which offered him the best view of his fellow passengers. Toby carefully walked down the narrow aisle, allowing his hips to correct the gentle swaying movements of the plane.

"Hi." Toby greeted the man waiting for the toilet ahead of him. The man nodded reluctantly, then turned his back on Toby. *Nice to meet you too;* Toby chuckled, shook his head, and then leaned on the flimsy wall of the toilet block, allowing him to better observe the comings and goings on the plane.

He watched as the soda-drinking lady seated in front of him left her seat for another trip to the rear of the plane, smiling as she approached him, "Hi." he tried once more.

"Hi." she greeted him back.

"Time to experience the world's smallest WC." he grinned.

"It really is!" she was instantly at ease, "Are you British?" she asked Toby.

"Guilty as charged, ma'am." He replied before giving her a new topic, "Were you in the UK on holiday?"

"I was, oh, and I loved it," she was positively gushing, "I went to Stratford on Avon, Bath, and of course London. It was all so beautiful and old."

"It's been old for ages. But was everybody nice to you?" Toby had to check on the behavior of his countrymen and women.

"They were. You guys are so polite."

Toby leant in, "Not all of us." he raised his eyebrows playfully, "And did you see the Crown Jewels?"

"I did, and whoah, they were real impressive."

"Did you take any? Tell the truth." he couldn't resist.

"Oh no. Ooh, you're cheeky, aren't you?"

"Well, thank God for that. I didn't want to have to throw you out of the emergency exit." he grinned again.

"Ha!" she was laughing uncomfortably loud now, "You're trouble."

Toby could do this all day long. He was dressed in civvies, wasn't performing any work duties, and it amused him. He grinned again, "You have no idea."

At that point, both toilets were simultaneously vacated, allowing the friendly bloke in front of Toby to take the first one, leaving the other for Toby to use, "Well, nice talking to you. I hope I don't get sucked out of the plane when I flush this thing." Toby left to the sound of her booming laughter.

Toby had long since finished in the micro toilet and resumed leaning on the wall, idly looking into the main cabin. He turned back, as he'd done several times, to see the flight attendant had finally re-taken her seat behind him, "You don't mind if I stand here, do you?"

She smiled, "Can't face going back to your seat?"

"Something like that. I booked late and ended up in the

middle seat of five." He rolled his eyes.

"I noticed, and no, I don't mind. I'd probably rather stand than sit there too."

She seemed nice. Toby flashed her a proper smile.

"So, are you coming to the US on a business trip? Or vacation?"

Neither. "Pleasure." He lied. Toby was surprised that she was keeping the conversation alive, "I had some leave to use up, and I picked New York City."

"NYC is fun, but if you've got time, you should get outta the city too. What are you taking leave from?"

"From the British Army, I'm a soldier." he was flying on his own passport, so for now, it made sense to stay close to the truth.

She nodded, "That figures, you carry yourself in that certain way." She smiled, almost dutifully, then continued, "Thank you for your service."

Toby didn't follow, "My service? Thank you for yours, you know." He mimed himself pushing the food cart.

Now she really smiled, a warm, infectious smile, "Very funny, but your service deserves real thanks."

Toby wasn't convinced. He nodded towards the other passengers, "You have to deal with these people, I couldn't do that."

"You seemed to be doing fine with the lady waiting in

line. She was quite taken by you."

"She just needed somebody to make her smile. The guy next to her was being a wanker." He flashed her another quick grin.

"You can use that seat if you want." she nodded to the only other seat in the crew's food prep area. Seeing his doubt, she added, "It's fine. Most of the passengers are asleep. We check on them, but most of the time, we're just as bored as you."

She actually wanted him to stay. Toby was taken aback. Never in his life had any beautiful woman shown interest in him, in fact, they usually treated him like he was diseased, visibly so. So what was going on? She was clearly out of his league. He tried brushing it aside; she must have been ridiculously bored.

He was also torn because typically on an op, he tended to slink along anonymously, minimizing any personal contact, but this wasn't like any other op. He wasn't on a uniformed deployment or a sanctioned job; he was on his own. He was also on holiday, at least in the eyes of the Top Brass back in the UK. Toby figured, *Why not?* Smiled and sat down.

"And you were the person for the job, a nice guy?" She asked cheekily.

"What? Oh, the Coke drinking lady? Uh," he groaned, then considered her conclusion, "I'm one of the good guys, yeah, but not a nice guy." He shrugged apologetically.

"What's the difference?" She looked intrigued.

"I don't know!" Another cheeky grin, "I just know that all of the lads in my regiment are good guys, they'd give their lives for their country, but there aren't many I'd consider nice guys."

"Very scientific." She pursed her lips provocatively, "Anyway, nice guys suck."

"They do, don't they?" He grinned again and then thought back to Damien and the smile evaporated. He was a nice guy, a seriously nice guy. But when things were at their worst, he just quit. He bailed on life itself. "They're weak," Toby spoke more quietly, as much to himself as to his new friend.

She paused to consider her own thoughts, then smiled warmly again, "I'm Mary-Ann, by the way."

"Toby," he replied. *Just not Toby, the nice guy.*

"So, where are you staying in New York?"

"Dunno yet." Another lie, he had a reservation for a cheap motel close to the airport.

"We all stay here," she wrote down a hotel name and handed it to Toby, "When we're at JFK. I'm flying out again in the morning, so it's only the one night this time around."

"Thanks. I'll check it out." He couldn't quite believe it but already knew where this was heading.

"We usually hang around in the hotel bar in the evening.

You should come join." She locked eyes on him much harder than before.

"I will." He returned the intensity, "But I have a question for you."

"Anything," she replied, her expression even more provocative.

Blood started flowing in unexpected areas, catching Toby off guard, "You're not CIA, are you?"

She burst out laughing, "I'll see you later, Toby. I should go walk the plane before you get me in trouble."

62.

Movement woke Toby. He opened his eyes to find he wasn't in his flat or the army barracks, then it all came back. He was in America. He turned around to see the beautiful naked flight attendant getting out of bed. He watched as she bent over to pick up her shoes, giving him a view that made his heart-rate soar, "How long do you have?" He asked.

Mary-Ann turned to him and busted out her beautiful sultry smile, "Long enough." She climbed back onto the bed, then on top of Toby. He started running his hands over her soft, warm body, she leant in and kissed him, and they resumed what they'd done for most of the night.

Toby stepped out of the shower, Mary-Ann followed him. He started toweling off her moist body and her back arched in response, then she snapped herself out of it, "We can't. I'm already gonna be in so much crap. I'm so late I'm gonna have to get my own ride to the airport." She ran into the bedroom and started working through her stuff, throwing yesterday's underwear into a bag, climbing into new ones, her boobs swaying provocatively as she wriggled her hips.

The only way for Toby to leave her alone was to turn away completely, and as he did, he realized he needed to get his own head back in the game. He grinned as he started gathering his own belongings.

"Here's my number, Toby," she scribbled it using the

bedside pen and paper, "If last night was all you wanted, that's cool. But I wanna give it to you, you know, in case you want to get together again."

Toby took the tiny piece of paper, feeling like a god. He was still baffled as to how it had happened; whatever she saw in him, it was something no English girl had ever noticed. He took the paper, slid it into the pocket of his jeans from the floor, and watched her finish up.

"I'm on auto check-out, so just shut the door when you leave. But I've really gotta go. I'm sorry to run out like this." She pulled up the handle of her wheeled suitcase, then leant in and gave Toby one last juicy kiss for the road, "Yum. Bye Toby."

Toby listened to the room door close and allowed himself a moment to commit it all to memory, then stood up, looked around the room with the same stupid grin, and headed out.

"Good Morning, British Consulate General, New York."

Toby was back in his own motel room, patting his freshly shaven face. "Morning, Mark Wilson, please."

"Who's calling?" Asked the voice.

"A colleague," Toby replied, slightly annoyed.

Mark Wilson was the one name in the Consulate who took anonymous calls. The receptionist remembered this and inhaled sharply, "Sorry Sir, I'm patching you right through."

"This is Mark." A gruff voice answered.

"Mark, it's Toby Miller." Toby threw the face towel on the floor and walked back into his motel's bedroom.

"Miller, I didn't know you were in town. You on an op?"

"I am, but this one can't leave a trail, none whatsoever. Understood?" Toby was playing with fire and he knew it. It wasn't unusual for a job to be undertaken with no communication in advance, but even Toby wasn't sure if that truly meant zero communications between home and an overseas post.

He'd thought it through at length, and this really was the only way he could do it. If this put him in the shit later, then so be it, as long as that shit was much later.

"I understand. What do you need?" Mark Wilson sounded reassuringly un-phased.

Toby sat down on the unused motel bed, "A standard observation bag plus a phone and wireless jammer, a good one. I need to be able to dial it in with a very specific radius."

"Okay, what else?"

"An electronic reader, one that can duplicate the code of a garage door opener and then a means of writing that door code onto my own opener."

"No problem, do you have a computer with you for the software?"

"I do. And finally, for now, I need a subject location."

"Of course, what's the subject name?"

This was the riskiest part. Toby took a deep breath before allowing the words to come out, "Name is Madyson Lutz, with a y."

Mark Wilson hesitated before replying, "I know that name."

"Of course, you do, Mark. Why do you think I'm here? Now you understand why they want no trail left. I'm putting my faith in you to keep this clean, coz I'm the one out there playing with fire, and I'm doing it with a huge bloody bullseye painted on my arse." Toby winced at such a bold lie.

"You've got it, Miller, not a word to anyone. Are you coming in for the tech gear?"

"No, Mark, we'll play it safe and use a drop point, ideally by JFK airport. How long do you need for that subject location?"

Toby could almost hear Mark think, "Uh, I think the end of the day should be more than enough time."

"Good, I'll call you back at five exactly, and thanks, Mark."

"Sure, I'll make sure everything is ready for you at five." With that, the line went dead.

Toby threw his mobile on the bed and ran his fingers through his hair. The call seemed to have gone unremarkably enough, it had sounded much like every other organizational request, but he couldn't be one hundred percent sure. Clearly, Mark Wilson didn't know the full back story, particularly the part about Toby's family relationship with the victim of Lutz's crime, or there would have been considerably more suspicion evident in Mark's phone manner.

But no matter how well the call seemed to have gone, Toby knew he'd crossed a forbidden line. From this point on, he was finished; because whether he was charged with just the planning of an unsanctioned job or charged after having completed the actual task, his career was well and truly over. Probably his life as a free man too.

He dropped his head into his hands and groaned. There really was no going back now.

What a bizarre twenty-four hours; the first half had been blissful, one of the best nights of Toby's entire life, and then there was the other half. With one single phone call, he'd ensured there would be no more fun nights like that, no more socializing, no more soldiering, and no more lurking in the shadows for the Government.

It was hard to understand if such an incredible last night had been a positive or a negative. It had certainly felt positive at the time, but since then, it had only served to illustrate just what it was that Toby had chosen to turn his back on. He'd spent too much of the day since then, hanging around waiting, and that had only served to trigger these unwelcome feelings of doubt. Hell, all feelings were unwelcome at this point.

Toby growled and committed to making an early start, busy hands and all that. He opened the box and unwrapped his new prepaid burner phone. He looked over at his UK mobile phone, wanting to shut it off and pull out the SIM card, but knew he had to wait until he'd made the call to Mark at the Consulate. He growled again.

Still stuck and with no option but to wait, he found himself picturing Mary-Ann's body writhing around in bed, then to how much laughter they'd shared the night before. Whatever had just happened, it was more than a physical thing. He reached into the pocket of his jeans and pulled out the piece of paper, finally seeing it was more than just her number too, 'I really dig you, Toby, call me, any time.'

"Bollocks!" He snarled out loud. Now what? Call her? Say I dig you too, but I just did something that's screwed up any chance at a possible future. He stared down at the floor and fought for discipline. He pictured Luke, pictured his sister, and then focused on Damien; of the day Damien was pushed over the edge by Madyson Lutz, that was where his mind had to stay. Toby sat up straight, scrunched up Mary-Ann's note, and threw it in the trash can.

He growled, composed himself, and then rummaged around in his bag and dug out a driver's license. He'd brought an American one with him, one of many he'd been given at work. This one in particular was useful, as he could go off-grid and function stateside without any English documentation. Toby slid his UK driving license out of his cardholder and then wrapped it up in tinfoil along with his UK passport and credit cards. Having some random chip reader notice his UK passport certainly wouldn't help anything, and the foil would prevent that.

The wrapped foil bundle went into the hidden bottom of his bag, and he put the US driver's license and a pair of matching US credit cards into his cardholder. He looked down at the credit cards, wondering if Mark Wilson really understood what he'd meant by zero trail; those US credit card charges should only be known to Mark, so Toby had to have faith.

His phone's time finally turned to five. Toby dialed and waited for the same receptionist to get through her greeting and shush.

"Mark Wilson, please."

"Of course, Sir, putting you through now."

There you go, Toby smiled.

"Miller?" Asked Mark's voice.

"Yep," Toby replied.

"Everything you wanted is ready. Drop point is JFK airport, baggage carousel for flight AE721, coming in at six this evening."

"Oh." Toby was pleasantly surprised at the drop's proximity, "Thanks, Mark, appreciate it."

"You've got it. Call me back if you need anything else, and uhh, good luck Miller."

"Thanks, Mark." *I'm gonna need it.* Toby ended the call and looked back at the time on the phone's display, "Wow. How civilized." He'd still got an hour to travel back to the airport, pick up his rental car and find the right baggage carousel.

Toby smiled. He could finally get on with some work. He took a quick look around his motel room and set to finishing up his tasks. Firstly he shut off his British phone, removed the sim card, and added both pieces to the hidden compartment of his bag.

While there, he double-checked that everything else British was well hidden and that everything American was close to hand. Then he headed into the motel bathroom, gathered his toiletries, and gave the whole room a quick once over. Satisfied, Toby picked up his bag and headed out of the door.

Toby carefully pulled the room door shut behind him, checked the time again, then walked down the corridor toward the elevator, where he pressed the down arrow. As the floor indicator counted from four down to three, Toby turned his head, looking back in the direction he'd just come from.

The elevator arrived with a pinging sound, and Toby stood there motionless as the doors opened, revealing three people waiting to continue their journey down.

After an uncomfortable silence, the oldest occupant finally asked Toby, "You going down, bud?"

Toby looked at him, smiled, then chuckled before replying, "No, not yet, mate. You go on, though."

As the old boy looked at Toby, he had the strangest feeling. It was as if the guy knew exactly what Toby was thinking, Toby's look of confusion turned back into a smile, and as the elevator doors closed, they grinned at each other, and the old boy nodded at him approvingly.

"What was that?" Toby mumbled in utter confusion, then shook his head and walked back toward the motel room.

Toby squatted down on the floor next to the room's trash can, "You knew I was coming back, didn't you?" He reached in and removed the only object inside, which he stuffed back into the same pocket of his jeans.

Toby stood below the huge airport arrivals board, waiting to see where flight AE721 was coming in. The flickering board finally updated to show baggage carousel number fourteen. Now it was time to put everything else behind him and get back into work mode.

As the herd of other people headed away toward carousel fourteen for their own bags, Toby paused to remind himself of how to operate: he needed to get back into reading people, minimizing the risks, watching his back and being ready for anything. As he stood below the arrivals board and gathered his thoughts, the Staffy Miller glare slowly but surely reappeared. He nodded, to nobody in particular, this was going to be a drop point in another country and he was now in the right frame of mind for it.

Toby strode over to baggage carousel fourteen and took up a suitable position near the back wall. From there, he could see everybody, and he'd left very little opportunity for anybody to come up on him unseen. He scanned the crowd. Some bags had already come around the carousel to be claimed, but you wouldn't know it by the number of people that remained; he continually scanned the crowd.

He noticed a middle-aged man looking over at him and met his eyes before consciously looking away again, but Toby kept half an eye on the man's movements with his peripheral vision. It was enough to notice the man move toward him, "Excuse me, Sir?" The man came to a stop right in front of Toby.

"Yup?" Staffy Miller locked eyes on him.

"I think I took your bag by accident. My apologies." The man rolled the bag toward Toby.

Toby nodded, "You're right. That is my bag. I appreciate it, Sir. Thank you."

"You're very welcome, have a nice day." The man said with an American accent, then walked away.

The American accent had initially caught Toby off guard, but sometimes local errand runners were used, people with no knowledge of what they were doing, or for whom. Toby took his new bag by the handle and wheeled it out of the airport, knowing he'd finally been given his destination.

63.

"Turn right in five hundred feet." Toby obeyed the old-school windshield-mounted GPS unit, swinging the rental car into the appropriate street. He looked at the unit's display which showed no remaining turns, and signaled to pull his car into the curb momentarily.

So this was the street where Madyson Lutz lived. Toby peered down the street, taking it all in, a small to medium-sized road, maybe a little quieter than he'd have ideally liked, but it could have been a lot worse.

Too small of a residential street always created problems, as any new car or person on foot tended to be instantly noticed by its residents and committed to memory. It made invisible observation of the subject, a logistical nightmare.

Contrastingly, too large of a street offered more traffic, both vehicular and on foot, which offered better camouflage for an observer. But it also increased the number of potential witnesses, and worse, it typically went hand in hand with more methods of video surveillance, which could later be accessed by law enforcement.

Toby looked at the large spacing between houses and nodded approvingly. This really wasn't too bad of a location. Now what he needed was a couple of observation points, so he signaled to pull back out from the curb and continued down her street, his eyes peeled for anything of use.

Having nobody behind him, Toby crawled along slowly,

looking left and then right, carefully taking in every house, one at a time. He knew his speed would be noticeably unusual, but he only planned on doing it once in this particular car, after which he'd trade it out at the rental agency for something totally different.

The GPS unit showed her house coming up on the left-hand side, which was a concern as he'd still found nowhere he could use for an observation point. Toby continued his slow progress, finally coming up level with the driveway of the Lutz house. It was a drab gray color, mid-sized by US standards, very anonymous, with no cars in the driveway. Knowing it was better not to pay too much attention, Toby continued on past without changing his speed.

As he turned his focus back to the road, Toby noticed a side street on the right, but even more importantly, a *For Sale* sign outside a house diagonally opposite the Lutz's and just a few doors down. "Hell yeah." Toby nodded to himself in approval.

He steered his car into the empty driveway of the available home, got out of the car and made a show of considering it from the front lawn, then he walked up to the front door and rang the doorbell. As Toby waited, he studied the lockbox hanging from the door handle. It was the older variety, requiring a simple code number to access the front door key contained within.

Having waited the appropriate amount of time at the front door, he walked along the house's front wall. There was only one front window, after which was a tall privacy fence. Toby looked through the window, seeing no furniture or possessions; the house was totally vacant.

Satisfied, he turned around, walked back to his car, and leant on the hood, ostensibly messing around with his US burner phone. From this position, he had a great view of the Lutz home, so he subtly fired off a couple of photos, then walked over to the *For Sale* sign and made a show of carefully framing the Realtor's sign with his camera; taking another photo with the Lutz residence as his backdrop.

Toby considered his options, deciding that it would be smarter to get a viewing of the vacant house before swapping out his rental car. That way, his current vehicle would only be associated with an uninterested home buyer.

That cautious line of thought made Toby decide to turn his back on the Lutz couple's house. This situation was far more complex than most: Madyson Lutz had just dodged a foreign extradition request, her husband was probably a CIA employee, and here he was in the state of Virginia, where there must have been thousands of US Government employees living locally.

Toby decided he'd spent long enough outside his first potential observation point, so he got back into his car in the hope of finding a second. Initially he continued in the same direction of travel, but having found nothing of any use within a useful range, he'd turned around and headed back toward the Lutz home, turning into the side street opposite.

As soon as he turned into this smaller side street, he knew

he'd found his second observation point because while one side was given over to housing, the other half was a busy public park. Toby pulled into a spot between some other parked cars and took it all in; there was a bright playground bustling with fast-moving kids, various benches containing people reading, chatting, or canoodling, and a fenced-in area with dogs chasing balls and their owners either chatting with, or carefully avoiding, each other.

Is this where they'd photographed Lutz playing with her dog? He frowned. And there was his newest potential problem; thinking about Madyson Lutz had made Toby care. Emotion never came into his work, so he would have to pay attention, not only to all of the usual external risks, but to any self-created ones.

"Mister Anderson was it?" asked the realtor, clip-clopping in her heels toward Toby's rental car.

"It is, but you can call me James." Replied Toby, trying out his new identity with the first test subject.

"It's nice to meet you, James, so what brings you to the area? Work, I assume."

"Oh yes," replied Toby with a polite smile.

"Is there a Mrs. Anderson, kids? Because the area has wonderful schools, which of course raises the prices somewhat, but it also ensures the stability of your investment."

"No kids yet. But there is a Mrs. Anderson." The only visual which came to mind was that of Mary-Ann. Everything about this job was becoming far too real and personal.

"Well, you're young. Enough." She smiled.

Was that humor? Toby didn't bother with a reply.

"I'm sure there's plenty of time for that. Oh, but did you find the local park yet?"

"Uh-huh, so..." Toby nodded toward the house, "can we take a look?" This lady clearly needed some nudging along.

"Of course, of course, James, let's go and have a looksee." She tottered toward the front door, where she lifted the lockbox. In anticipation, Toby had turned his body away, giving her the false sense of security he required. She started deliberately pushing on the buttons to open the box, oblivious to the fact Toby had turned his head back to watch her. As the box clicked, Toby turned away again and committed her numeric code to memory.

"So, as you can see, we have a very large entrance area, which leads into an open plan living, dining, and kitchen area. It's very contemporary."

Yeah, great, thought Toby, looking around slowly as if he cared.

She walked to some large sliding glass doors which opened to the back yard, pointing for Toby's benefit, "It's nicely surrounded by evergreen trees, giving you lots of privacy."

"I do like privacy." Replied Toby quite honestly. "What's behind the trees?"

"There's a creek and then further back, some more houses, but you can't even see them at this time of year when everything's got leaves.

"Very nice. Can we take a look upstairs too?"

"Of course, we can, James." She smiled, mistaking his curiosity as a potential buyer's interest. "I'll follow you up."

Toby led the way, dutifully walking around the large rear bedroom, then heading into its flashy bathroom, "Do you mind if I rinse my hands quickly?"

"I think the water is on, but there are no towels." Her delivery implied it wasn't really appropriate.

Toby barely rinsed his fingertips under the faucet then wiped them on his loose fitting khaki pants, "Thank you." He smiled genuinely, happy in the knowledge that running water would make his stakeout so much easier.

She nodded and then turned and led him into the front two bedrooms. Most noteworthy was the excellent view from the one facing Madyson Lutz's home.

Toby lingered by the largest window, then turned to the realtor, "It's a lovely home, but I don't think my wife would like all of these big trees being so close to the house. You know, coz of storms." It was as good a brush-off as any.

"Oh." she hid her disappointment poorly.

"But I'll leave you with my info. Maybe you can let me know if anything more appropriate comes up?" He had to, it's what everybody else would do, and he was all about blending in.

64.

Toby had gone back to his new Virginia motel, closed the blinds, and forced himself to sleep in the late afternoon. Grabbing some shut eye, even at the strangest times of day, had become quite normal after so many years of tactical sleep deprivation.

His bedside alarm rang, telling him it was ten-thirty at night, the time when most nine-to-fivers were hitting the sack. Toby got straight out of bed, stripping out of the dorky-looking office garb from earlier and replacing it with dark-colored exercise gear. He ruffled his hair to erase the uncharacteristically side-parted look he'd gone with for the realtor and then headed out to his new white pickup truck. He fired up the new rental vehicle's engine, put it into drive, and headed back to the public park just across the street from Madyson Lutz's house.

Even at this time of night, a handful of cars were parked along the side of the road. He didn't know why they were there, or care. Their presence was welcome as it helped divert some of the attention away from his own vehicle.

Toby locked the truck, pulled up his hood, and jogged over to the vacant home he'd chosen earlier. As he approached the property line, he scanned each way for any other pedestrians, and seeing nobody, he continued straight up the driveway. He stepped into the shadowy darkness of the house and entered the numeric code into the lockbox, taking out the front door key. But instead of using it, he pocketed the key, closed the lockbox, and jogged back to his truck.

Toby fired the truck back to life and searched for the nearest twenty-four-hour big-box hardware store on the GPS unit. There he'd buy himself a nice metal raccoon-sized animal trap and get the front door key copied, so that he could put the original back in the realtor's lockbox.

"Good Morning. I need to speak to somebody about the home on Fairview Avenue, the one you've got for sale." Toby was capable of a convincing Southern accent, and this call required it.

"I can help you with that. Would you like to arrange a viewing?" Toby could recognize the same realtor's smarmy sales voice.

"No, oh no. This is Jimmy from Ace Pest Control. The Fairview house is one of our accounts, and to be honest, we didn't know the Johnson family had even moved out. I guess they figured they'd just let their service lapse at the end of the year. You know, instead of renewing." Toby knew her interest would wane quickly, "So strictly speaking, we should deal with the problem, as they're still paid up. Unless you prefer to use your own people."

"I don't follow. You said you were pest control? What problem? I haven't seen a problem." The realtor sounded dubious and impatient.

306

Toby smiled, wishing he could be there to see her attitude change, "No, of course not, you wouldn't have. Skunks are primarily nocturnal. You'd be lucky to see one, well, really I should say unlucky as if you see one, you'll probably wish you hadn't. When they spray us, it's real bad. I swear we don't charge nowhere enough money for..."

"A Skunk?" She interrupted, "On Fairview Ave?"

"No, not a skunk. They live in a den, which means a whole family of skunks, like the family living under the rear deck on Fairview Ave. But you sound busy, I can let you go." He let the silence linger.

"No, no-no." The panic in her voice was delicious, "You say the Johnson family are paid up? Until the year's end? Well, I think you should carry on with your service."

It was time for him to turn on the reluctance, "Uh, I dunno, if you've people coming and going, and one of them disturbs the animals." He let the silence take over again.

"We can tell them to avoid the deck while you do whatever you do."

"Yeah, that would work. You can tell them there's a family of skunks, and it's best to keep a distance until we've trapped them. Coz if someone makes them spray, well..." he laughed, "the smell will still be there in the Fall!" Cue the pause while she independently dreamed up the appropriate solution.

"You know, maybe you should do your job."

"Trap them." He interrupted.

"Yes, maybe you should trap them, and we'll just put the viewings on hold while you do that."

"Hey, that's a great idea, coz then nobody'll ever know the critters were there. 'Cept us." Toby looked at his watch. She was really dragging this out.

"So, how long will you need?" she asked, her keenness to get the job done for free overriding her disappointment at losing valuable selling time.

"A week, tops, I'd have thought. It depends how well we bait them and how many there are in..."

"Thank you, Jimmy." She interrupted him now, "It sounds like you know your stuff. Say, would you mind letting me know when I can show the property again?"

"Sure darlin, I can call y'all back when I've got the critters caged up."

"Okay then, sounds good. Look, I've got another call, so bye for now." She sounded quite repulsed by his inappropriately affectionate ending, meaning she'd have plenty of reasons to stay away for at least a week.

Toby pulled his pickup into the driveway of his new observation point on Fairview Ave, stepped out, pushed his sunglasses up onto his nose, pulled his baseball cap down low, and straightened his coveralls. He checked the magnetically affixed pest control signs were still straight on the truck's doors and then made a show of walking around the property slowly. He was counting on the fact that stay-at-homers were usually uncontrollably nosey.

Toby walked back to the truck, singing some old country song he'd just heard on the radio, and opened the truck bed, pulling out the metal animal trap. Then Toby slammed shut the tailgate as loudly as possible and continued his awful singing as he carried the cage into the backyard. While there, he checked his freshly cut key in the back door, finding it worked as expected. Why Britain didn't have one key for all doors was beyond him.

Satisfied, he re-locked the back door and headed back to his pickup. As he approached the truck, a lady two doors further down walked out toward her mailbox, calling over "Good morning." As if the timing were pure coincidence.

There we go, he shook his head, hidden by the truck. *She'll be here in just a few seconds.*

"I couldn't help but notice you're pest control, nothing bad, I hope." she smiled unconvincingly as she appeared on the driveway

"Oh no." He needed to be the kind of man you kept away from, "Don't you worry, sweetheart, it's not termites or nothing bad like that. Just a few skunks under the deck."

"Oh." She looked horrified.

"Have you seen any wandering in your yard? At night?" He leaned in as if he didn't hear so well.

"Uh? No." She leaned back instinctively.

309

"Well, good, I was gonna check with the other neighbors too, to see if they'd seen any of the critters runnin around. Are folks at home in the daytime?" Toby kept his tilted head awkwardly close.

"Uhh, no. This is a commuter neighborhood for most people. I work at home some days, but the only other person who stays at home is the house over there." She pointed in the direction of Madyson Lutz's house. "But she comes and goes. I don't know if she's in right now. They both keep to themselves. Most people around here do."

Apart from you, thought Toby, who then raised both hands, "Oh don't you worry, the road probably puts up a barrier. They don't like crossing roads, not unless they have to. I won't need to bother her."

"Oh, okay." the neighbor looked close to squirming in discomfort, "How long, do uh..."

"It's real quick darlin, I'd say you might see me comin and goin for just a week, maybe less, and you probably wanna keep the dog in, if you've got one, that is. It's not real nice when they get sprayed, and then you've gotta wash off the stink. Like I say, a week tops, and we'll be good as new again." He nodded and smiled as she accelerated back toward the safety of her home.

Toby had changed out of his coveralls, removed the magnetic pest control signs, and buried his plain-looking pickup truck amongst the other cars by the public park. He'd

310

headed back to the vacant house on foot, approaching via the creek in the back. Now he was positioned a few feet back from the smallest of the upper storey windows, which offered the appropriate view.

Observations, known more commonly as obbos, were tedious work, whether they were your first obbo or your hundredth. Toby had only been at this one for a couple of hours and was already dreaming of more interesting tasks. He sat back from the tripod mounted camera to rub his eyes, when somebody on foot turned into Madyson Lutz's driveway and walked toward the front door.

Toby leaned his head back in and repositioned his eye, just in time to see the front door open. He'd begun to wonder if Lutz was actually at home, but there was the evidence, in the flesh finally. She looked very similar to the photos which had recently appeared in the British press; with dark hair and a pale face, he watched as she handed a dog leash to the visitor, who turned around and left. A dog walker, Madyson Lutz, was now using a dog walker. Toby watched the front door close and then made a note of the time. It was his first one, and the idea was to learn which events were predictable routines.

Only one sighting so far, but a surprisingly interesting one. The newspaper images had shown her taking her own dog for a walk, but now somebody else was doing it. So had she stopped walking her dog, or did she just walk it occasionally? And if she'd stopped, was it in reaction to the photos which had been made public? And were they taken here? If so, then the absence of any photographers meant the story had finally died a death back home, and that nobody cared about taking her photo anymore. Which meant the only remaining story was his unsuccessful idea for diplomatic change. He sighed, feeling like he hadn't achieved anything. Still, he could now, that's what he was here for.

65.

Toby was on his third obbo day of the Lutz household. He'd gained a decent understanding of which incidents were regular routine and which were random. America's standard practice of coming and going through the garage door had made things more complicated, in that he couldn't see what objects people were carrying whilst coming and going, or even their manner of dress. But he'd still compiled a very useful list.

Jeff Lutz left at the crack of dawn and came back home late; the times varied slightly but during the week he basically never saw his wife during daylight hours. So for now, Mr. Lutz was a known quantity; he went to work, probably ate out, and then came home to sleep. Assumptions could be drawn on his reasons for spending so much time away from home, but Toby wasn't ready to get overly confident about any theories that may yet prove to be inaccurate.

Madyson Lutz let the dog walker take her dog out at eleven-thirty every morning, and the walker came back around half an hour later. Madyson also left the house at about twenty to two in the afternoon every day and returned at twenty past three. For now, Toby was confident in the assumption she drove to a planned event, which was between fifteen and twenty minutes drive from her house, and that this unknown event lasted for one hour. Maybe she went to work out? That's what he'd started to see in his mind.

313

Mrs. Lutz also came and went at various other random times, but these other trips were probably errands such as grocery store runs, which due to their unpredictability, couldn't be used to Toby's advantage anyway.

Toby had started his own routine, arriving at the house before daylight to set up his gear and only leaving after dark, once he'd properly dismantled and hidden everything. The risk of a different realtor entering the house and seeing Toby's camera set-up was minimal, but it was still a risk, and as it could be managed so simply, that's exactly what he did—worrying about something which could be avoided made no sense to him.

But having learned enough of their routine to predict them, Toby planned on doing something different today. He'd already broken down and hidden his camera gear and was watching through the small window, unaided by magnification. He knew the dog walker should appear at any moment, but figured that twice doesn't make for a concrete routine so wanted to actually see the dog walker arrive before taking action.

Toby watched as the dog walker headed up the driveway, took the dog from Lutz, and then headed back down the driveway, from where he knew they'd head straight to the local park for half an hour. He sprinted down the stairs and headed out of the vacant home's back door. He'd have much preferred to use the front, but the risk of Madyson Lutz seeing him simply wasn't worth taking.

Toby jogged along the side of the creek, coming out on

the street corner directly opposite the park. He made a point of jogging on the spot, in his fresh brand-name workout gear, while waiting for a gap to cross, then finally headed into the park itself. Seeing that the dog walker had already entered and started a clockwise loop of the park's perimeter, Toby veered in the opposite direction and started a counterclockwise circuit.

It wasn't long before the dog walker came into view, Toby slowed his jog, looking at the dog and not its walker, before coming to a complete stop with a warm smile on his face. "Oh, you look just like Frodo." The dog didn't, but Toby went down to the dog's level anyway, "He was my dog, but died a couple of years ago. Can I say 'Hi' real quick?"

The young woman stopped texting long enough to look at Toby, then she looked around the park and seeing plenty of witnesses, she seemed to make a decision she was comfortable enough to allow the stranger a couple of minutes. "Sure."

Toby held his hand out, allowing Madyson Lutz's dog to get his scent. He then rubbed the big dog's ears, "What's his name?"

"Huh? What did you say?" The teenager was far more interested in her cellphone than some dorky jogger in Dad sweats.

"What's his name?" Toby looked up momentarily before turning his full attention back to the dog.

"Putz." The girl went back to her texting or posting.

"Putz, what a funny name." Unseen, Toby brought his other hand up to the dog and fed it the soft dog treat he'd been holding. The dog already loved him. Job done. "Thanks for that and sorry to bother you." Toby flashed her another quick smile and then took off to continue his jog.

Toby had repositioned himself back in the small window of the vacant house and was mulling over the risks of his next step. The main one was the uncertainty caused by Jeff Lutz's CIA status; more specifically, how that status related to the house Toby was observing through his long camera lens.

What Toby did know was it wasn't their house; the electronic subject file he'd been supplied with had told him that. Apparently, the Lutz couple had moved from their own house when the attention from the incident had picked up, and shortly after that, they'd moved a second time, making this their third house in roughly four months. Toby's assumption was it was a rental property. The other possibility was it had been supplied to the husband through the CIA. The frustrating part was how different those two options were.

A standard rental home would make it unremarkable in terms of security and technology, but if the house was CIA-owned, who knew what kind of systems it had in place.

Looking through the lens, Toby could see it had a digital doorbell with a camera that typically fed an image to the home owner's cell phone. Those monitoring systems only transmitted images when the bell had been rung, rather than streaming constantly, but if it were a CIA house, an always-on system modification wouldn't be too surprising.

He panned the long lens of his camera for what felt like the thousandth time but still couldn't see any other form of external surveillance. It was time to start taking some risks.

Toby took apart his camera gear and hid it inside the attic opening. He put his new tech gadgets into a small backpack and left the obbo house by the back door. He collected his pickup truck from inside the main parking lot of the public park. He turned it around, repositioning it backwards in the last spot of on-street parking, which gave him a clean line of sight to Madyson Lutz's house.

The truck had a small sliding window immediately behind Toby's seat, which he only opened far enough to use the handheld component of the scanner. Then Toby fired up the device and set it to 'read mode,' which in theory would copy Mrs. Lutz's garage door code.

He'd already familiarized himself with the device's operation, God knows he'd had the time, but it was still fascinating to see if it would work perfectly on the first attempt. He held the device in the window's tiny opening. He didn't know if its requirement for an unobstructed line of sight would be hampered by the automotive glass but was unwilling to risk failure for such a senseless reason.

Toby sat in the driver's seat; his body twisted

uncomfortably to hold the reader backward, waiting and hoping that Madyson would be doing her afternoon workout as normal. He took out and checked his phone for the current time, then looked back at the house to see the garage door already rolling upward. He glanced down at the screen of his device and could see it was reading the code as promised, "Cool." Toby chuckled.

Madyson Lutz backed out of her garage, then rolled down her long driveway and turned right as she'd done every other day. Now Toby had to instruct his device to send that unique code into the handheld garage door opener which he'd got ready and waiting. The device stopped, closed its 'write mode' display window, and returned to the start screen, it looked like it was finished, but there was only one way to really be certain. Toby put his truck into drive and took it back to the parking lot, but instead of re-parking it, he used the lot to make a big swinging turn and came back out of the lot, finally facing the Lutz home.

Toby continued past the park's edge to the stop junction located at a perfect forty-five-degree diagonal from the Lutz house. He checked the street was totally empty of both foot and vehicular traffic and then headed straight across Fairview Ave and up into Madyson Lutz's driveway. He pressed the little rubber button as he rolled his truck toward their double doors and beamed as the door obediently opened, "What a nice bit of kit." He nodded approvingly.

As the truck approached the open doorway, he suddenly noticed how close the overhead support looked to the windshield of his truck, realizing with a slight panic, he'd not anticipated the height of the garage opening versus the height of his own truck.

"You stupid muppet." He chastised himself, his head almost pressed against the windshield, desperately trying to see if he was going to hit the lower edge of the now fully raised garage door. A quiet rubbing noise passed over his head as he pulled into their garage, "Bollocks." He growled, knowing he'd just made contact. He hesitated for just a moment before mumbling, "Whatever. The ship's already sailed." He applied a last little nudge on the gas pedal to bring his truck fully into the garage. He pulled the front bumper as close as he could to the back wall, then pressed the button on his own garage remote and waited for the door to fully shut.

Now inside the darkness of the Lutz couple's garage, he activated his wireless jamming device, which he'd pre-calibrated to fifty feet, with a three hundred and sixty-degree radius. He was working on the theory that any monitoring devices the CIA might use would transmit the information wirelessly, or not, hopefully.

Toby pulled a balaclava over his head, swung the door of his truck open, and turned on the garage lights. He walked along all four walls of the garage looking for any sign of surveillance cameras, and then seeing none, he removed the balaclava.

He had two more things to do before leaving. The first was to figure out if the dog was allowed to roam the house freely, or if Mrs. Lutz locked the animal inside a kennel. Toby suspected the former, judging by the proximity of the dog's bark.

But a hunch wasn't enough; he had to see for himself. He also needed to strengthen his bond with the dog, so the next step was to see if the connecting door to the house was locked. Picking such a simple lock would be child's play, but he'd already pegged Madyson as too lazy and trusting to even bother locking her inner door.

Ever the prudent one, Toby removed a cloth from his pocket and wrapped it around the door handle to avoid skin contact. He took a dog treat from his other pocket and yelled, "Putz! No!" The dog stopped momentarily before re-starting the noise, but it was encouragement enough for Toby, who turned the door handle. And then the dog flew at him.

As Toby landed on his ass, he instinctively clenched his fists and protected his head, but instead of sharp pain, he felt the dog licking his face. Toby relaxed his hands and started laughing as he rubbed the animal's head. He sighed, pulled himself from under the huge beast, and gave him the dry gravy-covered biscuit that had been broken into small pieces by his clenched fist. Putz almost inhaled the treat before licking Toby's left hand clean and going at his face again.

"Okay, that'll do for today, mate." Putz barked at him in response and Toby grabbed his jaw, "No!" He commanded the dog. When Putz stopped his noise, Toby handed him another biscuit and massaged his head enthusiastically, "That's a good boy, no barking."

Then Toby took out his last dog biscuit, held it in front of Putz's nose, and reminded him, "No." before he threw the biscuit into the house and told him, "Good boy." Finally, Toby closed the connecting door as Putz took off in search of his last treat.

"Now, why would they call you Putz?" Toby couldn't help but feel that naming the dog in a way that mocked Mr. Lutz's last name had to be significant. Temporarily he put it out of his mind, knowing he needed to do his last task and get out of there quickly. There was a possibility, small admittedly, that by opening the inner connecting door, he'd inadvertently triggered a silent alarm. The other potential trigger would be a loss of power to any surveillance devices, so Toby walked over to the main breaker panel and flipped the top left switch, labeled 'Main.'

He held his finger on the breaker's switch as the lights went out in the garage, then unhindered by the sudden darkness, was able to flick it straight back into the 'On' position. He stepped back into his truck, paused the wireless jammer, and pressed his garage door remote again. Toby then backed out of the garage to the same overhead squeaking noise. He took a quick look at the door's lower edge through his windshield, and seeing no incriminating paint from his truck's roof, he pressed the door remote again and drove back toward the public park as the Lutzs' garage door closed behind him.

Toby arrived back at his preferred observation window

breathlessly and cautiously leaned in to look back over at the Lutz house. Any alarms he'd triggered would mean the arrival of people, and they'd almost certainly be scanning for anything strange in every direction. But there were no people. He exhaled cautiously. Their response times might have been slower than expected, so he leaned on the wall and waited for something to change.

Ten minutes in, it was clear no response teams were coming. None of Toby's actions had triggered anything, meaning he could go further next time, much further.

Toby walked into the closest bathroom and sat down on the countertop, intent on formulating the last part of his plan. Today was Wednesday, and following its successes, tomorrow would be even more educational. He was keen to see if that next stage triggered any responses. If not, then Friday would be the big one. It gave him a lot to think about.

66.

Toby was well fed, rested, and ready to go. The tediousness of the observation part was coming to an end, and the stimulating phase was about to begin; stimulating because there were no rules, uniforms, or commanding officers to interfere or hold you back.

Unfortunately, it was those same things that made it so perilous because you had no competent mates to watch your back, no option of diverting blame to a superior's orders, and having ditched the uniform, there was no protection under the rules of the Geneva Convention. Yet Toby still enjoyed his work, risks and all. Although he couldn't kid himself, this one was different.

Being given a target and sent on your way, removed the option of doubting the validity of your task.

Donning plain clothes and undertaking an unauthorized, emotionally motivated operation in your number one ally's back yard just wasn't comparable - it was beyond reprehensible, and he knew it. If Toby were caught, he'd be abhorred on both sides of the Atlantic. Although every time the thought had run through his head, he'd ended up comparing himself to Jeff Lutz. Lutz had been up to something very under the radar in Britain, but he'd just run to ensure he and his wife could dodge consequences for their actions.

Toby growled; reprehensible and abhorrent didn't come close to describing what they'd done. Anyway, the only way this would become an issue was if he were caught, and he had no intention of letting that happen.

How you ran your op and the risks you accepted differed, depending on where you were and who your target was. So while in some countries you'd quietly put a bullet in the target's forehead and leave, in others, you had to be much more slippery. As yet, Toby had no plan on how he would deal with Madyson Lutz because it would depend on what he discovered today, but he did know how to avoid getting caught.

In America, a country where the men and women of law enforcement really know their trade, Toby needed to be a ghost, more so than ever before. The identity he'd already used to rent his cars and book his motels would need to be scrapped. He'd also have to go through the formalities of closing anything he'd left open, including the most trivial details, like informing the realtor that all of his fictitious skunks had been removed. Toby needed to remove every trace of his existence, even from the house he'd been using for observation.

In anticipation of the demands of the next phase, he'd already started to clean any evidence of his presence, and then moving forward, he planned on restricting himself to the routes from the entrance doors up to his primary observation room.

Toby paced the obbo room, re-running everything in his head. The priority was to be a ghost, so even the manner of her death had to be unremarkable, which meant he wanted to be inside their house figuring out how to do it. And he wanted that right now. Fighting the impatience was getting harder by the minute.

He had to run through his checklist to maintain his composure: he'd already jogged the park and petted their strangely named dog again, surreptitiously feeding him another treat. He'd changed out of his jogging clothes back at his motel, where he'd left all of the camera equipment. Finally he'd packed the necessary tools for today's breach.

Toby lifted his backpack and went through the contents again; it was all good. He looked up and down Fairview Ave yet again, a road he'd come to know like the back of his hand. All the locals had left for the day, at least the residents within view of the Lutzs. Toby chuckled; even the nosiest neighbor who'd told him she "sometimes worked from home" had changed her routine, leaving every morning and only returning at dinner time. His skunk ruse had apparently been a runaway success.

Finally, the Lutzs' garage door opened and Toby watched as Madyson's car backed out. He fought his impatience, waiting until she'd totally disappeared from view before heading down the stairs with his pack. Knowing the vacant status of every single house within sight and that she'd now left too, he knew it would be safe to take the direct route via his own front door. Toby crossed the street and started walking toward the Lutz home as casually as possible.

Reaching the bottom of the Lutzs' driveway, he took a quick look over his shoulder and checked ahead one last

325

time, but then paused, squinting into the distance, "Oh, no bloody way."

Toby lowered his head and repositioned himself to walk more centrally on the sidewalk as Madyson's car drove back down the street toward him.

"You've gotta be kidding me," he mumbled under his breath, deciding the only way to appear benign whilst so close to her house was to wait for her to pass him and then cross the street toward the park. But that choice also meant allowing her to drive straight past him, at very low speed, and unless she was totally self-absorbed, Madyson Lutz had just seen his face.

Toby was back in the window of the obbo house, having had no choice but to take the long way back. This situation was turning out badly, because he'd not seen her leave since returning to his vantage point. So was she still inside her house? Or had he missed her leaving, while he was scurrying back to his obbo house?

Toby looked at the time. It had just turned two, which according to his suppositions, meant she should have just started her jazzercise, or whatever fad it was that she probably worked out to.

"What shitty luck." He shook his head, his eyes permanently searching her house for any sign of movement.

The longer he waited, the more he started to understand

326

how problematic this was, in terms of the implications. He needed to enter their house today and spend a good hour carefully looking around it, so he could learn everything possible about their lifestyle. This was Thursday, his planned reconnaissance day. It had to be today so that tomorrow afternoon he could re-enter the house and make any necessary preparations for his final entry later that night.

Toby's plan had always been to spend Saturday morning heading Eastbound at thirty thousand feet, before her body had even been found. But if he bailed on today, he'd have to write off the whole weekend because there was no point doing a recce on a Friday, for a hit on a Monday. It simply allowed way too much time to pass in the interim. So bailing now meant delaying today's recce job until Monday, and the job's conclusion until Tuesday. As a setback, that seemed more problematic than just pushing forward right now.

Toby growled, "Bollocks to this." Then took off down the stairs again. You minimized the risks wherever you could, but sometimes you just had to dive in and take one.

One risk he was unwilling to take, was Madyson watching him leave from the house on the opposite side of the street. So Toby had to jog along the creek yet again, before heading back to his truck and changing into the skunk trapper's overalls. Then he booted up his wireless signal jammer and set it to standby before putting it into his pocket. He put the garage door remote into his other pocket, flung his pack over his shoulders, and walked toward the Lutz house.

Standing on their doorstep, Toby pulled his baseball cap low, turned the wireless internet jammer to active mode, and then, knowing he'd rendered their video doorbell inactive, he rapped his knuckle on Madyson Lutz's front door.

Putz's barking sounded very close, meaning the dopey beast still had free run of the house, and even more encouragingly, Toby couldn't hear anybody yelling at him to shut up. Although casting his mind back, he could recall another job where he'd entered a house after knocking with no response, only to find its occupant home with their pants around their ankles, literally. Talk about an undignified ending.

Toby sighed, knocked on the door one last time, then looked in both directions and threw caution to the wind, pressing the garage door remote in his pocket.

The door started trundling its way noisily up the runners, and with it barely three feet off the floor, Toby skipped to the side and took a quick look underneath it. Seeing that Madyson's car was absent, he rolled straight under the door, and before it had even reached halfway open, he tapped the button again, triggering a reverse in its direction.

He checked the time as the door came to a stop, finding it was a quarter past two. This setback had cost him half an hour, but it still felt like a victory after having come so close to postponing the whole thing. Nonetheless, the clock was ticking, so Toby opened his pack and took out one of the ridiculous over suits that crime scene investigators wore in the UK. He was intent that neither US Law Enforcement nor the CIA would ever find any evidence of him being present. He pulled the facial drawstring tight and then dug out a handful of dog biscuits from his bag.

Toby walked to the back door and yelled, "Putz. No!" The dog stopped barking momentarily but then couldn't resist and started afresh. Toby yelled the same command again, and the dog stopped. Toby threw open the door and sat down with him, smothering the dog in praise and dog treats.

He gave the dog a couple of minutes to calm himself and then stood up and looked him in the eye, "You know what, Putz? It's all about perspectives, and from yours, I'm the bad guy. So you're a sweet boy but a bloody useless guard dog." He handed him a longer-lasting chew treat, and then, as the dog headed off to his bed to enjoy it, Toby finally stepped inside Madyson Lutz's house.

As suspected Toby had found a tiny camera facing the rear door of the Lutz home and another covering the front. Both had been temporarily put out of action by his jammer, but that success had created him some extra work.

He knew that everyone's wireless could go out from time to time, but if Jeff Lutz of the CIA noticed that his had gone out for three days in a row, at exactly the same time, it would trigger suspicion. So Toby's new workload would include having to sneak back to the house at various other points during the next forty-eight hours to randomize the wireless network's failures. It wasn't a big commitment, considering the jammer could work just as well from outside the home, but it was another task to add to his list.

Toby had already given the downstairs a quick but efficient sweep, prioritizing the places where people typically left personal items, such as the kitchen's miscellaneous drawer, but nothing he'd discovered had really inspired him. Upstairs was always where people's private lives played out, so he left the wireless jammer in a central location and headed up there.

The first room he came to was in a real mess, what his Mum would describe as a 'Shit tip' - a compliment she'd usually deliver at considerable volume and always in reference to teenage Toby's bedroom. The mess in this particular room was interesting, as the whole thing screamed single guy.

Toby stood at the foot of the bed, his face scrunched up in thought. He put aside the overall chaos and looked at the details. The bed wasn't made, and most interesting was the pillow situation - only one was caved in by someone's head. This was the kind of thing he'd been looking for. Could the Lutz couple really be sleeping in different bedrooms?

Rather than wasting his time taking in any more details, Toby hurried toward the next bedroom. It was a spare room, perfect and unused, offering him no useful information. Next bedroom again, much tidier than the first one, but this one was definitely a woman's room, with an abundance of decorative pillows, hair ties, earrings, lycra workout gear, and pink sneakers on the floor. *They're definitely living as two separate people.* This was great news, in so many ways.

The first thing to hit him was a glimmer of satisfaction at their apparent unhappiness; it's the least they deserved after killing Luke. Toby wanted to call Tracey and let her know, but nobody could ever know about this. *What a shame. It might give her a lift.*

The second thing was the seeds of a plan; the Lutzs were unhappy, and he could work with that. Hell, it made the possibilities better than anything he'd anticipated. He might even be able to swing something which took out two birds with one stone. After all, this was the CIA guy who'd been the driving force in their running from justice, and why should he get off without consequences?

"Oh yeah." Toby spoke softly to himself, "I can do something with this."

But he had so many more questions: Just how unhappy were they? Were they miserable enough to be self-medicating? Did Jeff Lutz keep a gun in the house? Toby needed to investigate these details, record everything he could and still leave enough time to exit before Madyson's return.

67.

Friday dawned, the big day. It was either the last day of Toby's life as a free man or his final opportunity to back out.

The occasion had woken him early and as he lay on his motel bed in the darkness, he could only think of the choice he'd been forced into. Toby had always had faith in society, you followed its rules, or you suffered the consequences. He thought back to his youth, of how he'd lost his dad young, and only now could he understand the effects of that loss. Without his father's strong guiding hand, Toby had started to believe society's rules didn't apply to him and had been drawn to others of a similar persuasion. Toby had guided himself into the Army, unaware of how perfect a fit it would be, and it had become his salvation. He still couldn't really understand how he'd been so fortunate in choosing the right course. It had been chance, pure and simple.

But his old crowd hadn't made such lucky choices. They'd grown up without that direction change and persisted in believing that society's rules weren't for them. The only restraint he'd ever seen in them, was caused by their fear of dramatic consequences. Since then, Toby had known that consequences were the glue that held society together.

Since he'd changed his course, the connection between actions and their consequences had come to fascinate Toby. On a domestic level, that order was kept by the Criminal Justice System, whereas internationally, it fell to the Armed Forces or the International Court of Justice. Unknown to most people, some tasks also fell to government employees working in the shadows, people like Toby.

But at every level, mankind had created and then continually updated a system of consequences as a punishment for and a deterrent to unacceptable actions. So how had society missed this one?

Luke had been killed by a useless driver who'd lacked the skill required to transition to such a different way of driving and who'd compounded the problem by being negligently distracted at the wheel. The combination of those two facts would have resulted in a conviction anywhere, the only uncertainty being its severity.

But this driver had been permitted to run from consequences, because she was married to a man who worked for the Government of our closest ally. It defied belief, and without some intervention, the woman who'd killed Luke would never see justice.

It's not like he expected Lutz to be hung by the neck until dead. If that were deemed the appropriate punishment, then so be it, but he'd have also accepted a lenient sentence - as long as it had followed a legitimate trial.

But there would be no trial for Madyson Lutz and no consequences. And so Toby planned on delivering his own, for which he would undoubtedly suffer far worse consequences. Just thinking about it made him furious. He sat up in bed, breathing heavily, nostrils flared and fists clenched.

Right now, emotion was the enemy, so Toby worked on calming his breathing. He relaxed his hands and then his whole upper body, trying to distract himself with thoughts of something more positive. Mary-Ann came to mind, a woman he'd spent only half a day with. He could only shake his head at what a farce his personal life was.

I'd told her I was one of the good guys, as opposed to a nice guy. Is that how I'll be seen after this?

Of course not, was the answer. *So back out?* Backing out would mean no justice for Luke and no consequences for Mrs. Madyson Lutz. Both, were equally unthinkable.

No, his doubts had to be suppressed and something had to happen. The Police had tried to use the justice system and failed. The Government had tried to negotiate for international justice and failed. The press had tried throwing their weight around to force a change, and even Toby himself had tried to push for some kind of diplomatic change, and still, everybody had totally failed.

One tool remained capable of achieving the desired results, but the government was unwilling to deploy it. So Toby would deploy himself, for Luke, Tracey, and Damien. It was time to put aside all doubts.

Toby ran back up the external staircase to the second story, where his motel room was located. He was totally out of breath and feeling better for it.

He'd jogged until he'd found a twenty-four-hour drug store, where he'd bought an energy drink, a protein bar, and an international calling card. The first two items had fulfilled their purposes, but he was having doubts about using the third.

Since his emotional episode, he'd had an overwhelming urge to call his family, either Tracey or his Mum, but to what end, he wasn't sure. Self-doubt probably, hoping for some validation; it was all very unlike him.

No, calling them was a terrible idea, for so many reasons. Although, he did have another idea, Toby took out his US burner phone and dialed in the information shown on the rear of the plastic calling card, then a US phone number. The dialed number rang.

"Hi, this is Mary-Ann Ellis. You know what to do." Beep.

Her voice had made him smile, but he had no idea what to say to her. Toby took the phone from his ear, resigned to hanging up, before having a change of heart, "Hi Mary-Ann, this is Toby, I uh. I finally saw what you wrote on the note, and it made me smile. And yes, I would like to see you again."

He had to gather his thoughts before finishing, "If the world allows it." he paused again before leaving her his UK phone number, smiling again as he hung up.

Toby was back in his preferred observation window,

allowing the wireless signal jammer to do its job. He'd had to lengthen its effective range due to his increased distance from the Lutz house, but he'd also narrowed its operating angle to fifty degrees to avoid jamming too many other local houses. There may have been some bleed into the two closest neighboring homes, but they were both vacant during the day, so aside from a few rebooted domestic devices, it wouldn't create too many waves.

During his early morning jog, Toby had done the exact same thing with the jammer, meaning the Lutz couple's wireless internet had suddenly gone to hell and for no apparent reason.

Having abandoned any thoughts of alternative options, he'd properly put his mind to work, formulating a suitable plan to conclude this whole mess.

The aim had always been to fit the method to the circumstances, and having finally familiarized himself with the Lutz's domestic situation, he'd decided that her death should be the culmination of their disastrous marriage. It was simple, but simple always resulted in less suspicion.

Yesterday's reconnaissance had revealed that Jeff Lutz kept a whiskey bottle and glass on his nightstand, plus a bottle of sleeping tablets inside its drawer. Underneath his bed was a portable gun safe, it had been locked during Toby's daytime visit, although whether it was locked or unlocked during the night made little difference to anybody who could work a lock. Jeff Lutz also kept some paperwork in his room, it had been locked inside a hard briefcase, which might have been a sufficient way to hide them from his wife's eyes, but again, not from anybody proficient. The documents had been internal job descriptions for alternative postings, and all of them were bleak, implying he'd been demoted since the UK incident.

One thing Toby had hoped to find was something relating to Mr. Lutz's duties in the UK. To have known what both governments were so intent on prioritizing over justice for Luke would have been valuable to Toby. But even in his broken-down state, Jeff Lutz apparently knew not to take such documents home.

Madyson Lutz managed to keep her bedroom in slightly better order than her husband, but a bottle of high dosage Prozac antidepressant implied she was struggling elsewhere. That discovery had been uplifting, at least momentarily, as up until that point, Toby had pictured her living the life shown in the most recent news photos, i.e., playing happily with her dog in public. That her fun had finally ended was good news, but not even close to good enough.

The more Toby considered it, the more easily he could see the news headline; Mr. Jeff Lutz, CIA operative, murders his disgraced wife, Mrs. Madyson Lutz.

Then the first summary chapter; Following the death of young British teenager, Luke Rigg, Mr. and Mrs. Lutz fled the UK claiming diplomatic immunity, but on their return to the USA, their relationship steadily deteriorated to the point where Mr. Lutz, a man with his career in free-fall following his wife's actions, murdered his culpable wife, Madyson,

337

during a heated drunken row.

Toby's plan required him to crush some of Jeff's own sleeping tablets into a bottle of the man's favorite whiskey and allow him to sedate himself. Suitably incapacitated, Toby could place his own silenced pistol into Jeff's hand and fire off a single blank round, ensuring the appropriate amount of gunshot residue covered Mr. Lutz's hand and wrist.

Then Toby would have to clean up all possible evidence of his own presence before firing one live round into Madyson Lutz using Jeff's own weapon. Finally, that weapon needed to be placed into Jeff's limp drunken hand, and Toby needed to make a rapid exit before the arrival of law enforcement.

All possibilities would be investigated, but the evidence would show a drunken, disgraced government employee with a crumbling marriage, who'd been finally pushed over the edge by a forced demotion, which mixed with whiskey and a caustic row with his wife resulted in a dead Madyson Lutz. Possibly even triggering the suicide of Mr. Jeff Lutz. Nothing would be found in the house to suggest anybody else's involvement.

Today's planned task involved waiting for Madyson to leave for her Irish jig class or whatever it was she did every day. And then reentering the house to swap out Jeff's whiskey bottle for Toby's doctored twin. Then after the hit, Jeff's original bottle and drinking glass would need to be traded back, ensuring the only trace of sleeping pills found by investigators would be inside Jeff's bloodstream.

But for now, it was a matter of controlling the impatience he felt by occupying his mind in any constructive way he could find.

68.

Situation Normal; All Fucked Up, that was what they said in the Army.

Madyson was meant to have left at twenty to two, but it was closer to four o'clock, and she'd gone nowhere, which meant that either hip hop yoga wasn't a thing on Fridays, she was sick, or maybe some other unknown had crept in to snafu his plan.

Still, all he could do was wait and adapt, and for now, 'Plan MK 2' was to wait until she left on one of her random errands before his re-entry, which of course carried its own risks. If that didn't happen before the evening tide returned all of the local commuters, then he'd probably have to come up with a Plan MK 3. But he was optimistic, for now.

Back at the motel, his international bag was already packed, he'd arranged for a local bag drop through Mark at the Consulate, and he'd even got himself a seat booked on the first flight out. But none of that had taken into account Plan MK 2 or the need for a Plan MK 3 or even 4. Toby stretched his upper body as he rolled his eyes, all the while grinning at the situation. It was a pain in the rear when people ruined your perfectly laid out plans, but it happened regularly, and from time to time, it could actually be quite stimulating.

That thought led him to the memory of how the youngest of the new soldiers had no ability or willingness to adapt to changing situations, about how it was a learned skill. This led him to wonder how they were all doing in Afghanistan and whether the lads were all still in one piece.

He frowned because with his UK phone temporarily off, he had no idea if there was already bad news waiting for him. He desperately hoped they were all okay, even the new kids he didn't know, because only a small element of what bonded them was friendship. Browny was a good example, he loved Browny, and it would break his heart if anything ever happened to him. But he'd also be gutted if any of the young kids bought it because they'd committed themselves just the same way as him and Browny; by unconditionally offering everything for their country. It created a bond no civvy could ever understand. They were his lads, and he would always be worried about them.

So what would they make of his current job? He frowned. It wasn't a real job because he hadn't been assigned it; he'd gone off on his own. That annoyed him all over again. Why couldn't he have just been ordered to do this job? It would have made all the difference.

But then his boredom-induced thoughts were interrupted by the sound of an electric garage door, Madyson's door. "And finally, we have a green light," Toby whispered, watching as she turned and accelerated out of her driveway.

What was the time? Four o'clock, which was cutting it really fine in terms of returning commuters and the risk of them seeing him, but Toby was still willing. Caution dictated that he at least needed to prevent Madyson from interrupting him. So Toby set the jammer to block her garage door's

341

wireless frequency too, then dialed it back into its original three hundred and sixty degree operating radius, before throwing it in his bag and running down the stairs.

Toby stood at the side of Jeff Lutz's bed, studying yesterday's phone image of the man's whiskey bottle. Overnight the level had dropped by a lot, meaning Mr. Lutz was almost certainly drinking to forget. It was good news for Toby because it implied that Jeff Lutz drank every night, and without that, Toby would have been forced into another plan. Even worse, Toby might have been faced with an unexpectedly sober Jeff Lutz and forced into adapting in the heat of the moment. Although an element of that scenario was strangely inviting, the guy was CIA after all, which would have made it an exciting confrontation for Toby.

Setting that thought aside, Toby noticed how the dosed bottle he'd brought with him had a higher level of remaining whiskey than anticipated. Would Jeff notice that difference? Or should he pour some out? But if he drained twenty percent, would the sleeping pill dose still be sufficient? *Decide, quick.*

Toby picked the lower-risk scenario, heading to the nearest toilet and pouring nearly half an inch down the pot, which he flushed away before heading back to Jeff's room. Then as the sound of the cistern refilling itself stopped, he thought he heard a door close.

Toby froze to the spot, he was wearing a Tyvek crime

scene suit again, and he'd left the wireless signal jammer downstairs on the living room table. So how was he going to get out of this situation? He took a step toward the bedroom door, and his suited legs made an audible swishing noise. Toby froze again, realizing he'd have to adapt his movements to the suit, so walking like an astronaut, he took the remaining couple of steps toward the bedroom door and listened.

"I know, Hi. I know, puppy, I missed you too but give me a minute to put the groceries down."

It was Madyson's voice. He assumed, never having heard it before.

"Come on, puppy, let's go figure out why the garage door wouldn't open."

Oh crap, the jammer, Toby's eyes widened. Then he realized that stupid dog could lead her right to him; 'Look, look, this is Toby, he's my new secret friend!' Toby had to act quickly. He strained to listen even more intently and heard another door gently click closed. Figuring the way was clear, Toby ran a few more awkward steps only to hear the door open again, and then, Madyson appeared right at the bottom of the stairs, having come back in through the garage connecting door.

"Weird. My phone won't work either."

He stared down at her in disbelief as she toyed with her phone's screen, oblivious to his proximity. If she were to turn her head right now, she'd instantly see him, and he'd have to... Toby would have to finish her in front of her own dog, which would not be a clean kill. Knowing that someone's peripheral vision was more likely to spot movement than a stationary shape, Toby couldn't risk moving a muscle.

Madyson simply shook her head in confusion at her phone's inactive status. "Let's go see if we can get a signal outside." And with that, she headed straight out of the front door with Putz.

Toby ran back into Jeff's bedroom, grabbed the correct whiskey bottle and his bag, then sprinted down the stairs, stashing the bottle inside it as he moved. He jogged through the living room, grabbing the wireless jammer as he passed the table, and continued on to the back door, which he unlocked and opened. He immediately turned the internal lock straight back to the upright, locked position, then stepped outside and pulled the door shut behind him. At the same moment, the front door re-opened, illuminating the house's interior. Toby dove headfirst into the closest cover, a tall screen of bushes in Madyson's back yard, and yanked in any visibly protruding parts.

He let out a sigh of relief, *Problem one averted. Next?* The jammer, he needed to kill the jammer so that she'd be temporarily preoccupied with getting her car back into the garage. He was still holding it, so he hit the button, taking it straight out of active mode. Then in a flash of inspiration, he also decided to open the garage door with his own remote. He could hear her talking to the dog again, then silence, followed by the sound of her car starting.

Toby took the opportunity to crawl back out of the bushes and relocate himself at the bottom of their fenced-in yard, placing himself further from her view and further from the dog.

He allowed himself a few minutes for the adrenaline to wear off, then slowly eased himself out of the crime scene suit, which had been ripped by his dive into the Lutzs' privet bushes. It had served its purpose inside the house, and so he scrunched it up and shoved it inside his pack. Without the weird suit on, Toby's manner of dress was quite inconspicuous, but there was still absolutely no way of leaving her backyard without attracting attention. So he was stuck there until the darkness arrived, which at this time of year was four or five hours away.

69.

Things hadn't gone to plan, but the complications were innocuous enough, and so none of it had really mattered. It had been twenty past ten before the overlooking houses had quietened down and started to close their blinds and drapes, at which point Toby had run like a jackrabbit.

Since then, he'd used the time to perform a full clean-up of the observation house, and as far as he was concerned, it was now out of bounds. He'd cleaned up his Motel room, too, leaving only his travel bags inside the doorway.

It was now two-forty in the morning. Considering that most people were in the middle of their nightly cycle, it was as good a time as any to do the unthinkable. He'd been sitting in his newest rental car, parked in the street alongside the public park, watching the clock. He took a deep breath, stepped out, and closed the door quietly before locking it and trotting over toward the Lutz residence. As Toby jogged, he reflected on how differently the job had turned out to be compared to his preconceived ideas. He'd expected Jeff Lutz to be a valued CIA operative, furtively watched by dangerously skilled colleagues. In reality, he looked to be more of a desk jockey whose career was dead, and as a result, his colleagues had left him to his own devices.

Madyson was meant to have been somebody living the good life, running through the local park with her dog, happily enjoying the sunshine with her hair blowing in the wind, like in some godawful drug commercial. Instead, she was the target market for the drug, self-quarantined inside her own house and too scared to even walk the dog in public. But screw them both, they deserved much worse and certainly weren't worthy of his pity.

When Madyson had caught him off guard earlier, he'd been surprised at how quiet the garage door's mechanism had sounded from inside the house, so he'd decided to risk an entry via that point again. Toby ran up the Lutz's driveway, and realizing the full moon illuminated him, he took shelter in the shadow of their house, kneeling on the floor just a few inches from the garage door. Then Toby set the wireless jammer to active, blocking all frequencies except the door's remote control wavelength and hit the door open button. The door had raised itself barely a foot before he'd rolled underneath it and hit the button reversing its direction.

His speed had minimized the door motor's noise to just a few seconds, but he still needed to take cover and wait for long enough to confirm he'd not woken anyone. As he waited in their garage, Toby realized he hadn't heard Putz yet. He nodded in approval; most dogs slept near to their owners, and the absence of any barking could only mean the dog hadn't even heard the garage door noise.

It was time to get ready, so Toby climbed into a new crime scene over-suit. Managing risk was a normal part of the work, just not to this extent. The goofy suits were a real drag, but so were the consequences of somebody finding a perfect sample of his DNA inside the Lutz's house. The uproar would undoubtedly outshine the original diplomatic incident.

Toby decided to move out of the shadows toward the connecting door, and with the house still silent, he turned the handle - only to find it locked. Toby smiled. At least Jeff Lutz had some understanding of the need for home security. Toby knelt, placed his pack on the ground, and located the two slender metal tools he'd need to open the door, then set to work on the lock. Locating the operating pins was easy, but doing so in a way that left no scratches wasn't.

Toby felt the right movement through his tools, so he turned the handle to confirm the lock was in the open position, but he made sure not to open the door yet. He took a deep breath, returned the lock picks to his backpack, then took out the silenced pistol Mark had included in his kit. Toby also located Putz's bribe, the biggest one so far, then put his pack back up onto his shoulders and entered the dark house.

He felt ridiculous walking around inside a house wearing a white crime scene suit with a pistol in one hand and a dog treat in the other. The look was part Arctic training, part assassin, part dog trainer. Toby shook his head at the thought, then paused to set down his wireless jammer in the same central spot he'd used during his other visits and started up the stairs.

He gently placed a foot onto the first step, then second, third, fourth, and strode over the fifth, the one with the loud squeak. Onto step six, followed by seven, when Putz finally appeared, looking groggy and confused. Toby merely offered the dog treat to the huge animal who started down the stairs toward him, sniffing Toby before taking the treat and continuing downstairs, no doubt to his bed in the kitchen. Toby now had one hand free. He continued up to step eight then passed over step nine for the same reason as five. You really couldn't overstate the importance of proper preparation.

Toby reached the top of the stairs and moved his pistol from his right hand to his left, he was a much better shot with his right, but it was a close-range method he favored to keep his dominant hand unencumbered and his weapon as far from his target as possible. He then placed his right hand onto Jeff Lutz's door handle, gently twisted it, and the handle turned without resistance. Toby continued into Jeff Lutz's bedroom, always rolling his feet gently from heel to toe. Jeff was lying on his back in the center of his king-sized bed, not quite snoring but breathing very loudly. Toby continued toward him, switching the pistol back to his dominant hand.

Toby took up a position next to Lutz's bed, looking down at the man, expecting to feel something, but he felt nothing. This was a man who'd managed to maintain the perfect anonymous digital life, with no photos and no professional history, and Toby was curiously interested in studying his face. The man was very plain looking, his face softer and more rounded than Toby had expected. Toby pulled his pistol back in toward his own torso and maintained aim with his weapon hand. He used his other to lightly pull down on the sheet exposing one of Jeff Lutz's arms, which was also soft looking, not at all muscular. It certainly wasn't the arm of a man who undertook physical work for a living.

Toby's stare narrowed. Maybe Lutz was just an analyst, a computer guy? He shook his head, disappointed in what he saw.

Setting aside appearances, this was still the guy who'd snatched his wife from the hospital back in England and loaded her onto the first transport plane out. Toby's primary urge was to simply squeeze the trigger and hear the beautiful crack and whoosh of a silenced round. As an urge, it was hard to fight; his finger rolled back and forth on the trigger, feeling the tiniest fraction of movement in the plastic mechanism.

Toby shook his head at the idea of squeezing the trigger as the man slept, but he couldn't resist giving Lutz a prod with the pistol's silencer. If Jeff woke and sprung into action, then Toby would have no option but to squeeze the trigger, Toby would be screwed later on, but he'd have had no choice - which he could have lived with. But Jeff Lutz's only reaction was to breathe more heavily and turn his head slightly.

Toby looked over at the whiskey bottle, finding it empty. *Christ mate, no wonder you're so out.* He smiled and quietly set his pack down on the floor. Toby maintained his aim with his right hand as he took the bottle and glass from Jeff's bedside table with his left. He replaced them with the originals and then had an idea, it was probably a terrible idea, but he didn't much care.

Toby placed the pistol on the floor at his feet and unscrewed the cap from Jeff's original whiskey bottle. The whiskey level was too high in that bottle now, and there was one obvious way to fix it. Toby leaned over Jeff's upper body and tilted the whiskey bottle until the tiniest amount dribbled out and into Jeff's mouth. With his eyes still closed, Jeff Lutz started moving his tongue, and while a little of the whiskey ran out of his mouth, some part of his comatose brain knew to swallow the remainder.

Toby waited a couple of minutes, all the while grinning like a child, and then repeated the act. He paused again, this time picking up his pistol to give Lutz another prod with the silenced end, with the same inert result. Toby set the weapon back on the floor and opened Jeff's bedside table drawer, taking out the sleeping tablets with his gloved hand. He pushed down and unscrewed the cap, then dropped a whole tablet into Jeff's mouth. He couldn't resist trying to wash the tablet down with some more whiskey, so he gently poured a little more into Jeff's mouth. It didn't work, but it was fun, so he placed another tablet into Jeff's open mouth and did it again.

Each time he poured, he allowed Jeff some time to settle down before pouring some more. The sleeping tablets weren't getting washed down by the whiskey. They were just partially dissolving in the fluid before getting stuck to Jeff's tongue, teeth, and lips. As Toby neared the end of the whiskey bottle, he decided the fun was over and poured the remainder onto Jeff's pillow before setting the clean and now empty bottle back in its rightful spot.

Toby's smile faded, the games were over, and he had work to do. He placed the contaminated bottle and glass into his backpack, then knelt down and slid Jeff's gun safe out from under his bed. Finding the safe unlocked, Toby removed Jeff's weapon, slid the safe back into its original spot, and silently exited his room.

Toby stood outside Madyson Lutz's bedroom. A hollow internal door was the only remaining barrier between her and the consequences she'd been running from. Toby squeezed his fingers against the stock of Jeff's old-fashioned revolver. It felt heavy and clumsy compared to the silenced pistol he'd just stashed inside his pack. Toby switched the revolver over to his left hand and placed his right on Madyson's bedroom door handle. Only then did he realize his hands were gently trembling. He took his hand back off the door handle and studied it in the darkness, confused as to what was going on. This was new. He paused, knowing he needed to regain his normal composure.

Up until now, he'd been going through the routine just like on any other op, but standing in the darkness, what he felt was far from normal. He squinted in concentration; of course, it wasn't normal; that was the whole point. Toby thought back to Luke, to the harrowing description of the poor kid's injuries, to WPC Bell's first responder account of the scene, to Tracey's ever-worsening mental state since, and finally to Damien's attempt to escape the relentless emptiness it had caused.

With that, the anger rose, his nostrils flared, the trembling stopped, and he shoved open the door, only to see Madyson Lutz sitting up in bed and looking straight at him. Toby jumped, but his instincts kicked in. He raised the gun blisteringly quickly and leveled the sights at her. He checked her hands for weapons, and finding none, he panned left, the gun-tracking with his eyes, then he scanned rapidly to the right in the same methodical manner. Finding nobody else present in the room, his aim returned to Madyson's forehead.

"I heard you come in through the garage," she spoke in a calm, soft voice.

What the hell? Her manner was completely disarming.

She sensed his confusion, "It's okay, I had a feeling somebody would turn up, in the end."

Toby's breathing was rapid, a reaction to the adrenaline rushing through his system - even though he could see she was no danger to him. As Toby worked on controlling the timing of each breath, he stepped closer to her bed, her husband's gun unwavering in its aim.

Toby was close enough now to see how relaxed her manner was, but it didn't fit. People were never relaxed when death came; they fought, they argued, or they begged. They didn't calmly start chatting, because they were never at peace with it.

"Please, just do it. I deserve it." She tilted her head

sideways and held his gaze, almost as if she were begging him.

"What?" Toby was taken aback.

"I can close my eyes if you'd prefer." She did as she said, then quickly reopened them, "But can I ask you to do one thing first? For after, I mean."

Toby was struggling. He'd never expected this. He stared at her, swallowed hard, and lowered the gun slightly. "I dunno, try me." He spoke with his natural accent for the first time since arriving in Virginia. The act no longer served a purpose.

The tiniest trace of a smile appeared on her pale face, then faded before she continued, "Would you please find the parents and tell them how ashamed I am?" Tears were welling in Madyson's pleading eyes; then, she swallowed hard and calmly closed them for the last time.

And as Toby looked at Madyson Lutz, his resolve started to waver. He lowered his aim, then snapped it straight back and started to apply pressure to the trigger. She patiently waited for him. Her eyes still closed, and then Toby realized that doubt was the only thing he hadn't planned for, true doubt in his whole damned plan.

Toby lowered his aim, switched gun hands, and raised his free hand up to his forehead, rubbing away the sweat. Still, her eyes remained closed.

What am I thinking? He shook his head in disgust, looked

down at her bed, then just came out and said it, "Why don't you tell them yourself."

Madyson's eyes re-opened, but her expression only showed confusion.

"The parents, tell them yourself." His tone was snappier this time but he lowered the pistol a little more as he repeated himself.

"But?" Her expression was frozen in confusion. She looked down at the bed, thinking through what he'd said, then looked back at him, "I can't leave."

"Of course, you can bloody leave." He barked furiously. The idea that she'd been hiding behind that shitty excuse this whole time and was now using it to decline his uncharacteristic offer of redemption helped him to close the gap between them. He shoved the end of the stubby little barrel hard into her forehead, his finger pad pressuring the cold metal trigger even more than before.

"No, I really can't, they told us, his bosses." Madyson subtly tilted her head toward her husband's room in explanation, making no effort to break the contact between the revolver's barrel and her own head.

Toby squinted in confusion, the gun's barrel lost contact, and his aim wandered again, "Well." the room fell silent as he fully lowered the gun, "What if I could get you out?" He looked confused by the words which had just exited his own mouth.

Madyson's upper body slumped as she started to cry silently, "Please. Do it." She wiped at the tears streaming down her face. "Get me out, just help me finally make this right."

70.

"All you need is your passport. Do you only have one? Or do we have some choices?" Toby asked.

Madyson didn't understand, which in itself was an answer to his question, "Just bring your passport, that's all you need. And get dressed, quick."

Toby left Madyson's room and headed back to Jeff's. He had no particular reason to do it anymore but still chose to place the revolver in Jeff's limp hand before retreating from his room and closing the door.

"Let's go." Toby watched as she wriggled into a pair of jeans, and realizing she still needed a couple of minutes, he started on his own checklist. The crime scene suit, he was still wearing it, but even though this change of plans made it seem redundant, at this point, he'd rather keep it on until the very end.

What else? Jeff's glass, the one laced with sleeping pills, Toby took it back out of his pack and headed into Madyson's bathroom, filling it with water and repeatedly rinsing it out under the faucet. Once clean, he left it upturned on her bathroom counter. He looked in the mirror and caught sight of her putting her arms into a bra, instantly looking away in disgust. She was undoubtedly beautiful on the outside, but her personality had made her repulsive to Toby.

He walked back into the room and waited as she laced up her sneakers. Finally, she looked up at him.

"Come on then." Toby tilted his head toward the stairs and waited as she passed him, then Toby followed her down. At the bottom, Putz was waiting, his tail wagging at speed.

Madyson lowered herself to his level, rubbing his big bony head, then looked up at Toby, who was retrieving his wireless jammer from her table, "What will happen to him?"

Toby didn't care, "Don't know." But he was also starting to realize the fragility of this new situation. Madyson might start experiencing doubt at any point, so it was vital he became her ally, not her captor. "Does your husband love him too?"

She nodded unhappily.

"Then he'll look after the dog. It'll be alright."

She nodded again, then stood up, "See you, Putzy boy, I love you, and I'm sorry for what a mess I've made for everyone."

Toby watched her as she spoke to the dog, "You know, if you've got doubts, I'm not interested in doing this." He locked his eyes on hers.

She shook her head firmly, "No, no doubts. Not anymore."

"Good, then let's get going." Toby gave the dog a pat on the head too and gestured toward the garage. Madyson led the way again, and once in there, Toby raised a flat hand to stop her, "One second." He unzipped his over-suit and stepped out of it before bundling it up and putting it back

358

into his pack. He pressed the garage door button on the wall and gestured for her to step outside, then took the broom from the corner of the garage and swept the spot where he'd just removed the suit. He placed the broom back in its place, finally took off his gloves, then stepped outside her garage, where he took out his cloned remote and closed her garage door.

He looked over at Madyson and could see how spooked she was at his methods. She was also looking him up and down, studying the man who'd been hidden inside the weird protective suit.

"Can I ask your name?"

He didn't want to tell her, but it was futile as she'd find out at some point during the journey, whether he liked it or not, "You can call me Staffy."

"Staffy," she repeated quietly.

Toby nodded and then pointed toward the park, "This way."

Toby drove in the direction of his motel, for now, it was the only direction he was sure of. He held his US burner phone to his ear, waiting for the night-line to go to its answering service. Finally, the message played, Toby let it finish, then left his own, "This is an urgent message for Mark Wilson, it's Miller. I need an out for two people, and I need it as quickly as possible." He left his number then hung up as he steered his car into the parking lot of the motel, where he needed to retrieve his two big bags.

Toby hesitated while contemplating the best course of action. He could either force Lutz into coming inside with him or use this stop as a test. If she bailed on him here, then she'd only get a short distance, and he was confident he'd be able to relocate her. Whereas if he postponed that risk until later in the journey, the possibility of finding her again decreased dramatically.

"Stay here. I'll be right back." He took the keys from the ignition and took off for his room. He'd parked in a spot that gave him a clean line of sight, so as he ran up the stairs, he watched her using his peripheral vision. He unlocked his room door, stepped in, and picked up his two bags, then decided to properly enter and watch her from the unlit motel room. Madyson Lutz didn't even move her head. She just sat and patiently waited for him. Okay, the games were over. For now, she was trustworthy enough, so Toby reopened the room door and trotted back down the steps with his bags.

With the trunk closed, he lowered himself back into the driver's seat and started the engine. The only problem was he didn't have a destination. Part of Mark Wilson's job was to handle logistics like this, for any operative, at any time of the day or night, so how long was he going to take? Toby decided that in the meantime, he'd head towards Dulles International. It was the closest possibility for a British flight.

Toby's phone started ringing, but he didn't want to talk in front of her, so he steered his car to the side of the highway and came to a stop on the hard shoulder. "Mark?" The caller ID showed 'Unknown,' but nobody else had this number.

"Yeah, Hello Miller, what have you got?"

Toby stepped out of the car to talk, "Need a way home, as soon as. For two."

"Mm, I got your message. So where are you leaving from?"

"Virginia," Toby responded.

"And who is traveling? I mean the name you're traveling under."

Oh dear, Toby had to use his own UK passport as he'd officially been here on vacation, which would probably strike Mark as odd, "Toby Miller, I'm using my own name."

"Oh." His reaction was as expected. "And the other name?"

This would be even better, "Lutz. Madyson Lutz."

Silence.

"Mark, are you still there?" Toby asked. He really didn't have time for this.

"Um, is she still alive, or are you returning with..." Mark went silent once more.

Toby shook his head. Why would he take a dead body home? "She's alive, Mark."

"Oh." He sounded even more surprised, "We have a Royal Navy carrier off the coast right now, they're training with the new fighter jets. I could probably get you airlifted onto that."

Initially, it made no sense to Toby, then it came to him, "No, Mark, she's with me willingly. So I need a form of transport that can do four hundred miles an hour, not twenty-five knots."

It took Mark a while to reply again, "So, just let me clarify; you've got the diplomatic immunity runner with you, right now, willingly?"

"Yes, Mark, I do, and we need to get the hell outta here as quick as possible."

"Jesus Christ Miller, how did you manage that? You know what, don't worry about it, tell me another time. I'll get you guys onto a flight. What's your closest civil airport? Dulles?"

There we go, that was the efficient Mark that Toby had been waiting for, "Yeah Mark, Dulles."

"Okay, head there now and I'll get back to you with your travel plans. You both have passports? And they're current, valid, and all that?"

"We do, mate." Toby smiled as he stepped back into the rental car.

"Then get going, Miller, you don't have time to waste."

Toby rolled his eyes and accelerated back onto the highway.

71.

"They flew me back here on one of those Army planes." It was the first time Madyson had spoken since they'd left her house.

The US Army didn't fly her back, that was the US Air Force, but being pedantic would serve no purpose at this point. Toby looked over at her, "I heard."

"The pilots were mean to Jeff, they weren't happy. With me, I guess, with us running."

The smallest insights had a way of changing the whole picture. Toby had never contemplated that. Considering his biggest concern was that she might change her mind and cause him problems, he decided to continue with the theme of enlightenment, "I have a friend, a master sergeant in the US Air Force, and to be honest, he took it the same way."

Madyson wiped her eyes again, "I really let everybody down. My family, my country, and the poor young boy's family too. But I didn't understand that, not for the longest time."

Toby considered what must be going on inside her head, trying to understand it from her perspective as he followed the signs into the rental car returns area of Dulles International Airport. "Then, from now on, let your actions speak for you."

Madyson nodded and wiped away some more tears, "I've never felt so ashamed in my life. You're English, and so I'm sorry, I want all of you to know how sorry I am."

I'm more than just English. I'm his bloody Uncle. Toby experienced an unexpected rise in emotions, the most surprising of which was sympathy.

"I tried killing myself, you know," Madyson said the words but couldn't look at him.

Toby's jaw dropped. He turned to study her face but had to turn back to the road or risk wrecking the car.

"They pumped my stomach." she laughed bitterly, "They wouldn't even let me die."

Toby's head was spinning. This wasn't how things were meant to pan out. He pulled into the side of the road, too flustered to drive. "Well, the boy's father tried killing himself too." Why had he just told her that?

Madyson looked at Toby, and for the first time, he really looked into her eyes, realizing they were just as defeated and exhausted as Tracey's. Toby was starting to realize how wrongly he'd read it all.

Bwap, sounded a siren behind them, "You can not stop here." A voice boomed through the vehicle's loudspeaker. Toby checked in the rearview mirror, seeing a cop car had come to a stop behind them. "Oh fuck no." He hissed. His car was rented in a fictitious name. His passport was issued in another name, and sitting inside the car was the famous diplomatic runner from UK justice, for which they'd probably assume kidnap. Toby was absolutely screwed.

"Move the vehicle, now." The voice ordered.

Toby looked in the rearview to see the driver wasn't getting out, which confused him. So he decided to try and gently accelerate away from the curb, using his turn signals like a teenager putting on a show for the driving examiner. As Toby reached normal speed again, only half of his attention was on the road, with the other half still in his mirror, so when the cop pulled around them to accelerate away, he could not believe his luck.

It was too early in the morning for them to buy hot food inside the airport, so Toby bought them some packaged crap from a vending machine. They walked in silence until they found a nearby gate with no imminent flight and sat down in the middle of a long row of vacant seats.

Toby had chosen a spot that backed up against a wall, allowing him to size up every passer-by. He'd never known a situation quite like this. A part of him despised this woman more than anybody he'd ever encountered in his life. While another part of him would probably be willing to die to protect her from being seized back by the American authorities.

"Is Jeff dead?" Madyson asked, looking down at the floor as she spoke.

Toby cast a quick glance in her direction. "No. And that's not a conversation we should have in here."

Madyson nodded, then after a pause, she continued, "Marrying him was the second biggest mistake of my life."

Toby was starting to understand the real Madyson Lutz wasn't completely sub-human, "When he wakes up, which might not be until this evening, he's gonna have the worst headache of his life, though." Toby turned to her, grinning.

The tiniest glimmer of a smile briefly formed on Madyson's face, but Toby looked away, feeling uncomfortably conflicted at sharing even the smallest of positive moments with her.

As the silence settled in again, an overhead voice called their flight, "We are now boarding the last group for flight A-B one-one-two to London Heathrow, again that is the last group for London."

Toby nudged her, "Come on, we've left it as long as we can."

Madyson and Toby walked toward their gate. It was a short walk as it had only been two gates down from where they'd eaten their pauper's breakfast. Toby habitually checked the other travelers, only seeing what you'd expect inside an international airport. People were gathering at the gate across from theirs. He looked at a family heading off on holiday, judging by their clothes. Then he looked at the group of young friends sitting a little further down the same row of seats; some of them were sleeping due to the early hour. There were three uniformed off-duty soldiers, one

366

napping with headphones in his ears, the other two just chatting to pass the time. They reminded Toby of his own men. He smiled and then finally looked over at his own gate.

The uniformed flight attendant took people's boarding passes, fed them into her machine, and then allowed them to pass through to the jetway. Behind her were two suited men, carefully looking around the boarding area. Toby's eyes opened wide. One guy had a visible curled cable running from inside his jacket up into an earpiece. *They put out an alarm on her passport.* Toby inhaled sharply, which caught Madyson's attention. She looked at Toby, then followed his stare, seeing the two men.

Toby listened as her breathing fell apart, "Stay calm, Madyson, it's okay."

"It's not. They won't let me leave, I told you."

At that point, one of the men met Toby's stare. He nudged his colleague then they stepped out from behind the ticket machine and started walking towards the couple. Toby went into work mode. He looked at the men, noticing their suits obscuring their belt area; and while he saw nothing, it was obvious their jackets were cut loosely enough to hide weapons. Toby looked behind, seeing there were no suited newcomers there, then ahead, and in every other direction, scanning the airport for more suits, but there were only these two. As he looked back toward the men, he saw they had now panned out, meaning one was approaching from his left, the other from the right.

Madyson grabbed Toby's arm, "We need to run."

Toby shook his head, he wasn't running, and neither was she. "We're not running, Madyson. We don't have to."

She looked at him, doubting his words, then back at the men who'd come to within just a few feet of them.

"Mrs. Lutz, you need to come with us." The man to Toby's right spoke.

"No." She was still squeezing his arm, and he could feel Madyson shaking as she replied, but her response was surprisingly firm.

"Sir, please come with me." The one to Toby's left reached for Toby's other arm.

Toby whipped his one arm out of Madyson's grasp and the other out of the man's reach, stepping to the left and grabbing the man's elbow with his right hand and the man's wrist with his left. He then pivoted and jerked the arm up behind the man's back, holding it there at a ninety-degree angle with just his one arm. All it would take was a quick upward jerk of a few more inches, and the man's elbow would snap. But what would it achieve? Would it help them to board the plane? Toby realized he had to put his own version of normality behind him. He took a long breath and spoke calmly, "I'm going to let you go, but trust me, you don't want to try that again. I'm a representative of Her Majesty's British Government, and you have no authority to detain me."

The man to his right replied quietly, "Then step back, Sir, because Mrs. Lutz is coming with us."

No, she wasn't. It was time for Toby to step out of the shadows and into the spotlight, "This woman is a US citizen who has requested to be taken to Great Britain, where she has an outstanding warrant for her arrest. I am her official escort, and again," now Toby really raised his volume, "you have no power to detain her."

The man to Toby's left pulled his suit jacket outward, revealing a holstered pistol, "You think?"

Toby turned, seeing the whole airport was watching the bizarre scene unfold. He decided to take it up another notch, playing to the crowd, "These men have approached us without any attempt to identify themselves and are trying to take this woman, a US citizen, against her wishes. And now this man," Toby pointed, "Is flashing his service weapon. Is this America, or some kind of dark dictatorship?"

The suited men looked ready to kill Toby.

"Did you say she wanted to leave?" Toby turned to look where the voice had come from, seeing one of the US servicemen walking toward him. But instead of replying to the soldier, Toby smiled at Madyson, "Tell him whatever you want. It's all up to you now." He put his faith in her and stepped back.

Madyson's face contorted, the tears came forth, but she purposefully wiped them away and found the strength to speak, "My name is Madyson Lutz, and I am choosing to return to Britain. I should have done it a long time ago, but I'm doing it now. It's my choice, and this man is only here to help me get safe passage."

The soldier, wearing the rank markings of a lieutenant, looked at Toby, "Madyson Lutz? The CIA wife who claimed diplomatic immunity?"

Toby nodded, then as he looked at the officer's uniform, his eyes nearly popped out of his head because just above the man's name tape was a tan-colored 4DC badge.

"So, who are you two?" The Lieutenant asked the suited men, who looked at each other with some doubt finally registering on their faces. Their silence empowered him, "I asked you men a question, now identify yourselves." Unknown to the Lieutenant, his two uniformed colleagues had got up from their seats and joined him as he spoke.

The cockier suit to Toby's left spoke, though quietly. "We're from a higher part of the Government than you, ya dumb fucking grunt."

The Lieutenant turned to the Corporal at his side, "You've already got your phone out, Jimmy. Can you get a photo of this clown?" He turned straight back to the suit, "Well, you must be real high up if you can stop a US Citizen from coming and going, without any explanation of why or who you are." The Lieutenant turned up his volume now, too, "But how high up do you think you really are? High enough that this incident won't kill your career? Coz that's what you're doing, creating a new diplomatic incident. And it

370

won't be your boss who's blamed, and not your secret little department of suits, but you." He provokingly prodded the man in the chest. "And I'll take my US Army uniform over that cheap-ass suit any day, bud."

"Careful about touching him, or he'll flash that little gun again." Toby nodded to the soldier, then turned to goad the same suited man, "So are you gonna start shooting innocent American soldiers too? Or just the unarmed Brit?"

The man glared at Toby with an impressive intensity, before turning and truly taking in the size of the unwelcome audience he'd attracted.

"Well?" Toby growled. "Coz we've got a bloody flight to catch." then leaned in uncomfortably close to the face of the man, who was already struggling to resist Toby's verbal prodding. The second suit finally broke the stand-off by tugging at the arm of his colleague's jacket, "Look at this shit storm, we really do gotta go."

Toby shook his head at the arrogant suit, "God, you catch on fucking slow, don't you?" Then took the calculated risk of turning his back on the unresolved situation, offering his hand to the Army Lieutenant. As Toby and the US Army officer shook hands, the two suits retreated with as much dignity as they could muster, under the circumstances.

"For Diplomatic Change." Toby nodded at the soldier's badge.

"Oh, you've heard of that?" The Lieutenant looked genuinely surprised.

371

"Yeah." Toby beamed, "I came across it a while back. But that's not important, thanking you is. So, thanks mate, I mean it."

The officer shrugged. "As you say, bud, for diplomatic change. Y'all have a safe flight."

Madyson had stood to the side of the whole event, and now that the time finally seemed right, she approached the ranking soldier and gave him a gentle hug, "I'm so sorry for what I did, but I'm going to fix it now, I promise." She looked up at him with pleading eyes.

The Lieutenant stood to attention and saluted Madyson Lutz, a gesture that the two other US soldiers immediately duplicated. Toby found himself standing to attention too and saluting the men in the open-palmed British manner, "Sergeant Toby Miller, Sir." It was an international gesture of respect, one which the smiling officer clearly appreciated.

Toby relaxed his salute and turned around to see the boarding agent franticly beckoning for them to hurry up.

72.

"Hi, how are you this morning?" Asked the flight attendant.

"Good thanks. You?" Toby responded politely, although considering he'd navigated so many obstacles, to say he was good was an understatement.

"I'm doing okay, considering the early hour. May I see your boarding pass?" She took a peak at Toby's document, "Oh, but you've already gone too far."

Toby had just entered the coach section, "Sorry, you mean I'm back there?" he didn't dare hope.

"Yes Sir, this is a business class ticket, so let me show you where your seats are." The lady gestured for them to back up and smiled kindly at Madyson.

"Oh!" Toby was gobsmacked by the two large leather seats he'd been pointed to. Mark had really hooked him up. "Do you have a preference?" He asked Madyson, who shook her head in response, "I don't believe you. I think you'd prefer the window seat." Toby gave her a polite half-smile.

"Thanks." Her lips curled, but her eyes were still filled with doubt.

"Ma'am?" The flight attendant leaned in so as not to be heard by the general population, "I think what you're doing is very brave. I admire you for it."

Madyson attempted the same unconvincing smile before

edging over into the window seat. Then Toby sat down in the adjoining one.

"And I'm glad she has someone like you watching out for her." The attendant spoke more quietly to Toby, "We all heard about the incident outside."

Toby smiled, riddled with inner guilt, knowing he hadn't been looking out for Madyson until a couple of hours ago.

"Just let me know if you need anything. We'd all like to make this journey as relaxing as possible for the both of you." The attendant smiled, and Toby seized the opportunity.

"I do need to make a phone call, an urgent one."

The attendant seemed conflicted. She looked away and called one of her colleagues over, "The gentleman needs to make a call while we taxi. I've said it's okay." The second attendant nodded their understanding and walked back through to the next partitioned area. "Go ahead." She smiled at Toby.

Toby had listened to their conversation and so was already powering on his UK phone, "Thank you. I'll be really quick."

"Please do, and I'll have to stay close so the other passengers don't complain about you breaking the rules."

"That's fine. I appreciate it." Toby was scrolling through his contacts, then having found the right one; he hit the call button. The other phone rang in Toby's ear, then clicked, "This is WPC Bell."

"Bell, this is Toby Miller, I need to be quick, but this is very important. Are you ready?"

Bell's line of work had given her a similar ability to deal with the unexpected; quickly and efficiently. "Go ahead, Mister Miller."

"I'm flying back to the UK, from America, on flight A-B one-one-two coming in at Heathrow."

"Okay, I've got it." Lucy sounded reassuringly organized.

"With Madyson Lutz." He heard Lucy Bell gasp, "Who has decided to return to the UK of her own free will. That point is vital, Bell, she reached out to us, and I'm bringing her in."

For the moment, Lucy was lost for words.

"And I want you to meet her on arrival, Bell. I know it's not your Constabulary's patch, but you need to be there because this is your case, and she's earned the right to be greeted by a friendly face. And in my opinion, also the right to be treated fairly. We all need to put the past behind us."

Toby heard snatched breathing and turned to see Madyson looking at him, with tears streaming down her face. He tried to put it aside and finish his call, "Meet us in the secure area Bell, not out in the arrivals area. It's a bloody zoo out there. Oh, and you need to help her through immigration too so that she can enter with some dignity."

"Of course, Toby and I agree about all of it. I'll make it happen, no matter how hard. And Toby?"

"Yes, WPC Bell."

"Good job, mate."

"Uh yeah, okay. Gotta go, I'm getting the stink eye on the plane," and Toby hung up his phone.

"Phoah," the flight attendant fanned her face, "I feel like I'm present while history is being made." She placed her hand on Toby's arm, "You're a good man." She held Toby's gaze for a moment and then turned to Madyson, "Good luck, Mrs. Lutz. As I said before, I admire your bravery. Although I suspect you're gonna be treated very fairly." The flight attendant smiled at them both, then left to take her own seat for take-off.

Toby saw that some voicemails had come in whilst on his call. One of the IDs was Mary-Ann, but as excited as that made him, now wasn't the time, so he powered off his phone. He slid it into the seat back and looked ahead, trying to wind himself down emotionally for the long flight ahead.

"I didn't reach out to you. You made me sound better than I deserve." Madyson was trembling as the tears flowed.

Toby looked into her sad, scared eyes, "And I didn't come to America to bring you home." He whispered, "But, this way is better."

Madyson leaned in and gave Toby the most gentle hug, trembling as she did it, "Thank you." She let go and slid back into her own seat, still looking at him. Madyson obviously had more to say but held back. Finally, she swallowed hard,

"I'm really scared." Her bottom lip trembled.

For five months, all Toby and his family had wanted was some remorse from Madyson Lutz, now here it was, and gloating seemed unimaginable, "I know." He searched for reassuring words but could only think of one response, "But you have to put faith in the justice system."

Madyson attempted the same smile, which only involved her mouth, then her sad eyes looked away, she scrunched up her body and took the blanket from the seat-back.

Toby turned his gaze ahead as the plane accelerated along the runway, thinking back to the previous night's events. It suddenly hit him that with another quick phone call, he could send responders to the Lutz house, where Jeff would be found full of whiskey and sleeping tablets, with a gun in his hand. It would probably be the final straw, ending Jeff Lutz's career. But it was reminiscent of the situation with the CIA agent in the airport, whose arm Toby could have snapped in an instant - sometimes it was better just to let it go.

Epilogue.

"I'm really not sure about this, Toby." Tracey's breathing was way too fast, Toby needed to calm her down but it was Damien who stepped in first.

"It's the right thing to do Trace, you can manage it, and we're all here with you. Luke would want this, especially with everything that's happened recently. You know he would."

Tracey squeezed Damien's hand so hard it hurt him, "You're too like him, that's why I pushed you away." Her breathing continued as before. "You know that, right? You even look like each other."

"I know we do, babe, so you'll never be able to forget him. It's a good thing, not bad."

"I don't think I'm there yet." It was Tracey's attempt at a joke.

"I hope you know what you're bloody well doing, Toby Miller." Toby's mum didn't look at all convinced.

"I do, Mum. I know exactly what I'm doing." And he did.

"Oh my God, is that her?" Tracey started trembling.

Instead of replying, Toby walked toward Madyson, who was accompanied by WPC Lucy Bell. Toby stopped in front of Madyson, who whispered to him, "I can't believe you never told me he was your nephew."

"It never seemed relevant." Toby smiled kindly and then turned toward Bell, "Lucy." he nodded his greeting.

"Toby." She smiled back.

Toby looked back at Madyson, "You really are doing a brave thing now. Are you ready?"

Madyson nodded, "No, but it's something I've gotta do."

"I know. Come on. I'll introduce you." Toby led the ladies toward Luke's headstone and as they approached, Tracey collapsed in Damien's arms, convulsing in the same way she had when the initial news had been broken to her.

Now Madyson's mouth started trembling, and the tears started flowing, but she didn't slow her pace, "Mrs. Rigg and Mr. Rigg." She stopped walking and Toby could see she was shaking pretty hard too, "Nothing I say can help, I know that. But I have to tell you how sorry I am and..." the tears were invading her nose, which started running too, but she wasn't done. "How ashamed I am, how full of remorse I am. And if there was anything I could do, if I could trade my life for his, I would." Maddy had to fight the sobbing, which was threatening to stop her flow. She held her head high and took another breath, "I wish I could give my life." She snatched another breath, "For that of your son's." and another snatched breath, "And I'm so very. Sorry. It took me so long. To understand."

Tracey let go of Damien and sped toward Madyson, who flinched defensively just as Tracey wrapped her arms around her. "Come here, girl, thank you. Thank you so much for coming." And the ladies held onto each other tightly as the rest looked on in disbelief.

"Oh my bloody God," whispered Toby's mum.

Damien merely took his long arm and pulled Toby in close, "Bloody nice work, Tobe."

Toby couldn't manage a smile yet. He just turned to Lucy, "What's gonna happen to her?"

Lucy shrugged, "The courts will decide that. But the change in her," she nodded in the direction of Madyson, "it's going to help her a lot. You did a really great thing Miller."

Toby's mum beamed with pride, but Toby appeared to slump on hearing Lucy's comment.

"But what's wrong, love?" Asked his mum.

"I think I just ended my career." He stared into space, "I wasn't sent over there Mum. I went on my own. That's serious indiscipline, and it'll catch up with me." Toby shook his head at what he'd set himself up for.

"I wouldn't be so sure about that." Lucy was grinning, "It doesn't sound like you've seen today's papers."

Toby, his mum, and Damien all turned to look at Lucy. None of them having seen what she had.

"It's on the front page, a story about how some unidentified British Government agent brought back the diplomatic immunity runner, against the odds apparently. It said that in a public airport, some CIA agents tried to stop

380

them, seriously overstepping boundaries. That the Americans are officially okay with the way it's turned out, as Mrs. Lutz made her own choice, and because her return here has re-strengthened our international bond. Even the British PM was bragging about the sophisticated skill of his valued agents, who are always at work in the shadows for our country. Blah blah."

"Wow, Tobe." Damien looked staggered.

But Lucy wasn't done, "So I reckon some orders are gonna be backdated for you and a commendation is more likely than the sack. But Toby," Lucy looked confused, "I thought you were in the Army?"

"He is, plain clothes." bragged his mum.

"Oh, about that, Mum." Toby grinned.

"Now, if he could only meet a nice girl." Toby's mum rolled her eyes for Lucy's benefit.

"But I did, I actually did! It's early days, but we've had a few dates, and we really like each other." Toby's smile was real, and it was infectious.

"So you might make me a grandmother again?" His mum locked her eyes on his, "I hope you're not going to take forever about it."

Toby groaned, "Oh for God's sake, Mum, really? Here?"

"Well, excuse me, Toby Miller, I'm not getting any younger, you know."

"I hardly know her Mum. What do you want from me? 'I know you haven't met my mum yet, but she wants me to knock you up...' "

"Oh, Toby, sometimes I wish your father were still here to knock some sense into you."

Damien shrugged at Lucy, who, despite the circumstances couldn't suppress the radiant smile illuminating her face.

Toby's story will continue in the follow up book,

Rescue & Redemption

Connect with the author at

https://www.facebook.com/SimonGreen.US.UK.Author